The Trigger

Joe Joyce

For Molly

One

The patrol moved into the shallow valley and he breathed deeply and slipped the Winchester in between the long stems of the grass on top of the ditch. He slid the bolt forward and down and took a last look over his shoulder at the valley behind him.

The sun was high in the sky and flared down on the vibrant greens of the still fields, on a far-off herd of black and white cattle munching slowly with their tails twitching, and on cocks of buoyant brown hay. The air hummed with heat and insects and the leisurely chirping of birds.

The escape route was clear.

He turned back to the valley before him and watched the string of camouflage uniforms moving slowly by the grove of upright evergreens and thought methodically of the distance and the absence of wind. He settled comfortably into the dull undergrowth where the sun never penetrated and eased the butt into his shoulder and his eye settled naturally on the telescopic sight.

The crosshairs were superimposed on a red-bereted head and he breathed carefully and rhythmically and followed the target until everything was ready. Then he squeezed the trigger. The bullet roared away and the barrel jerked and he held it steady and thought, perfect. A hit.

He eased the rifle slowly back into the ditch. There was no need to look down the valley: he knew it was a hit, a perfect shot. The exploding bullet had deadened his hearing and stilled the valleys and was fading as he heard a new sound and his heart raced into a heightened, pounding rhythm.

Helicopter rotors were thumping through the air like a frantic housewife beating dust out of a hanging rug. He raised his head to look into the valley behind and a helicopter was sweeping down the opposite hillside, pulling into a tight turn and settling down. Soldiers were out and fanning into a line and a burst of fire snapped and snarled through the hawthorn bushes over his head.

They can't have seen me, he thought, disbelief trying to overwhelm panic. They can't have known. He risked a glance down the valley in front and saw nothing and then the patrol rose as one man and dashed towards him in a series of scissoring movements. Another burst of fire splintered the twigs and bullets sloughed into the ground, reaching for him.

He sank down into the ditch, hugging the useless empty rifle and wished there was some going back. Wished he had one more round. But the bullet was gone and couldn't be recalled. There was no going back. There was no way out. He was trapped.

This is it, he thought. It's over.

He felt cold, as if the life was already running from his body in unseen rivulets, and he shivered uncontrollably. He tried to think but there was nothing to think beyond the refrain that this was it, it was over. There was nothing he could do but wait, numb. The bullets whining overhead sounded almost leisurely in their flight, knowing they would find him eventually. There was no escape.

The firing stopped and his eyes swung around the top of the ditch, waiting for the muzzle that would kill him, willing it to appear and get it over with, terrified he would see it. An unseen voice gave a crisp order to fix bayonets and he closed his eyes and clamped his hands over his head and shoved his twitching body deeper into the earth against the horror of the sharp steel stabbing and slicing.

He waited.

Fergus Callan woke from the nightmare with a start and saw the grey wispy cloud swirling past the window. The cabin was silent and he thought for a terrible moment that the plane was falling but it shuddered as the air brakes again slowed its descent and he heard the clunk of the landing gear coming down. He closed his eyes and sighed and shook a cigarette from the Marlboro pack on his tray.

An elderly nun at the edge of the row watched the terror drain from his face and coughed politely and pointed at the no smoking sign. 'Almost there,' she smiled tightly.

He forced a rueful smile in return as he squirmed in the narrow seat and found the belt and snapped it shut. His shirt was soaked with perspiration. Christ, he thought, what a time to have that dream.

He felt disoriented: everything but the here and now of the aircraft seemed to belong to a long time ago. Just like it used to be in the old days when endlessly changing houses, forgetting the place he had been somewhere along the road to the next one.

The dawn had been rushing to meet them, spreading sunshine like melting butter into the indigo sky, when he had passed that point. Boston had already been a long way back and he had wondered suddenly what Sharon was doing and seen her sleeping in the large bed under the sloping ceiling. Then he had drifted off to sleep with the soothing sun on his eyelids.

The plane lurched a little to the left and then to the right as it corkscrewed into position. There was no sound but the rushing of air through the ceiling nozzles as though they were breathing for all the tensed bodies around him. He looked through the window, rain flecked now, and saw the dull green land and the murky water and mudflats of the Shannon estuary as they came down through the cloud base. Home.

Inspector George Keerins crossed the staff canteen to the corner table where the three detectives were grouped in silence, concentrating on their breakfasts. The grey light of the murky morning seemed to deaden the neon brightness of the room. A scattering of airport workers watched him with undisguised interest.

'It's bang on schedule,' Keerins said as he sat down. 'Be here in forty minutes.'

The others gave no indication that they had heard. Keerins poured himself another cup of cool tea and watched them devour their bacon and sausages. His stomach felt queasy from tiredness and the jittery tension of the waiting. He had been up at four and the fast drive from Dublin had used up any benefit of his few hours sleep.

He sipped at the tea, acutely conscious of the slight shake in his hand and of his youth relative to their crumpled middle-age. Keerins was tall and thin with quiffed-back brown hair over an earnest face that made him look even younger than he was. They were local Special Branch men, dragged out of their beds too early by his nervousness to get everything into place in plenty of time. They were probably bitching about nervous newcomers, he thought, about a recently jumped-up officer trying to make his mark at their expense.

Fuck them, he decided. It was just another job to them but he couldn't afford to take any chances, to cock it up. It was his first big operation in security, based on his own information. He had to do it right.

A group of chattering maintenance men came in at the end of the night shift and lined up at the self-service counter. They fell silent as they glanced at the untalking group in the corner. Keerins stared back at them, unseeing, his mind going back over the plan again.

His main fear was that he wouldn't recognise Callan. The picture in his pocket was nearly ten years old and he must have changed a lot. He wondered again if he should show the photograph to the others but decided against it. Better that they concentrate on the physical description, on the things that wouldn't have changed: five foot nine, medium build, brown eyes, brown curly hair.

It'll be all right, he reassured himself. We have the edge on him. He's not expecting us. And we know the name he's using. Cleary.

The fields began to flash underneath and Callan saw the outlying airport buildings and the start of the runway. She's still asleep, he thought as the wheels hit the tarmac. I should have told her. But that would have been making a big deal out of it and it was no big deal.

Still, he thought, I could have said I'm going back, just for a week. And she would have asked why and I couldn't tell her that. I could have given her the ostensible reason, told her about Willy. And she'd have argued that that was ridiculous, too ridiculous to be true. Which it was, in a way. But not as ridiculous as the real reason would sound if I tried to explain it.

The engines roared in reverse and the plane slowed and he knew he should have told her something, anything. Anything would have been better than nothing. I can phone, he thought.

The elderly nun made the sign of the cross and he gave her a wan smile and turned back to the window. The mist billowed across the forlorn grass and the greasy tarmac and the grey terminal. The plane came to a halt and the silence broke with the mechanical loosening of seat belts as the passengers regained control of their own fates. The nun began to struggle with the overhead locker and he rose to help her retrieve a black hold-all.

'You had a bad dream,' she said as they waited in the choking aisle.

'Flying is a bad dream,' he said lightly. 'I'm surprised I managed to sleep at all.'

'I wish I could have. I've come from Vancouver.'

A red-uniformed stewardess said goodbye as they stepped through the covered ramp and into the terminal. 'Let me take it for you,' he offered as the nun stretched for her bag.

'Are you going home to your folks?' Callan asked, slowing his pace to her painful-looking walk as they passed the empty cavern of the duty-free shop. Most of the other passengers filed into it, awaiting onward flights to Dublin.

She told him she had been visiting her sister and he listened with half his attention as he looked around, apprehension threatening to give way to anxiety. The early morning air was damp and cold and the building felt like it, too, was waking from a bad dream. He glanced back at the empty corridor and the Air Canada plane and the rainswept apron and stopped for a moment to swop her bag with his duty-free drink and cigarettes. There was nobody in sight other than the straggle of disembarking passengers.

'Do you have family here?' the nun asked as they slowed into the short queue at the immigration desks.

'Maybe,' Callan gave a short laugh, thinking himself into his cover. 'I'm hoping to find some relatives. My grandmother came from County Cork.'

He watched a plain-clothes detective standing by a wall to one side as he chatted. He had persuaded himself the risks were negligible but the price would be high if he were wrong. Very high. The detective looked bored. There was nothing to worry about, he told himself. Nobody knew he was here.

He yawned involuntarily and let his body sag into the nondescript pose of a tired traveller as the nun handed her passport across the desk. The ashen-faced immigration officer barely glanced at it and passed it back again.

Callan handed over the Canadian passport and the officer turned it sideways to read the personal details and examine the picture. He glanced up and saw a tired version of the same square face with dark hair cropped into tight curls. He leafed through it without haste and went back to the start.

I knew it, Sharon had said when he admitted he was Irish, I knew it the first time I saw you. How, Callan had asked, taken aback. Because you've got a mick face, she had laughed, it's written all over it. He had smiled a surface smile. And I thought I was a master of disguise, he

8

had said truthfully although she hadn't recognised the truth. Maybe you should put on some clothes, she had giggled.

'What's the purpose of your visit, Mr Graves?' the immigration officer asked.

'A short vacation.' Nobody in Ireland recognised the mick face, Callan thought. It was so common they couldn't see it. Besides, I have an honest face, honest and unmemorable. The kind of face and undistinguished presence that people forgot instantly. Both had saved him many times.

The official stamped the passport and handed it back. 'Have a good holiday,' he said automatically.

The nun was waiting for him and he went with her into the baggage hall, relieved and slightly elated. It was going to be all right. It was just the dream that had unsettled him, momentarily.

In the staff canteen Inspector Keerins looked at his watch and said: 'Right, let's get into position.'

One of the detectives stubbed out a cigarette and they all got to their feet slowly. 'We take him in the corridor,' Keerins looked at each in turn. 'As soon as he comes off the plane. A nice clean lift. And put the bastard where he should have been a long time ago.'

One of them nodded automatically: they didn't need to be reminded how much they wanted him. They trooped out in single file.

Callan got a trolley and loaded the nun's cases on to it and retrieved the large backpack he had chosen in Toronto for its maple-leaf symbol. They went through the green customs channel and into the arrivals area where an elderly couple greeted the nun.

'This young man has been very kind,' she told them. 'Could we give him a lift somewhere? Into Limerick, maybe.'

'That's not necessary,' he said, hefting his backpack off the trolley. 'I'm going to hire a car here.'

'Are you sure?'

'Yes,' he nodded. 'Thank you.'

'I hope you find some relatives.'

He watched them leave and checked the terminal. A group of elderly tourists were gathered patiently around a tour guide who checked their names off her list. Most of the other disembarking passengers had dissipated. There was no sign of any watchers.

He went over to the one car-hire desk that was open and selected a Ford Escort from the chart a young woman showed him.

'Can I see your driving licence, please?' she asked as she filled in the forms. Her make-up was heavy and recently applied.

He handed her an Irish licence and she glanced at him uncertainly. 'Do you have any other identification?'

He smiled and produced the Irish passport that they had given him with the licence in Boston. She obviously did not expect him to have Irish documents but she took down the passport number and asked if he had a contact address or telephone number in Ireland. He gave her a ready-made phoney address and number in Cork and she wrote them down too.

'Credit card or cheque?'

'Travellers' cheque?' he inquired.

'That'll be fine, Mr Cleary,' she said.

She brought him outside under a large umbrella to the car park and he shivered in the chill air and felt the insistently wetting mist as she completed the formalities. He tossed the backpack on to the back seat and sat in and adjusted the driver's seat.

The dashboard clock showed eight-twelve and he waited for the wipers to clear the smudge of drizzle from the windscreen and then he drove into the dank morning past the squat modern blocks of Shannon town. Off to his left the green Aer Lingus jumbo from Boston floated heavily down to the runway, watched by the detectives waiting in the terminal.

Callan didn't give it a thought.

Two

The afternoon sky had cleared and was now a clean blue. Puffed white clouds scudded in along the horizon from the Atlantic and the sun was beating down, drying the road and the stone walls and the dark-green fields. Fergus Callan felt as refreshed as the washed landscape.

He slowed down and let a distance open up between him and the lumbering truck in front as he caught sight of the inner reaches of Galway Bay, an unremarkable inlet of blue sea drawn back from the jagged tide marks of the land. A line of impatient cars flashed by as he glanced at the sea and saw his own tide of memories.

He used to compete with his brother to be the first to see the sea here when they were on their way to the seaside as children. He had always won, more aware of the landmarks than his younger brother and confusing him by pretending they were nowhere near it until he let out the ritual shout of 'I see the sea' and claimed victory.

The road wound inland and he tried to remember the last time he had been here. Ten years ago at least. Probably more but he couldn't pinpoint his last visit. Nothing much must have happened. Nothing much seemed to have changed either, except that everything looked smaller now; the fields, the cars, the road and the buildings on the outskirts of the town. Smaller and squatter.

He turned off the main road before he reached the town centre and drove into Renmore. Lines of suburban houses radiated in all directions, momentarily confusing him. In his memory, the house had overlooked Lough Atalia, green fields running downhill from the garden to the water's edge. But the fields had been covered by rows of more houses and he drove back from the water's edge, searching for the right street.

He found the house and went slowly by, automatically checking the parked cars and the pavement for anything suspicious. A group of small children chased one of their number on a bicycle but there were no other signs of life. He continued round the block and stopped near the house the second time round.

He sat in the car for a moment, thinking about what he was about to do. The risks would be higher once anyone knew he was here, the word would inevitably get around. But it shouldn't filter too far before he was gone again. At least, that's what he was banking on. The risks were negligible, he reminded himself. This is what I've come for. I've got to do it.

He got out and went briskly to the house and the door was opened by a woman wearing an apron and looking harassed.

'Peggy?' he said uncertainly. Her hair was greying and tied back in a tight bun and her face was beginning to break down into lines.

She nodded, watching him with a weary wariness. 'I'm Fergus,' he said. God, she has become middle-aged, he thought.

'Fergus?'

'Can I come in?' He didn't want to stand on the door-step any longer than necessary. This was probably a marked house.

'Of course,' she said. 'I didn't recognise you.'

He watched her closely as she shut the door and brought him into her kitchen, wondering suddenly whether her attitude concealed unease at his presence. She moved a bowl of dough and a wooden platter to one side of the table and wiped the floury surface.

He sat down as she filled a kettle from the sink and asked him if he would have a cup of tea. 'I wasn't expecting you,' she said with a weak smile over her shoulder.

'I was going to phone,' he said. 'But . . .'

'Better not,' she agreed. She untied her apron and sat down opposite him and shook her head. 'I really didn't know you from Adam.'

'It's been a long time,' he said. 'We're all getting older.'

'You're looking well.'

'The easy life.' He smiled to try and put her at her ease, still worrying about her lack of enthusiasm. It was too late now, though; he had committed himself. 'How are things with you?'

'Getting by. Jimmy was made redundant but he's got another job, driving a lorry. It's not much but it's better than nothing. The children are growing up.'

She got up to make the tea and he declined her offer of something to eat. He asked her about the children while she set two cups on the table and sat down again.

'And Willy?' he asked about her brother, the reason he was here.

'Willy,' she sighed as she poured the tea. 'He's disappeared. Like I told you on the phone.'

'No word of him since?'

'Not a whisper.'

'Have you contacted anybody?'

'Only yourself. He told me to call you if anything happened to him. I didn't know what else to do.'

He sipped the brown tea which tasted flat and bitter, a taste that was now strange to him, and resisted the urge to ask the question that was uppermost in his mind. 'How was he before he disappeared?'

'Up and down,' Peggy said. 'He has his good days but he still gets very down in the dumps. Maybe it's my imagination but he seemed to be more depressed recently.'

'Was he working or anything?'

'No,' she said sharply. 'Sure, how could he?'

Callan imagined Willy in his wheelchair and thought that that was not necessarily a bar to work but he said nothing.

'He's still involved in the movement, if that's what you mean.' Peggy added. 'Not that he tells me anything about it, of course. Just the odd hint.'

'Doing what?'

'I haven't a clue. I don't ask.'

'Do you have any idea why he might have been more depressed?'

She shook her head. 'He's changed a lot from the time you used to know him. He's very edgy and touchy a lot of the time. I suppose he feels life's been unfair to him.'

Not life, Callan thought. Me. She must know how her brother came to have a bullet by his spine. There was nothing in what she said which imparted any blame to him but maybe that had something to do with her air of reserve. Or maybe I'm just being super sensitive, he thought, imposing my own guilt on her.

'How did you find out he was missing?' he asked.

'I usually drop down to see him every couple of days, do some shopping and cleaning up and so on,' she said. 'He wasn't there for about a week and I began to get worried. After the second week I called you.'

'When did he tell you how to find me?' Callan inquired, the question he had been waiting and wanting to ask.

'A couple of months ago. He gave me a slip of paper with a phone number and said it was yours. And I was to phone you if anything happened. You'd know what to do, he said.' She looked at him speculatively.

I'd know what to do, he repeated silently. But I don't. And I don't like the idea that anyone would think I do. 'What did he mean by that?' he asked aloud, for something to say.

'I thought you'd know,' she said.

He shook his head. 'I'm out of it now,' he said. 'I don't know anything.'

They lapsed into an uneasy silence, she disappointed by his response, he troubled by the feeling that somebody was trying to draw him back into things, into something he didn't understand. The phone number, he thought, how did Willy know it?

'When did he say this, give you the number?'

'Around Easter,' she said. 'Just after Easter, I think it was.'

'And that's all he said? That I'd know what to do?'

She nodded wearily, giving up on him. A pounding of running feet came round the side of the house and the back door burst open with a young boy demanding something to eat. Peggy snapped an irritable 'no' at him and got up and pushed him back outside. Callan could see some other children outside and then they all disappeared in another pounding of feet.

'Things have not been easy,' she said as she sat down again 'Willy is a constant worry at the best of times. He can't do a lot for himself, you know. And he resents anyone trying to help him, treating him as an invalid.'

Callan nodded. He could imagine Willy's anger: it must be very difficult for someone as active as he used to be to find himself in a wheelchair. But surely he had adjusted after all this time.

'And Jimmy doesn't want to know,' she added. 'He doesn't want anything to do with them. Wouldn't let Willy move in here with us. Doesn't even want me going to his flat to look after things. I have to do it without him knowing.'

Callan touched the back of her hand. 'I'll see what I can find out,' he said.

He sat down on the breakwater above the incoming tide, half-dozing as the jet lag caught up with him. The waves broke into slow eddies beneath him, lapping and overlapping on the beach, their rhythmic sound lulling the shrieks of children. The heat of the sun was fading as it dropped down to the west and the raw edge of the breeze from the sea kept him awake. Callan was not thinking about anything.

14

He shivered slightly and idly watched a boy of maybe twelve dancing delicately on the swirls of the broken waves. The boy was concentrating hard, his bare feet splatting the thin films of water in some intricate pattern. He tired of his internal game eventually and Callan watched him run along the tide line and up the dry sand to an elderly couple who looked like his grandparents.

It was only then that Callan realised what was unusual about him. He was wearing well-pressed grey trousers, obviously the bottom half of a suit, rolled neatly above his knees, and a white singlet. His formal dress made him stand out from all the other children in their jeans and teeshirts, a reminder of the past.

Callan watched, fascinated, as the elderly woman towelled his feet while the boy pulled on a shirt and began replacing his tie. That could have been me, Callan thought, that's how I looked here once. In my Sunday suit, the embodiment of my mother's image of a proper little man.

The elderly couple shook the sand from their rug and packed their towels and newspapers and a flask into a wicker basket. The woman smoothed the sand from the boy's clothes with her hand and jerked his jacket properly on to his shoulders. He walked by her side as they made their way up to the promenade

Callan watched them go and felt an urge to follow as they reached the promenade and merged among the strollers. He had a sudden certainty that they would go to an upright 1950s Ford Anglia for the drive home and that, if he followed, they would lead him back to the farm, to his own home. To once upon a time.

He didn't move for a long time; not until the sun was glaring levelly at him and it was time to meet Eoghan. The day trippers were gone and the holiday makers had retreated indoors and there were few people about as he followed his long shadow down the promenade towards the centre of Salthill.

The bay was an unmoving blue calm reaching over to the blue hills of Clare, broken only by the little outcrop of Mutton Island with its white lighthouse blinking ambitiously at the evening sun. The garish facades of the amusement centres and the singing lounges and the fast-food places were limbering up for the darkness, aware that their time was coming.

He followed the extension of the promenade curving round the unadorned backs of the buildings, wasting time, and turned back into

15

the resort's main street towards the hotel. He was five minutes late but he strolled leisurely past the building before doubling back and entering.

The compact lobby was empty and a mutter of conversations and clanking cutlery came from the crowded dining room. Callan went down a corridor to the copious bar and saw Eoghan sitting stiffly in a corner behind a round table. He was the only person there but disapproval seemed to radiate from him like a temperance preacher forced to witness convivial drinking. A metal teapot, jug, sugar bowl and two cups stood on the table.

Eoghan leapt to his feet as if he had seen his saviour. 'Fergus, a ghra.' He grasped Callan's outstretched hand with both of his own. 'Conas ata tu?'

'Fine.' Callan smiled back. 'And you?'

Eoghan nodded his round head repeatedly as though the question was particularly apt. His hair was shaved to a severe length and as grey as his bland face. He was wearing an over-used navy suit with a Pioneer pin flashing from the lapel like a beacon of rectitude. He looked like a nondescript clerk, worn out by a lifetime of drudgery in a large public body.

'I ordered some tea for you,' he said as he sat down. 'Unless you'd like something stronger?'

Callan glanced at the deserted bar, overhung with fishing nets and floats, and shook his head. 'Tea is just right,' he said, smiling inwardly at the memory of the time he provided protection for a briefing session at which Eoghan had a group of hard men sitting around sipping tea like a guild of the Irish Countrywomen's Association.

Eoghan stopped in mid-pour and looked at Callan, the teapot poised. 'It is good to see you,' he nodded and went back to filling the cup. 'You're making out all right?'

Callan nodded. 'Surviving.'

'That's the main thing.' Eoghan put the cup in front of Callan and passed him the milk and sugar. 'That's what it's all about now. Survival.'

A black-jacketed waiter raced in from the dining room, saw no one behind the bar and left in a hurry. The piped piano music tinkled a melodic ballad about Derry's troubles and Callan sipped his tea. The barman emerged from a door and lined four brandy glasses on the counter and the waiter returned and waited for him to measure the drinks.

'You're just visiting, I presume?' Eoghan was eyeing him through his round glasses.

Callan lit a cigarette. 'I need your help. I'm trying to find Willy Boyle. He's disappeared.'

'Disappeared?'

Callan told him briefly what Willy's sister had said. 'I've got to try and help her.'

Eoghan nodded absently. He knew how Willy had been crippled by an RUC bullet, saving Callan after a cocked-up ambush had turned into a chase. Callan was driving, headlights off, squinting down the speeding, winding road through the frosty starlight. The lights of the police car swept back and forth over them as it twisted between the high hedgerows, unshakable. Willy and another man were low in the back seat under the window, spider-webbed into crystals by a glancing bullet. Then they were in a short straight and the pursuit car had its lights full on them as Callan swung into another bend, momentarily blinded by a flash of light from the tilted wing mirror He reached for the light switch but it was too late.

The car cracked against a hedge and Callan jerked the wheel and it went out of control, twirling in a slow-motion half circle until it was going up the road backwards. It slunk into another hedge and a rear wheel dropped into a drain and the car jerked to a violent stop. Willy and the other man were out and into the ditch with the Armalites on automatic, blasting at the police car as it came round the bend. Callan was still slumped in the driving seat, stunned. The police car skewed to a sideways halt, one of its lights shot out, the other beaming into a frozen field, as Willy pulled Callan out. Callan staggered as his unprepared feet took his weight and Willy bent to grab him and was knocked on top of him by the bullet.

'That's why you're here?' Eoghan sounded surprised.

'Partly,' Callan said. 'Mainly. I owe it to Willy.'

'You're taking a terrible chance.' Eoghan shook his head.

'I've been careful,' Callan said defensively. 'Nobody knows I'm here. And I'm not staying long.'

'Still.' Eoghan let the word hang like an accusation while he poured himself another cup of tea. 'Don't misunderstand me,' he added as he tested the tea, 'it's admirable that you should be so concerned about an old comrade. But foolhardy, as well. You cannot take personal responsibility for things like that. The fortunes of war.'

Callan nodded, slightly embarrassed at the suggestion of his nobility. The older man's presumption was what he had expected from Sharon, was why he hadn't told her. It sounded too corny to be true. Which, of course, it was. Too corny to be the whole truth. Still, he did owe it to Willy.

'He did save my life,' Callan said uneasily.

'Yes. And you saved his, too. Don't forget that.'

Callan remembered their flight across the low hills into Monaghan, he and the other man half carrying, half dragging Willy along by the cover of the hedges. Willy had the sleeve of his combat jacket gripped in his teeth as he tried to silence the pain and way behind them they eventually heard the clatter of helicopters dropping in reinforcements. Yes, they had maybe saved Willy's life but it was not exactly a balanced equation.

'Besides,' Eoghan went on in his paternal tone, 'it was all a long time ago. There's been a lot of water under the bridge since then. Whatever Willy's problems are now, they're not of your making.'

Two couples came in laughing and sat up at the bar. The barman drew back from them with mock horror and said he never expected to see them back for more. Just for one, one of the men said in a strong Northern accent. The two women giggled.

'And you've got to remember your own situation.' Eoghan cast a disapproving glance at the bar and dropped his soft voice a further notch. He shook his head in sorrow. 'A bad business.'

'That was a long time ago, too.'

'Yes, but not forgotten.' His tone hardened. 'There are some things that can't be forgotten. Or forgiven.'

Callan shrugged. He didn't particularly want to get into a discussion about the past. What had been done had been done and couldn't be undone. He had long ago pushed the whys and wherefores of it all to the back of his mind and opted out. Understanding what had happened didn't change the consequences. Not for him.

'You know you were set up?'

'I know,' Callan said evenly.

'A bad business,' Eoghan repeated, disappointed in the way of the old at a younger person's lack of interest in reliving something from the past. 'A bad business.'

The bar was filling up as the dining room emptied and Callan turned the conversation to the fates of people he used to know. They sat among the holidaymakers talking of those who were dead, in jail, on the run. It wasn't only a lot of water that had passed under the bridge, Callan thought.

'You know that I've been, ah, retired?' Eoghan said with a slight smile that carried a cutting edge rather than humour. 'The movement took a wrong turn. Misled by people who think they know better than the lessons of history.' He sniffed. 'They will find out in time, of course. We can only hope they'll find out before they destroy everything, all the sacrifices.'

Callan said nothing. These weren't his battles any more: he had made his own decision a long time ago or, rather, it had been made for him by circumstances. He had no desire to become embroiled in the internal debates again, yet he felt an odd sense of loss at not being part of it any more. There was still a residual sense of companionship and common purpose with all the people they had talked about. He felt suddenly detached as he listened to Eoghan recite his well-worn cares.

'But,' Eoghan said, bringing himself back to the present, 'I still have some friends. I'll see what I can find out about Willy.'

'Thanks.'

'You'll be going to see your family,' Eoghan added, a statement of fact. 'I'll send word to you there.'

Callan was about to suggest some other arrangement but a burst of raucous laughter from a group of determined-looking drinkers drowned him out. Eoghan's assumption made up his mind, made a visit to his family seem such a natural and obvious thing to do. Anyway, he thought, that is part of why I'm here, too.

'You'll make it as soon as possible,' he pleaded. 'I don't have a lot of time.'

'I understand,' Eoghan nodded reassurance.

They parted in the corridor outside the bar and Eoghan disappeared towards the back of the building. Callan left by the front and strolled down to the seafront towards his car. The streets were busy with the roaming nightlife and the promenade was occupied only by couples. Beyond it, the bay was dark but the sky to the west still held a lingering light. His watch, still on Eastern Standard Time, showed it was almost five-thirty and he thought again about Sharon. She should be home from work about now and he stopped at a phone box, undecided.

He waited until a young woman finished her call and stepped into the box, still undecided. Slowly he read the instructions on how to make a long-distance call and rooted in his pocket for change. He found only one fifty-pence piece and realised with relief that he didn't have enough. It was probably too risky anyway, he told himself as he abandoned the booth to a group of teenagers. You never knew who might be listening in to international calls.

He reversed his car out of its parking space, his mind made up, and drove in through the city, heading eastwards, going home. On the radio, a news summary led with the wounding of two British soldiers by a roadside landmine in South Armagh. Suddenly, for the first time since he left Boston, he felt he was really back.

Three

Inspector George Keerins looked out the window over the superintendent's head to where the afternoon sun washed the parade ground. The flags around the memorial to gardai killed in the line of duty drooped as limply as his spirits. He still felt hot and tired after the three-hour drive back from Shannon and he shifted uneasily from one foot to the other, trying not to look and sound as stupid as he felt.

The superintendent was not making it any easier: he sat behind his desk and listened, unmoving, to the report about Callan's non-appearance. He did not invite Keerins to sit down.

Keerins finished with an account of how he had checked the passenger lists for the past week and the coming week's reservations from Boston. There was none in the name Callan was supposed to be using.

He stopped and the superintendent continued to look at him impassively, as if he might be suspect in some way. That was his style, Keerins reminded himself, or so everybody told him. He specialised in a taciturn formality, keeping everybody at a sceptical arm's length. It was nothing personal but it was difficult not to feel that it was. Especially when Keerins was still trying to get to grips with this job.

He had been promoted into the security section of garda headquarters two months earlier, thanks to one piece of good fortune and his former mentor in the central detective unit. Security is where it's all at, his mentor had advised him, you should do a stint there if you want to get anywhere. Keerins did want to get somewhere but his initial delight at the transfer had turned to doubt. He had been left to his own devices, given nothing much to do and told practically nothing about what was going on. He felt like an unwelcome intruder in a long-established club.

'I'll get back to my informant,' Keerins said to break the silence. There was nothing else he could do. He had always known Callan was a make or break job, a high-profile operation that would either establish his reputation or leave him even more isolated. 'Find out what went wrong.'

The superintendent stirred. He lifted a photocopy from his desk and held it out. 'Arrived this morning,' he said.

Keerins glanced at it quickly. It was an extradition warrant from the RUC and asked that Fergus Callan be sent to Northern Ireland to be tried for the murder of a member of the Ulster Defence Regiment twelve years ago. The warrant had been sworn before a magistrate in Belfast the previous day.

'How did they know?' he blurted out in surprise.

The superintendent nodded.

'Were they informed officially?'

The superintendent shook his head and held his questioning gaze while Keerins tried to formulate the implications of that into another question, feeling his way mentally. He didn't want to appear ignorant or, worse, naïve.

'Does that mean,' he began but was interrupted by a phone ringing. The superintendent listened for a moment and put his hand over the mouthpiece. 'That's all,' he said to Keerins, dismissing him.

Keerins took the photocopy with him and made his way slowly back to his own corner of the general office, still trying to work out what the extradition request really meant and what he was supposed to do about it. It had nothing to do with actually capturing Callan. It was a red herring, as far as he could see.

Sergeant Pursell watched him approach with a crooked smile that seemed to say, I knew it. Pushing fifty, he responded to everything with the knowing air of someone who had seen it all before and always knew it would be a fuck-up. 'Good journey?' he asked with a smirk that turned the question into sarcasm.

Keerins shook his head quickly with the wary formality which he had adopted towards Pursell. The sergeant was a reminder of the days when policemen were recruited for their intimidating presence, physical symbols of law and order. His heavy face was dominated by a large nose which had been broken several times, more often as a disco bouncer than in the course of his official duties. He delighted in a crude physicality which made Keerins uneasy: he didn't know what to make of him most of the time.

'Touts,' Pursell nodded, as if the word explained everything. 'Archie was just giving you the old run around.'

Archie was the weedy little Dubliner, part-time musician, part-time drug dealer, who was the source of Keerin's information about Callan.

Keerins nodded vaguely, not sure whether Pursell was offering his commiserations in his elliptical way. He took Callan's file from the drawer of his desk and slotted his picture back into it with an air of finality.

'Maybe we should pay him a little visit,' Pursell grinned, stretching his fingers. 'Tune his strings for him.'

'I'll handle that,' Keerins said quickly. Vicious thoughts about Archie had occupied his mind all the way back from Shannon but Archie was still his. When it came down to it, Archie was the only thing he had going for him. Which might be pathetic. But he had to deal with him himself.

The direct phone on his desk rang and he grabbed at it as thought it would answer all the unanswered questions that were piling up around him.

'You're back,' Deirdre said brightly, as a greeting. 'I've been listening to the news all day but I haven't heard anything yet.'

'There's nothing to hear.' He made no attempt to curb the impatience in his voice, wishing she wouldn't talk about his official activities over the phone. He told her more about them than he should because he felt he owed it to her to relieve her house-bound isolation. And anyway he had to talk to someone: there was nobody in the office with whom he could properly discuss anything.

'Oh,' she said.

'How are things?' he softened his tone. It wasn't fair to take it all out on her. He passed the extradition warrant to Pursell who had perched himself on the side of the desk, making no pretence at not listening. Deirdre talked about the children's doings and he told her he would be home for tea.

Keerins straightened himself to his full height and looked down at Pursell. 'What do you make of that?' he nodded at the photocopy.

'They'll be fucking lucky,' Pursell snorted.

'It seems strange,' Keerins said tentatively, trying to draw out Pursell's advice without asking for it directly. He knew Pursell did not approve of him, didn't consider him to be one of the lads because of his degree in business administration and his early promotion. 'That the RUC should send us a warrant now for Callan's extradition.'

'Politics,' Pursell shrugged. 'Probably sending us a load of pointless warrants so that some politician can get up and accuse us of being bad boys. Letting terrorists roam the streets with impunity.'

'Some coincidence, though,' Keerins added, 'that it should turn up the very day that Callan was supposed to come back.'

23

Pursell nodded pensively. 'Archie,' he said. 'You think he's flogging them the same information?'

'Maybe,' Keerins replied. At least that possibility was more reassuring than the other obvious one – that someone in the gardai had passed on the information. That the RUC had a spy in the gardai. Presumably that was why the superintendent had given him the warrant, to check it out with Archie.

'I don't get it anyway,' Keerins added. 'The RUC must know we couldn't extradite him. We want him too badly ourselves.'

'Sure,' Pursell nodded. 'They're welcome to him in forty years' time. What's left of him.'

Forty years in jail without remission was the price the government extracted for commuting the mandatory death sentence for the murder of a garda. Keerins looked at Callan's file and added forty years to his age: he'd be nearly eighty when he was released. It was like talking of millions of pounds, Keerins thought; beyond any meaningful comprehension. Extradition would be pretty academic by then, for him and for me.

'Forty years is too good for him,' Pursell added. 'Scum like that should be hanged by the neck. Like the law says. And they would be too, if the politicians had any balls.'

'Did you know Maher?' Keerins asked, wondering at his vehemence.

'A decent man,' Pursell nodded. 'And a very good detective. Which was why they shot him down in cold blood. Without a moment's notice.'

'I remember the murder,' Keerins said. He had been a young uniformed garda, doing his degree at night, when Maher was killed by a single bullet fired from a vantage point a hundred yards from where he was standing by his car near the border. Keerins remembered the shock throughout the force and the initial fears that it was the start of an IRA campaign against Southern policemen. 'But I didn't know him.'

'He was a good footballer one time,' Pursell said, inconsequentially. 'Someone told me recently that his eldest lad's joined the force, a recruit in Templemore.'

He would have been younger than his own son when his father was shot, Keerins calculated. He thought he remembered television pictures of a grieving boy at the graveside buy maybe that had been another funeral.

'Ah, well,' Pursell took a sudden interest in his watch and lurched to his feet, 'you win some, lose some.'

'We might get Callan yet,' Keerins offered grimly.

'Worth a try,' Pursell assured him as he left.

Keerins sat down at his desk and leafed idly through the file, a catalogue of suspicions about Callan's subversive activities. He was known to be a sniper, probably responsible for a dozen deaths or woundings. There had never been any hard evidence, however; nothing substantial enough to get him before a court. He had been hauled in for questioning five times under the Offences Against the State Act, spending the forty-eight hours in custody with his eyes fixed on an imaginary spot on the wall, blanking out his interrogators behind his impenetrable concentration.

Keerins sighed and took the file and the copy of the extradition warrant and locked them in a cabinet. There was no doubt that Callan had murdered Maher: informants said so and, more importantly, he had left his thumb mark on a five-bar gate beside the sniper's position. They had him on that one. If they could catch him.

He made one brief phone call before he joined the tail end of the rush hour as the city emptied into its suburbs.

'So, what happens now?' Deirdre inquired, concern shadowing her naturally happy face.

'Find you what went wrong,' Keerins said. 'It's not finished yet.' Not by a long shot, he thought. There might be more ways than one of getting Callan. Find out where he was and have him deported or extradited from the US. And he had to check out this other extradition matter.

Deirdre got up from the table and stood behind him, resting her bare elbows on his shoulders and her chin on his head. Her caramel hair, still youthfully long, fell down over his eyes and enclosed him behind a protective curtain.

'You've done everything you could,' she said.

He tipped his head back and kissed her lightly on the lips, upside-down. There was a bang on the window and James and Fiona were smiling in at them, faces squashed against the glass. They ran away with whoops of delight as Keerins shook his fist at them.

He sat at the table for a while, feeling lethargic, as Deirdre cleared away the remains of the salad. He stirred himself eventually and told her he was going out for a short run, to wake himself up. She looked at him quizzically.

'I've got to go into town in a while,' he explained. 'Get to the bottom of all this.'

He changed into his running gear and went out the front door and jogged up the footpath. All the children of the neighbourhood, as old as the semi-detached houses, seemed to be out on the paths and the lawns. A neighbour was peering under the bonnet of a car, standing immobile in the calm stillness. Someone somewhere was pushing a lawnmower, its grating blades adding to the stretched peace of the perfect evening.

James broke away from a group of children and ran a short distance with him, offering to race. Keerins shook his head and let his steady footfalls set the pace of his thoughts. He always found jogging to be an aid to thinking.

Maybe I would have been better off sticking with ordinary crime, he thought, getting more experience there. He had enjoyed the work and the sense of camaraderie that existed in the unit: in retrospect, it seemed satisfyingly straightforward. At least, they were not burdened with the excessive secrecy that seemed to dominate the security branch where nobody seemed to tell each other anything. Nor with the intricacies of battling with well-organised conspirators like the IRA. The stakes were a lot higher and the work a whole lot more bewildering.

He reached the end of the cul-de-sac and ran down a small embankment to the fence that separated the estate from the public playing fields. He vaulted the wire, one hand on a wooden post, without breaking stride. The shouts of players from a distant game of energetic soccer carried clearly across the fields. Nearby, two men were smacking a hurling ball high to each other up and down half the length of the Gaelic pitch.

He wondered if he should have a chat with his former mentor in the ordinary crime unit, seek his advice. But it would not be politic, he decided: his mentor's close identification with the present leadership of the Garda Siochana was a double-edged sword. It had ensured his promotion but might also be a factor in his present problems. The superintendent belonged to the other unofficial, but clearly defined, camp within the force. It didn't help to be too closely identified with either group; especially if you didn't want your long-term ambitions to be thwarted by the vagaries of internal politics.

There was nothing for it but to slog it out on his own, he decided. But it would be a great help if the superintendent ever told anybody what he really thought. That was supposed to be the secret of his success: he gathered everything to himself and shared nothing. But it made life very difficult, especially for a newcomer.

He completed a circuit of the pitch and vaulted the fence back into the housing estate. Back home, he had a quick shower, gathered the children from the road and left the house as they went to bed 'Be careful,' Deirde said lightly, a semi-superstitious admonition she had adopted since his promotion.

He drove slowly but still arrived in the city centre too early. He crossed over Butt Bridge and took a delaying loop up Cathal Brugha Street and down O'Connell Street where the traffic lights finally halted him on the bridge. The low sun stretched lazily down the Liffey from the west, splitting the city in two like a natural divide between Dublin's fashionable and unfashionable halves and brightening the shabby quays into a golden picture postcard. It shone in his eyes as he turned into Dame Street and checked the time: he was still a few minutes early but no longer too early.

Up near the city hall, the bulk of Christchurch cathedral finally blocked out the sun and he could see Archie already waiting at the bus stop. He was swaying impatiently against the narrow pole and holding his guitar case upright as though it was a weapon. Which, Keerins thought, was the way he played it; hammering out the chords like he was laying down a field of fire.

The brake lights glowed on the car in front as the traffic lights at the city hall changed and Keerins stopped. He watched Archie's wiry frame and wondered idly if he was still carrying pot in the case. A double-decker bus careered out of Parliament Street just as the lights changed and heaved itself up the hill in a cloud of diesel smoke.

Keerins cursed aloud as it stopped and Archie got on board. It would take almost half an hour to get to the second pick-up point. His irritation grew as he cruised behind the bus. When it came down to it, his whole career now rested on this little fucker who was about as trustworthy as a stick of weeping gelignite.

Keerins had stopped him one night when Archie was riding a light motorbike with the guitar case propped precariously between the handlebars and his shoulder. He had no helmet, no insurance for the borrowed bike and inside the guitar he had a small cube of foil-wrapped hashish. Keerins took him to the station and into an interview room and questioned him about the drug.

'Ah, it's only a little bit for myself,' Archie twitched and screwed up his pinched face in a hopeless attempt to make it look honest. 'Swear to God. It was a Christmas present.'

'From Santa Claus?'

'The girlfriend.'

'What's her name?'

'I couldn't tell you that,' Archie pleaded. 'I don't want to get her into trouble. It's only a little bit.'

'Balls,' Keerins snapped. 'You're a courier.'

Archie shook his head vigorously. 'I'm a singer. I swear to God, I've got nothing to do with drugs. I never touch them and I haven't even touched this little bit. I've had it for weeks and never even looked at it. Look at it yourself. Hasn't been touched.'

'I think,' Keerins said solemnly, 'we better get the drugs squad over here.'

'Hold on,' Archie leapt in the chair as if it was electrified. 'Listen.' He settled down. 'I can get you some good information. If we can forget about this.'

'No deals,' Keerins said. 'You're in deep shit.'

'Really heavy stuff,' Archie squinted at him, holding his eyes.

Keerins shook his head. 'There's nothing judges like more than jailing pushers these days. They're competing with each other to give the longest sentences.'

'About the IRA.'

'You're in that too, are you?' Keerins snorted.

Archie denied it impatiently and something in his demeanour made Keerins hesitate. Archie told him that an IRA arms shipment was due from the United States and he could get the details. Keerins still wasn't sure why he had gone against all his own instincts and let Archie go. But Archie had turned up the information and the arms had arrived in a container, documented as machine parts like he said. The gardai had got an M60 machine-gun, twenty-five Armalites, two men and a lot of publicity. Keerins had got promotion and his transfer to security.

28

Keerins slowed down and let the bus draw away from him. Archie was walking up the footpath as he turned into the road of terraced corporation houses and stopped beside him. Archie went through his usual ritual, bending down to see who was in the car, feigning surprise, and then tossed his guitar on to the back seat and sat in the front.

'How's it going,' he said chirpily and blew a cloud of cigarette smoke at the 'no smoking' circle on the dashboard.

Keerins ignored him and swung the car into a tight U-turn. He accelerated back the way he had come.

'Hey,' Archie yelped. 'Where're you going?'

'Down town,' Keerins said grimly.

'But we're on stage in half an hour.'

'You'll be charged in half an hour.'

'Ah, Jesus, Mr Keerins,' Archie whined. 'You can't do that. We have a deal.'

'Had.' Keerins snarled at him. 'You broke it.'

Archie fell silent for a moment. 'The fucker didn't show,' he nodded to himself.

'Surprise, surprise.'

'I wasn't bullshitting you. I swear to God.' Archie turned and almost stuck his face between Keerins and the windscreen. 'The information was good.'

'That's only the half of it,' Keerins growled.

'What do you mean?'

'You've been selling this so-called information to other people too.' Keerins glanced at him with disgust. 'Trying to maximise your profits?'

'What profits?' Archie flicked his eyes nervously over Keerin's face. 'What the fuck are you talking about?'

'You're playing a dangerous game.'

'What?' Archie screamed.

'Passing stuff across the border. To the RUC.'

Archie started at him, dumbfounded. 'You think I'm mad?' he asked.

'Just greedy.'

'You must be fucking joking.' Archie sank back into his seat and shook his head in amazement. He dragged on his cigarette as if it contained something more potent than tobacco. 'Look,' he added without any of his usual exuberance. 'I don't know what you're talking about. But I don't like the sound of it. I'm taking enough of a chance talking to you without talking to anyone else.'

Keerins stopped the car suddenly and stared through the windscreen at the road ahead, his hands over the steering wheel. 'I have to meet your source,' he said after a moment. 'Face to face.'

'Oh, no,' Archie recoiled. 'That's not on.'

'I've got to,' Keerins turned to him.

'No way.' Archie squirmed with the defeated air of someone accustomed to life's unfairness. 'Take me in, if you want to. But that's not on.'

Keerins sighed in frustration. It was ridiculous that his whole career should be dependent on this little gurrier, that he didn't even know where his information came from. Archie, as far as was known, was just what he seemed to be; a small-time drugs dealer. He was not involved with the IRA but claimed to get his information from someone who was. The arms seizure supported his story and proved that the real source of the information was very well placed. But it was still an unsatisfactory arrangement, as the Callan case proved.

'That's what I'm supposed to do. Take you in,' Keerins lied. 'Charge you with passing information to a foreign government.'

'Jesus Christ! You'll have us all killed. Is that what you want?' Archie squinted at him. 'Have me found up the fucking mountains with a bag over my head? Some thanks for all I've done for you.' He wound down his window a crack and tossed out his cigarette. 'You know what these fuckers are like. Think nothing of plugging me and the source. Is that really what you want? Two deaths on your conscience?'

Keerins forced himself to laugh. 'You don't worry about my conscience, Archie. I've told you what I want. I've got to meet this source. That's the only way out of the mess you've landed me in.'

'I'd love him to do that. Let me out from under all this shit.' Archie lit another cigarette and coughed on a lungful of smoke. 'I've pleaded with him. Talk to Mr Keerins yourself, I said. He'll look after you.' He waved his hands in despair at being caught in the midst of such unreasonable people.

'And what'd he say?'

'No way. It's not safe, he said The Provos have their own contacts in the guards. Which makes me feel very fucking happy,' Archie added bitterly.

'Who?' Keerins swore silently. That was great: the bloody force seemed to be riddled with spies. He quickly ran through the handful of people who knew about Archie and told himself that there was no cause for alarm. Still, the RUC had got to know about Callan which was hardly reassuring. Maybe he should learn a lesson from the superintendent: tell nobody anything in future.

'I don't know.'

'Well, you don't need to worry,' Keerins said with more confidence than he felt.

'And what's all this about the RUC?' Archie demanded. 'I don't like the sound of that.'

'Somebody told them about Callan,' Keerins shrugged. 'I thought it was you.'

'It wasn't.'

'Then you've got nothing to worry about.'

Archie seemed to accept that, although Keerins didn't feel so sanguine on his behalf. He had a lot to worry about. And so have I, he told himself. It wasn't beyond the bounds of possibility that Archie's source was also the RUC's. Nothing seemed beyond the bounds of possibility: the whole business was turning into a tangled mess.

'The source,' Keerins said. 'Ask him again to meet me.'

'OK,' Archie sighed. 'But it's a waste of time. He won't take any chances.'

'Tell him he owes it to me. He volunteered the information about Callan in the first place.'

'OK. Right.'

'And ask him about Callan,' Keerins added. 'Why he was supposed to come back. Why he didn't turn up. Where he's living, what name he's using, what he's up to these days. Anything he can tell us about him.'

'OK, OK,' Archie said doubtfully. 'But don't blame me if he doesn't say anything. I'm only the messenger. Right?'

Keerins reversed the car into a driveway and drove back towards the pub where Archie's group were playing their weekly gig. 'There is another way you could get out from under all this,' he said slowly and glanced at Archie. 'Tell me where to find him.'

'Sure I will.' Archie gave a humourless laugh. 'As soon as I want to commit suicide.'

'Why does he do it?' Keerins asked, hoping to wheedle some kind of pointer out of Archie to the source's identity.

Archie shrugged. 'I don't know. We don't have any heart to hearts. He just tells me what to tell you.'

Keerins pulled into the curb near the pub. 'You'll come back to me? As soon as possible?'

'Yeah, yeah,' Archie said impatiently, like a child being told something by a teacher after class had officially ended.

He got out and opened the back door to retrieve his guitar. 'You know what?' he grinned across the back of the seat, once more his bouncy self now that the troublesome business was over. 'There's a talent scout coming to see us tonight. From a London record company. A Mr John Amber.'

Keerins stared at him. He had gone out of curiosity one night to watch the Rambling Boyos perform and listened to Archie belting out the ballads in a reedy voice that he fancied was plaintive. There were as awful as he had suspected and he decided they'd never rise above venues where most of the audience was drunk.

'What d'you think of that, now?' Archie winked broadly. 'The Dubliners better watch out.'

He slammed the door and Keerins watched him swagger away.

Four

Callan woke to the clanging of milk churns and lay listening to the guttural chugging of the tractor until it had gone down the lane and faded. He looked around slowly at the faded pink floral wallpaper, the picture of the Sacred Heart, the parallel lines of the two bookshelves. The room was airless and filled with the reflected glow of the sun, already well up in the sky.

He slid out of the bed and drew back the thin curtains and let down the top half of the window. The cool morning air came in, carrying the chirping of birds and the sweet smells of the farmyard. The fields were a heavy, almost luminous, green, squared off by dense hedges. A line of evergreen trees stood stiffly to one side as a windbreak, temporarily redundant A large oak stood alone on an exposed rise, its leafy branches leaning away from the western winds that had smoothed one side like the back of a head.

It was like he had remembered it, tighter but brighter, more vivid.

He dressed in jeans and a sweatshirt and went downstairs to the kitchen. A place was set at one end of the table and his mother was working at the sink. The endless middle-age in which she had always seemed to be had given way to old age: her hair was grey, her body had shrunk and her movements slowed down.

'You're up,' she turned to him as if she, too, was examining him for the first time.

'I heard Brendan going off to the creamery,' he said.

She dried her hands and hobbled over to the range. 'I don't know what got into him last night.' She shook her head.

'It was a shock for him, I suppose.' He sat down at the table as she moved a pan on to the hot plate and laid some bacon and sausages on it.

His mother had shown pleasure rather than surprise at his arrival, a glistening in her eyes as she hugged him, as if her prayers had been answered. But Brendan had come home from the pub, slightly drunk, and turned aggressive when he found Callan there. 'What the fuck do you want?' he demanded. She had tried to quieten him but her upset had only fanned his anger. 'You have some neck,' he said. 'Coming back after all this time.'

Callan had said nothing, taken aback by his brother's appearance more than his words. Brendan had turned into a big-framed farmer and seemed to have settled into a dour middle-age. He looked years older than Callan rather than the other way round.

He had stomped off and left them alone. Callan asked his mother about relatives, neighbours, anyone he could remember; keeping her talking to smooth over the awkwardness. Eventually, he went to his old bedroom and spent an hour fingering through the bookshelves and the old school and college notebooks.

'I don't know what's the matter with him at all these days,' she sighed as she put the breakfast in front of him. She poured a little milk into two cups and filled them with steaming tea, automatically. 'He's getting very fond of the drink.' She sat down.

'No sign of him getting married?' he asked lightly and immediately regretted it. That was not a subject he should have brought up.

'He was doing a line with one of the Brady girls but that's fallen through. He spends most of his time in the pub now.' She paused and studied the oil cloth and he knew what she was going to say. 'Do you ever see Maire and Shay?'

He shook his head and ate some bacon.

'It's strange,' she said, 'to have a grandson that you've never seen.'

'I know,' he said sympathetically. It was strange, too, to have a son you had only seen once as an infant, a bland relaxed face in a zipped-up sleeping bag. Maire had been lifted and jailed in Northern Ireland shortly after they married and Shay was born in Armagh prison. Her parents brought him up in the North and it had always been too risky for Callan to visit. At least, that had been his excuse.

'I sent a birthday card last month,' his mother said, matter of fact. 'His eleventh. I send one every year but I've never heard anything back.'

Callan nodded absently. That didn't surprise him. He had last met Maire's parents, the only time he had seen the child, at a tense meeting in the lounge of a hotel in Dundalk. They had made plain their disapproval over his treatment of their daughter: made it plain, too, that he wouldn't see the baby again unless he mended his ways. Somebody had been telling them stories, Callan thought.

'You haven't married again or anything?' his mother asked.

He shook his head, preferring to leave her in ignorance.

She was determined, however, to find out something about his present life. 'What are you doing for a living?' she persisted.

This and that, he told her; mostly construction work, decorating, landscaping. He tried to make them sound more interesting, more substantial than they were, covering up the succession of menial, under-the-counter jobs with excessive enthusiasm. It was a good living, he nodded sombrely, as if he was playing down a high-powered appointment.

'It's a pity you never finished your degree,' she said, not fooled.

'It's a living,' he shrugged, dropping the pretence. 'I get by.' Which was all that could be said for his life in Boston. It was an achievement of sorts, surviving so long as an illegal immigrant with no hope of ever becoming legal, forever facing a harsher penalty than the simply prospect of deportation. Except that getting by wasn't enough any more.

After breakfast he strolled through the farmyard and the fields, spotting childhood landmarks in the hay barn and the turf shed and among the trees and the ditches. Places where they had played hide and seek and cowboys and Indians and set snares for hares and sometimes for foxes. A warm breeze swept audibly over the land, rippling across a field of barley like squalls on the ocean and humming in the telephone wires by the road at the edge of the farm.

A youth went by on a bicycle, a Walkman clipped to his belt and headphones clamped to his ears. He nodded to Callan and burst into a robust song as he rounded a bend, singing along with his private music. Callan smiled at the incongruity of it: he hadn't expected the Walkman to have taken hold here. It didn't seem right somehow.

He settled down on the bank of a small stream and watched the current trickling among the stones as energetically as if it was a major river in full flood, undeterred by its minuscule power. A little cloud of dust rose in a still pool to one side and when he looked closely he could see the darting shadows of the pinkeens.

He lay back in the rough grass and looked up into the huge blue cavern of the cloudless sky, letting his mind roam free, feeling totally at peace. The thin white streak of a jet trail seemed to be climbing straight upwards as it cruised towards North America and he remembered watching those trails as a young teenager, wondering what it was like to be up there, if he would ever find out.

Maybe this is all I need, he thought. A holiday. A change of scene to relieve the listless dissatisfaction, the overwhelming pointlessness of everything.

I was right, he told himself, totally certain, to come here.

'It wasn't Archie,' Inspector Keerins said emphatically. 'I'm ninety-nine per cent certain he didn't do it.'

The superintendent grunted. They were walking briskly across the parade ground, on their way to the superintendent's car. He was off to an unspecified meeting, wearing an executive pin stripe and carrying an expensively new briefcase. He looked and behaved like a managing director.

'So it seems,' Keerins offered cautiously, 'that, ah, it may have been somebody on our side who passed it on. A mole.'

'That's a polite word for him,' the superintendent said grimly.

Keerins nodded, not sure what to say but satisfied that he had been right. 'Do we know who it is?' he asked.

'Not unless you do.' The superintendent gave him an inquiring glance and Keerins shook his head quickly.

'Find out,' the superintendent said in an executive tone. 'List everybody who knew about it. When they were told, by whom. Anyone anywhere who might have overheard anything.'

'Right,' Keerins said eagerly.

'And don't let anybody know,' the superintendent said. 'Not anybody.'

Keerins nodded. They were still a short way from the Ford Granada and he wondered if he should mention Archie's fears about IRA spies within the gardai. The Super seemed to be in an unusually receptive mood but he decided not to: there was nothing concrete to say. Instead, he told him he had tried to persuade Archie to put him in direct contact with his IRA source. 'I suppose I can't blame him,' he added as they reached the car. 'It's more than his life is worth.'

'That's what they always say.' The superintendent unlocked the door and tossed his briefcase onto the passenger seat. He straightened up as if he had something on his mind.

'We could put surveillance on him. Let him lead us to his source,' Keerins suggested quickly, to show that he had been thinking about the problem. 'But that'd be risky. I think we owe it to him not to put him in danger unnecessarily. He's given us good information before.'

The superintendent merely nodded and got in behind the wheel. Keerins stepped back as he drove off and watched the security barrier at the gate rise to let the car out.

He walked back to his office with a sense of satisfaction and purpose. That was the first half-decent conversation he had ever had with the Super. And he now had something definite to do other than wait helplessly for Archie to come up with some snivelling excuses.

Callan crossed the field with a flask of tea and a packet of ham sandwiches, heading for the groaning drone of the tractor. It was cutting another swathe through the long grass, spewing it out through a high spout into the high-sided trailer behind. The scent of newly cut grass rose as densely as a fog from the cropped meadow.

Another man was standing on the step of the tractor and Brendan was driving. He could hear their voices raised in laughter but they stopped talking as he approached. Brendan killed the engine and they both jumped down.

'Fergus,' the man said, automatically wiping his hand on his trousers before offering it. Callan shook it, recognising the slyly deferential look while he searched the man's face for some clue to his identity. It had been a long time since he had been given that knowing look the unspoken recognition of a kind of celebrity status. Brendan poured some tea and passed a cup and a sandwich to the man. He leaned against the tractor and ignored Callan.

'You brought the good weather with you,' the man offered.

'Isn't it always like this?' Callan smiled.

'Not around here it's not.' The man cleared a sheen of sweat from his forehead with his sleeve. 'No weather to be working.'

Callan thought he recognised him now; one of the Bradys, a brother of Brendan's former girlfriend. He searched his memory for a first name but failed to find it. 'How's your family?' he inquired politely.

'Grand,' the man said. 'You remember Sean? He was in your class in school.' Callan nodded uncertainly, trying to visualise him. 'He's in the States too.' A shadow of apprehension flitted across his face at what he had said and he turned his attention to his sandwich.

'Yes?' Callan said, to put him at his ease. He wondered idly if the man had known about his general whereabouts before or had just picked up on it now from his accent. 'Which part?'

'New York.'

Callan said nothing and the silence stretched out like the long afternoon. The breeze had died and they could hear a rumble of traffic from a distant main road.

'Does anybody cut hay around here any more?' he asked, his mind on dead days like this when they used to sink down to rest against the prickly cocks and drink tea and listen to his father re-tell his well-worn stories.

Brendan snorted disdain and climbed back into the cab. The man shook his head and said it was all silage now. The engine fired with a cloud of dirty diesel smoke and Callan took the flask and the discarded paper and walked away. They were talking again as the tractor lurched into gear.

The house was cool and gloomy and he went into the kitchen and rinsed the flask into the sink. He balanced it upside down on the draining board and leaned back against the counter. A vacuum cleaner hummed upstairs and he wandered slowly through the ground-floor rooms, ending up in the parlour.

The air was musty and the furniture seemed to have grown tired from lack of use. A Paul Henry print of purple mountains and lakes hung over the fireplace, a polished cabinet and bookshelves lined one wall and an old-fashioned radiogram rested against the other. It all seemed to belong to another time. His father's time.

He switched on the radiogram and the radio dial lit up and began to hum as the valves warmed up. He picked the first record from the small pile stacked at one end of the player and lifted the lid and settled it on to the long finger. The machine clicked and dropped the record on to the turntable.

Callan moved around the room as John McCormack sang 'Down By The Sally Gardens', his scratchy voice creating a tangible nostalgia. His father had come in here alone every Sunday afternoon and spent reverential hours listening to his records. Nobody ever sat in with him and Callan wondered whether that had been his wish or just the way it was, an accepted fact in the way family things became accepted facts. The music had been a permanent part of Sundays, suffusing the whole house and seeping into the yard, like football commentaries on the radio were in neighbours' houses.

He stopped at the cabinet where his parents' wedding photograph rested in a dark frame: they looked younger than their years, his mother's broad smile, his father's earnest expression giving them an aura of trusting innocence. He opened a drawer underneath and saw a pile of remembrance cards piled neatly in a corner. Blessed are they that mourn, the cover said, for they shall be comforted.

He took one and settled into his father's chair and turned the folded card over, examining the picture of the Virgin Mary on the back as though it contained a clue to something important. Then he opened it and studied the small, slightly fuzzy picture of his father, cropped from a group photograph. His strong features were faded into vague outlines under a heavy shock of dark hair. He was wearing a flower in his button hole.

My Lord and my God, it said. In loving memory of Thomas Callan who died on 28 November.

Callan looked at the date, sinking back in memory to that time. It was the day after the Maher operation but he hadn't heard about his father's death until a couple of days later, informed, almost casually, by a man who was driving him to another safe house. The bare countryside had been powdered with frost as he was bundled time and again from one place to another, like the prize at the centre of a real-life game of pass the parcel.

His father's death had seemed almost a minor matter then, of lesser importance than his own immediate fate. Everything had suddenly slipped out of his control; he was hunted for killing a target whose real identity he hadn't known, sheltered by people who had misled him into thinking he was sniping somebody else. It was a chaotic situation and he was running so hard he had no time to strip away the layers of deception. All that seemed irrelevant now, less immediate than his father's death as he sat in his armchair with the crackling music washing over him. He felt a rugged of regret for his own past insensitivity.

Callan sighed and glanced through the pious phrases in the card. Crucified Lord Jesus, have mercy on the souls in Purgatory. The words, once familiar from their automatic incantation, seemed to have a distant, alien quality, like something from a barely understood culture. Jesus, Mary and Joseph, assist me in my last agony.

He closed his eyes and drifted back into childhood memories of religion, of serving mass and being a small acolyte in the sombre rituals of funerals and of holy week ceremonies, remembering the smells of incense and the sounds of coughing, crowded congregations.

'There you are.' His mother stood in the doorway, taking in the remembrance card in his hand, the clicking of the finished record. 'The tea is ready.'

He pushed the card into the back pocket of his jeans and followed her into the kitchen.

The telephone shrilled in the dark and Deirdre shook him out of a confused dream in which a phone was ringing and he fumbled at the receiver.

'Mr Keerins?' Archie said in a breathless whisper. 'He's here.'

'What?' Keerins pulled himself up on one elbow and squinted at the radio alarm as if it was important to know the time. The green figures shifted almost imperceptibly and said 2:37.

'He did come after all,' Archie said in triumph. 'Like I told you.'

'Callan?'

'The one and only. He's here.'

'Where?' Keerins swung his bare legs from under the duvet and sat up, alert. 'Where are you?'

'Not right here,' Archie said quickly and went quiet. Keerins could hear animated voices in the background and a snatch of a woman's voice saying 'not in a million years'. Archie breathed deeply and whispered: 'He's in the country.'

'Where?' Keerin's raised voice broke the bedroom stillness.

'I don't know exactly.' Keerins swore. 'Hold on, will you?' Archie said. 'But I know where he's going to be tomorrow evening. At seven o'clock. He's supposed to meet somebody, another' – Archie's voice dropped – 'one of them.'

'For fuck's sake, where?'

'Connemara.'

'Connemara?'

'Yeah,' Archie said as if he was dealing with a particularly dense person. 'A lay-by beside a lake. Near Maam Cross.'

Keerins thought for a moment. 'Can't you be more precise?'

'I don't know that neck of the woods myself,' Archie said. 'That's what I was told.'

Keerins sighed. 'Where's he coming from? Which direction?'

'I haven't a clue. That's all I was told. But you better be careful. I mean I was told to tell you to watch out. He's . . .' Archie stopped as another voice called his name and demanded another joint: he muffled

40

the mouthpiece quickly. 'He's desperate. Know what I mean?' He put down the phone.

Keerins reached for his clothes and began to get dressed.

Five

The sun was still hidden behind the barn and Callan shivered in the cool morning shadows of the farmyard. The sound of running water and the scraping of a yard bush came from the milking parlour and he went over and watched Brendan at work.

'Can I give you a hand?' he asked after a while.

Brendan continued pushing a small tide of dirty water towards a concrete channel. He stopped and watched it drain away. 'You can take her to the church,' he said. 'If you want something to do.'

Callan sighed. His mother had mentioned the funeral over breakfast, some old man whose name he had already forgotten. He had a good innings, she said, would have been eighty-four next month.

'I can't do that,' he said.

Brendan snorted as if he had just proved a point. 'I see your friends struck another blow for freedom this morning,' he said sarcastically.

'What?' Callan didn't want to get into this kind of discussion but he did want to talk to Brendan.

'Maimed a young girl on her way to school.' Brendan looked at him aggressively. 'A bomb in a litter bin.'

Callan thought about the inevitable casualties of guerilla warfare. No doubt it had been an unfortunate accident but he said nothing. There was no point getting into an argument about the IRA.

Brendan walked across the yard and Callan followed him to a shed where he put the brush alongside other implements.

'Do you remember the time you were nearly smothered by the turf?' Callan asked. They had climbed up on the turf, up under the galvanised roof of the shed and scooped out a deep hole. Brendan had been in it when the sides collapsed and almost buried him.

'No,' Brendan said. He turned to face Callan and put his hands on his hips in an unconscious gesture of defiance. 'She's signing over the place to me.'

Callan almost laughed aloud. So that's it, he thought. That explains everything. He's afraid I've come back to claim my inheritance. The idea was so impractical as to be ludicrous.

'I assumed you'd taken it over years ago,' he said.

'I've been doing everything myself since the old man died.'
Brendan's tone was enlivened by his sense of grievance. 'But she refused to sign it over for a long time. She said you had a right to it too. Even though you never showed the slightest bit of interest in it and they sent you to university instead.'

Callan felt a flush of love for his mother and her futile hope that he would return, could return, and settle down here again.

'But she has seen sense at last,' Brendan was saying, too wrapped up in his own problems to share his brother's perceptions. 'A couple of her friends pointed out to her that she isn't getting any younger. They've persuaded her to make the proper arrangements.'

'That's fine by me,' Callan said.

'Has she mentioned anything about it to you?'

Callan shook his head. Their mother came out the back door, dressed in her overcoat and carrying a handbag. She called to Brendan and sat into the car.

'Just so you know what the score is,' Brendan said quietly, so she wouldn't hear, 'you have no claim to any of it. You have no rights here.'

'I'm not looking for any.'

'You can always take me to law,' Brendan said with a vindictive grimace. 'If you change your mind.'

He hurried into the house to change his boots and emerged a moment later and drove away. Callan waved to his mother who smiled back as the car went out the gate and threw up a layer of dust from the driveway.

He wandered down the fields and stopped to look at the herd of fat Friesians browsing on the dense grass. The sun was warm here and the air heavy with the smell of fresh cow dung. Brendan was right: he had never had any interest in farming, had never felt like a farmer. But he still felt a sense of loss now, knowing he could never come back here again. No matter what had happened or where he was, it had always been home; always there, as certain and unchanging as its landscape. But it wouldn't be home any more. He wouldn't be welcome in his brother's house.

After they returned from the funeral, he sat at the kitchen table while his mother washed a pot of potatoes and relayed the minor gossip she had picked up at the church. Who was having another baby, whose health was deteriorating and who was home on holidays from

43

England. He listened with half his attention, not taking in the specific details but hearing the once familiar litany of happenings. Apart from the names, he was thinking, nothing seemed to have changed.

She stopped in mid-sentence as a car drove into the yard and he tensed suddenly. 'Sean,' she said in a bemused tone as she watched a young man get out and talk to Brendan. Callan relaxed and she resumed her monologue.

There was a sharp knock on the back door and a fresh-faced young man walked in. 'Morning, ma'am,' he said. 'Great weather.'

'Glorious, Sean.' She dried her hands on a towel. 'You'll have a cup of tea or something.'

'No, no thanks. I won't be delaying.' He looked at Callan and gestured to him with his head to come outside. His mother caught the signal and glanced quickly from one to the other. Callan got up and gave her a reassuring smile as he followed Sean. The messenger, he thought.

Outside, Sean grasped his hand and shook it enthusiastically. 'Great to have you back, Fergus,' he said.

Callan recognised him now. He had been a whiny, snot-nosed kid the last time he saw him.

'I've left the stuff in the boot of your car. And I've got a rendezvous for you.'

'What stuff?' Callan demanded suspiciously.

'Just something to deliver to the man you're meeting,' Sean said coyly.

Callan walked over to his car and raised the boot lid. A black plastic garbage bag lay inside and he eased back its mouth with the nails of his index fingers. The dull black barrel of a Kalashnikov weighed heavily against the shiny plastic.

He shook his head emphatically. 'I'm not carrying that.'

'It's just a matter of convenience,' Sean argued. 'The man you're meeting wants it. And since you're going to see him we thought you'd deliver it. That's all.'

'Who am I meeting?'

'I don't know,' Sean began to look confused. 'I assumed you knew.'

Callan shook his head and stared at him.

'I wasn't told,' Sean shrugged. 'All I was told was to give you the rendezvous. And ask you to deliver this. It's no big deal.'

'Where's the rendezvous?'

Sean shifted from one foot to the other and avoided Callan's eyes. So, it was a big deal, Callan thought. Either he took the Kalashnikov or he didn't get the meeting. He sighed inwardly and took his time working out the implications. It was either a test or a trap. They wanted to confirm his continuing commitment by giving him a simple task or they were setting him up for something nasty. It had to be a test, he decided. There was no reason why they'd want to set him up, especially after facilitating his return with the passport.

'Who gave this order?' he demanded with an air of authority, trying to exploit the reputation he obviously had in the young man's mind.

'Jesus, Fergus, I can't tell you that,' Sean said plaintively. 'Security's very strict these days.'

Callan paused. He didn't like it but he didn't have much choice. 'OK,' he said. 'Where's the rendezvous?'

'You'll take it?' Sean asked.

Callan nodded and noted the relief in Sean's voice.

Sean took a map from his pocket and ran his finger along the main road from Galway to Clifden and stopped at Maam Cross. 'Turn off there and less than a mile down this road there's a lay-by beside a lake,' he said. 'That's the spot. Seven o'clock.'

Wide-open countryside, Callan thought automatically. Full of tourists this time of year.

Sean folded the map and put it back in his pocket. 'Good luck.' He shook Callan's hand. 'And I'm really glad to see you back with us.'

Callan watched him drive away, thinking that if it was a trap nobody had told Sean. He seemed genuine. But that didn't necessarily mean anything.

He slammed down the boot and went back inside. His mother gave him a desolate look, her drawn face revealing her thoughts. He said nothing and sat down at the table again, wondering about the gun. 'You'll stay for dinner?' she said after a while. 'It's nearly ready.'

'Sure,' he replied, trying to think of something to talk about but he couldn't find anything. The atmosphere had been poisoned, suddenly and irretrievably, by the intrusion of unstated reality.

He went down the fields to summon Brendan when the meal was ready and they ate in silence, listening to the radio news. Brendan glared an unspoken challenge at him as a reporter said from Belfast that a twelve-year-old girl may lose both her legs after she was hit by shrapnel from a bomb exploded as she and a British army patrol were passing. None of the soldiers was hurt.

Brendan went back to work afterwards and Callan sat with his mother over a second cup of tea.

'Brendan tells me you're going to sign over the farm to him,' he said. 'I think that's a good idea.'

She looked at him and asked when he would be back again.

'I don't know,' he said and she looked away. 'Why don't you come and visit me?' he asked suddenly, wondering at the same time how he could arrange it. It would be risky but with proper care it could be done.

'How would I do that?'

'Simple.' He smiled, determined to raise her spirits. 'I'll send you the ticket. And you get on the plane, Simple as that.'

She searched his eyes with a mixture of hope and doubt.

'That's all there's to it,' he repeated but she didn't seem convinced.

'I don't have a passport,' she said.

'Apply for one,' he suggested lightly. 'Then you'll have it ready.' There was no point in prolonging the agony, he decided, and he stood up and patted her shoulder gently as he passed by and went upstairs to his room.

He gathered the few clothes he had unpacked and stuffed them back into the backpack and stood for a moment looking at the room. Then he went back down and out to the car and threw the backpack into the boot beside the black plastic bag.

His mother stood at the back door, watching him with her eyes red and her arms folded tightly as if she was holding herself together. Callan walked quickly over to the barn where Brendan was doing something to the tractor's tow bar and held out his hand. Brendan straightened up slowly and wiped a hand on his trousers.

'I've told her she's doing the right thing,' Callan said.

Brendan nodded. 'Good luck,' he said brusquely.

Callan went back to his mother and put his arms around her and kissed her on the forehead. 'Don't worry,' he said. 'I'll see you again.'

'Will you write?' Her voice broke. 'Sometime.'

'Yes,' he promised. 'And I'll send you that ticket.'

He got into the car and swung in a quick arc round the yard and waved to her and went fast down the drive. He stopped at the road and glanced back through the dust haze and she was standing, a slight figure, at the side of the house. He let the clutch out like a quick release of emotion and sped down the road.

The car bounced over the small hump of the bridge across the stream at the edge of the farm.

After Oughterard the road rose and fell and twisted uneasily as if it was reluctant to go deep into the primal landscape of Connemara. The land opened into a wide undulating vista of brown bog and stretched away into the barren, brooding mountains. The high sun soaked some of the underlying menace from the elemental mixture of hills and water and pieces of the flawless sky shone from ruffled lakes.

A caravan swayed at the head of a long, slow line of cars like it was leading a convoy into hostile territory. Callan, far down the line, drove easily. He was in no hurry, content to be part of the convoy and that most of the cars had foreign number plates. The place was even more full of tourists than he had expected. Which was good, now that he was once more a tourist too.

The convoy crawled into Maam Cross, a perfect joining of two routes with nothing else but a haphazard clump of craft shops, petrol pumps, a sprawling bar and a traditional thatched cottage. It looked like the last outpost of consumerism before the looming mountains and it drew most of the cars in.

Callan parked on the other side of the road behind an empty tour bus and looked around methodically. Three cars waited for petrol; a group of elderly American women came out of the gift shop; a couple lifted a young child on to a jaunting car outside the thatched cottage and tried to steady her long enough to take a picture.

He got out of the car and strolled across the road and drifted around the buildings. Nothing troubled him and he went into the long lounge and ordered a glass of beer. He took it to a window seat and scrutinised the only two men who might be out of place among the families and couples scattered around. They both wore jeans and teeshirts and sat with their bronzed arms resting on a table, talking in a desultory way.

He dismissed them as workmen and sipped at the beer and listened to a tape playing some indeterminate Irish music. My life is too compartmentalised, he thought. A series of unconnected boxes, carefully isolated from each other. That's the problem. I'm all boxed in.

Sharon knew something of his past but not much. Most of the other people he knew in Boston knew nothing, didn't even know her. He kept his distance from her friends. And his family and his real friends were a world away, in a hermetically sealed box or in jail or dead or disappeared, like Willy. Anyway, they probably weren't his friends any more.

A flashing blue light caught the corner of his eye and cut short his thoughts. He turned in time to catch a glimpse of a garda car disappearing from view and he drained the beer and went outside. There was no sign of the patrol car.

Callan got back into his car and took the map from the glove compartment and studied it. Then he started the engine and drove past the crossroads towards Clifden. A short distance away he pulled on to a section of old road and parked in a tiny disused quarry beneath a wall of sheared rock.

He got out and looked around furtively and relieved himself against the rock. Then he looked around again, casually this time, and was satisfied he was almost hidden from view. He opened the boot of the car and emptied some of the clothes from the backpack and replaced them with the plastic bag.

He hoisted the backpack on to his shoulders, feeling the extra weight of the Kalashnikov, and went round the side of the quarry and climbed the small hill. On top, the wiry grass levelled off for a bit and then the land began to sire, gradually at first and then more steeply. Ahead of him, a brown mountain rose up to a bald peak of bare speckled stone.

He tramped steadily upwards alongside a loose stone wall which seemed to run like a vein straight up the mountain. After a while he stopped and shrugged off the backpack and leaned against the wall and felt the sweat cool on his body.

He was several hundred feet up and he could see a long straight stretch of the road to Clifden running west and back towards the east a distant, looping length of the other road where the rendezvous was to take place. He checked his watch. There was still more than two hours to go.

He went on again, keeping an eye on the rendezvous road as it disappeared and reappeared with the contours of the land until, suddenly he saw what he wanted. There, between a gap in two low hills, was the road and the lay-by and the lake beyond it. He smiled. It was almost perfect, better than he had hoped for.

He pulled off the damp sweatshirt and sank down in a hollow behind the wall and closed his eyes. The cool wind from the west sighed steadily overhead and the warm sun dried his body. I'll go back with a tan, he thought idly and his mind drifted on to going back.

The sooner the better, he decided. He had done the main thing he had come here for. And this meeting was as much as he was going to do for Willy. Having to deliver the gun had made up his mind on that. He didn't like the idea of his former comrades testing him: it implied that they might want him to do something else and then something else. And he wasn't part of it any more.

Call Air Canada tonight, he thought, and bring forward the reservation. And if that's not possible, get another flight. Better do that anyway, he decided. Just in case anybody had tracked him.

He lay there in the warm sun, relaxed, hovering on the edge of dozing. Curiosity began to nag at him and he resisted it for a while and then thought, what the hell. He sat up and glanced around. There was no one in sight and he opened the backpack and pulled out a teeshirt. He put it over his hands and dragged out the plastic bag and tipped it sideways.

The short assault rifle slid out on the ground, followed by two curved magazines and a telescopic sight. Both magazines were full.

Callan stared at them.

An eddy of wind carried a sweet whiff of gun oil and he was back in the training camp in the Wicklow mountains and the first time he handled an Armalite, the first time he had discovered his talent as a marksman. They were all fired up with theory and camaraderie and purpose and he had thought: this is the life, this is living. Not the smug, inane existence of his college associates with their boastful drinking, ineffectual attempts at screwing women and agonising over whether to join daddy's engineering firm on graduation or go abroad for a few years first. And all the time there was a brutal, dirty war being waged on their own people . . .

He dropped the teeshirt from his hands and picked up the Kalashnikov and balanced its stubby length on one palm. It was the

49

first time he had handled a weapon since the Maher operation, the first time he had ever handled one of these. He flicked the bolt back and forth and fitted the butt into his shoulder and looked down the sights at a tuft of grass.

He suddenly lowered the gun and glanced about apprehensively. He picked up the telescopic sight and wondered why it was with the rest. It was cheap and low-powered but it was a godsend. He raised it to within a couple of inches of his eye and scanned the far side of the valley. The crosshairs centred on a small white cottage, apparently in the middle of nowhere, and he tried to pick out a road or track leading to it. He couldn't find one.

He swung the scope round to the mountain above him and several grey rocks turned into grazing sheep. Up near the summit he made out the movements of two tiny climbers. He swore at himself for playing with a gun in full view of anyone with a decent pair of binoculars. He quickly wiped down the Kalashnikov with the teeshirt and packed it and the magazines back into the backpack.

After six o'clock, he rested the scope on the wall and lined it up on the distant lay-by and slowly and methodically swept over as much of the immediate area as he could see. A few sheep grazed unperturbed on the hill overlooking it. Cars went by in indistinct blurs. The sun shone and the wind barely ruffled the cowed carpet of scrub. Everything looked normal.

He was about to go when a car stopped at the lay-by.

He steadied the scope and looked carefully. It was a brown estate car and had a yellow number plate which indicated it was Northern or British. The sun reflected off the windows and he couldn't see inside.

Both car doors opened in unison. A brown-haired woman got out of the passenger seat, on his side, and walked round to the back. A man joined her and raised the tailgate. The woman seemed to be wearing blue jeans and a blue top: the man had on a light-coloured shirt and grey trousers. They were too far away to make anything of their features.

Callan calmly cursed the scope's tantalising lack of power and watched the man set up a small table and pull two folding chairs into position. Then he walked over to the edge of the lay-by and looked out over the lake while the woman bent into the back of the car.

It's Maire, he thought suddenly, irrationally. He waited for her to straighten up and carry a box to the table but her features were still an unidentifiable fuzz of floating brown hair and a blob of pale skin. It couldn't be, he told himself. It could be anyone. And anyway, he realised, he had no idea what Maire looked like now. If they were his contacts, however, the were using a perfect cover for the meeting.

He glanced at his watch and it was a couple of minutes to seven. Time to go. He pulled on his sweatshirt and stuffed the teeshirt he had used to wipe the gun into a gap in the stone wall. He was heaving the backpack on to his shoulder when a sudden movement on the Clifden road caught his attention.

Three navy-blue cars were going down the middle of the road, pushing other cars aside. Their headlights were on, hazard-warning lights flashing. Racing towards Maam Cross. There was no sound of sirens but their identity was unmistakable.

He swung the scope back towards the lay-by and there was a second car there now, parked away from the picnickers.

Trap, his senses screamed.

He headed downhill with long, careful strides, going fast but not running, speeded up by the gradient. He slid down the last hill, one hand stopping him from falling, and pulled off the backpack as he ran to the car. He took out the plastic bag and tossed it on to the passenger seat and started the engine.

The main road was empty and he pulled across it and accelerated towards Clifden, away from Maam Cross. The adrenalin was pumping cleanly and he concentrated totally on the immediate problem, getting away. With a bit of luck, he'd be gone before they realised they'd missed him.

He surged past two French cars, driving fast but not recklessly. They might have another checkpoint ahead but he had to take that chance. The road behind was certainly sealed. In the village of Recess he caught up with a short line of cars.

He breathed deeply and slowed down and settled in behind them. It was OK: he had covered nearly ten miles. They went through the village and passed a lake on their left. The wind built up sharp little waves and long lines of foam ran with the hidden currents. He didn't notice, alert only for threats.

The cars rounded a bend and all the brake lights ahead of him came on, one set after another. There was some kind of hold up but he couldn't see beyond the car in front. They all came to a stop and he sat still for a moment.

He let down his window and stuck his head out. Two uniformed gardai stood in the middle of the road up ahead. A patrol car was parked on the opposite side.

Callan watched the garda checking the other lane halt a car and then wave it on. He seemed casual. The garda on his lane was examining documents from somebody in a small covered-in van.

He opened the door and stepped out to see what was on his side of the road, hoping the move would signal impatience rather than anything else. There appeared to be nothing more to the checkpoint than the two gardai and the empty patrol car. There was no sign of an armed back-up. Callan sat in again and decided to bluff his way through.

A small girl waved at him from the rear window of the car in front and he smiled back. She watched him for a moment and then began to roll a coloured ball along the parcel shelf. He glanced in the rear-view mirror and saw the two French cars he had overtaken come round the bend and line up behind.

He reached over and eased the Kalshnikov from the plastic bag and laid it across his knees and took out a magazine. He clicked it into place and checked that the safety was off. When he looked up again the girl was watching him and he winked at her. She looked away shyly and he put the gun under his seat, stuffed the bag under the other seat and angled the backpack behind his seat to conceal the barrel if it protruded.

The cars began to move forward, slowly but steadily, and Callan could see the garda slowing the second car ahead of him and then waving it on. He barely glanced at the car ahead of Callan and then raised his hand.

Callan rolled down his window while the garda looked at the tax and insurance discs on his windscreen. 'Hi, officer,' he said brightly, exaggerating his accent.

'Where are you coming from?' the garda asked. He had a spotty chin and looked ridiculously young.

'Galway,' Callan drawled the name. 'Going back to Clifden. My family and I are vacationing there.'

Another garda car came from the opposite direction and stopped to talk to the other garda on the checkpoint. Callan could hear the indecipherable chatter of its radio in the background as the driver spoke to the second garda. He kept his attention fixed firmly on the young garda.

'Can I see your driving licence, please?'

'I'm sorry, officer,' Callan said. 'It's with my things in Clifden.'

'Do you have any identification?'

Callan patted his pockets and shook his head. 'I'm afraid not. My passport and everything else are in our hotel.' He became aware that the other two gardai had fallen silent and were looking at him. 'You see I went into Galway to pick up some things and I'm going straight back. It just didn't occur to me that I'd need to carry anything like that.' He shrugged apologetically. 'I'm sorry.'

The young garda looked perplexed and then nodded and stepped back. The driver of the patrol car said something to the other policeman who came towards Callan with a hand raised. Callan smiled politely at him.

He looked in the back of the car and pointed at the backpack. 'What's in that?'

Callan twisted in the seat to look behind him. 'Oh, that,' he said. 'That's one of the kid's bags. Clothes and stuff, I guess.'

'Just pull in to the side there for a minute, please,' the second garda said.

'Sure,' Callan said.

Someone in the queue behind them tooted a horn hesitantly and the policemen glanced back. Callan eased the car into gear and was moving down the road, gathering speed, before they realised what he was doing. As he rounded a bend he caught a glimpse of the patrol car's reversing lights.

Fuck it, Callan muttered aloud as he swung into a narrow road. He took a tight bend at speed and thought for a moment he wasn't going to make it. Two wheels mounted a slight ditch and the side of the car screeched off a rock. He got it back on the road and slowed down a little.

There was no sign of pursuit but he couldn't get a straight view far enough back to see if they were following. The road was as twisted and bent as an ocean-sprayed bush and its surface deteriorated as he went on. The car bounced and leaped over bumps and potholes and hit the ground in a series of jarring, scraping thuds that constantly threatened to put him off the road.

He came to the start of a long lake and mountains reared up on either side of the flat wide valley. Patches of shadow were beginning to spread in the hollows of the mountains on the left. There was no sign of human habitation for miles and he tried to work out where the road would take him. He saw a sign for a picnic area and a small wood of evergreens appeared before him. He turned in and drove as far as he could into the clearing, trying to get the car out of sight of the road. He turned off the engine.

Fuck it, he said to the silence.

The wind raked through the tops of the trees and the sunshine was speckled by their branches. He got out the map and traced the road he was on. It was no good. They could block that off easily.

He gathered the weaponry and took the magazine from the rifle and put it in his pocket. He stuffed the Kalashnikov and the spare magazine into the backpack and set off on foot towards the mountains without a backward glance.

It would take them more than an hour to get a helicopter up, he was thinking.

Six

Galway held the silent evening atmosphere of a small town in the trappings of a city. The yellow orbs of pedestrian crossings flashed unnecessarily. Sodium lights shone on shuttered shopping streets and on dark, parked cars. Overhead, the sky was translucent with a drawn out half-light that was neither day nor night.

Inspector George Keerins came down Shop Street and crossed the bridge over the Corrib, walking fast, and headed back towards the garda station. He passed the open door of a pub, feeling its warmth fug splash out over him like the wake from a passing truck.

The exercise had cleared his head and relieved some of the frustration that had set in after Callan's escape and deepened with the lack of developments during the long evening. In the station, a detective was coming from the room Keerins had been given to use and the inspector looked at him inquiringly.

'Just left details of the car on your desk,' the detective said. 'Hired at Shannon the other morning. By a Mr Cleary.'

'Cleary?' That was the name Callan was supposed to be using.

The detective nodded grimly. 'He hired it about half an hour before he was supposed to get off the plane.'

The fucker's one step ahead of us all the time, Keerins thought. Almost like he's teasing us.

'He hired it for a week,' the detective said.

'Check the earlier flights that morning,' Keerins ordered.

'There were two,' the detective nodded with the satisfied look of someone already ahead of the boss. 'From Atlanta and Toronto. We're getting on to the airlines now.'

Keerins went down the corridor wondering if Archie's information had been right. Or was it deliberately inaccurate enough to allow Callan to get away twice? And, if it was designed to let him escape, what could be the purpose behind that? That didn't seem to make any sense at all.

He stopped outside the interview room. There was no point building huge conspiracies on speculation: life was complicated enough. Anyway, Callan's escape this time had been a simple cock-up. That was all. The man watching the meeting site had given the signal when two cars arrived at the rendezvous. It was just one of those things that an English couple had stopped for a picnic at the lay-by at the same time as Blinker arrived to meet Callan. If they'd had enough manpower to mount a proper outer cordon they'd have got him. But, at least, they had flushed him out.

Keerins sighed and opened the door and everybody glanced at him like he was the latest arrival in a slow-moving doctor's waiting room. Sergeant Pursell sat at one side of a table, his heavy head propped on one hand: Blinker was sprawled in an upright metal chair across from him and a second detective lay back against the pale-coloured wall to one side. The window was covered with closed horizontal blinds and the fluorescent light was a harsh white, washing out the colours. The policemen looked bored but Blinker stared Keerins up and down with interest.

'Who the fuck are you?' he demanded in a strong Northern accent.

'Watch your fucking manners,' Pursell growled automatically.

'Ah,' Blinker nodded knowledgeably at the sergeant. 'The brain after the brawn.'

Keerins walked slowly round behind him, looking down at his crinkly black hair, parted in the middle. Blinker wore dark cord jeans and a teeshirt which said 'Discover Ireland' and stretched tightly over his tubby frame. His nickname came from his habit of blinking constantly which added a permanently perplexed look to his round face. Keerins had never seen him before but he knew all about him.

He looks like a lost coal delivery man, he thought. But he was a senior member of the IRA. Had been involved since the early days as a young teenager, moved South after being interned for a while. He had served one jail sentence years earlier but was above being likely to be found with anything incriminating on him these days. He now rotated around a number of border towns from where he controlled several IRA units.

Keerins stopped at the window, at the edge of Blinker's vision, and leaned against a cold radiator with his arms folded. Blinker swivelled round to face him and they stared at each other in frank and silent appraisal.

'I must be getting old,' Blinker swung back to Pursell. 'When the peelers are looking so young.'

'You're a long way from home,' Keerins said.

'I've told your elderly minion all about it.' Blinker looked back at him as if he was anxious to please. 'I'm on holiday.'

'That's where you're going,' Pursell intervened. 'On a long holiday.'

Keerins caught Pursell's exasperated signal that he had got nothing out of him. 'R and R,' he said.

'What's that?' Blinker blinked innocently at him.

'Soldier talk for holidays, isn't it?'

Blinker stifled a laugh. 'What would I know about that? I saw this ad on TV. Discover Ireland, it said. It's there to enjoy, or something. And I was happily enjoying it until your heavies came swarming all over the place. Spoiling the scenery. And scaring the shit out of those English tourists.' The English couple who had stopped at the lay-by were already on their way to the ferry home, their holiday cut short by their fright at the arrival of the armed gardai. 'They thought you were terrorists,' Blinker laughed. 'Maybe they were right.'

'What are you working at these days?'

'What's that got to do with anything?'

'Holidays,' Keerins said. 'What are you taking a holiday from?'

'Just because I'm unemployed,' Blinker said sadly, 'is no reason why I can't take a holiday. The unemployed have rights too.'

'Must be hard to maintain that car on the dole.'

'Is that a crime? Being unemployed and having a car?' Blinker looked from Keerins to Pursell as if the sergeant would support his tone of injured innocence. He turned back to Keerins: 'Anyway you lads should be more concerned about the damage you're doing to the tourist industry. Terrorising honest, decent holidaymakers. When the Free State needs them so badly. To keep your little puppet economy afloat.'

He's enjoying himself, Keerins thought, he knows we've got nothing on him. He walked back slowly towards the door. 'I'm going to lodge a formal complaint with Bord Failte,' Blinker said as he passed behind him. Keerins stopped at the door and told the detective to lock him up.

'What are you holding me for?' Blinker demanded. 'To stop me complaining?'

Pursell got up as the other detective took Blinker by the arm and hauled him to his feet. 'Haven't you heard the news?' Pursell asked sweetly. 'Internment's been introduced. You're being locked up for ever.'

Blinker laughed at him as he was led away, a short portly figure. 'God bless,' he called back over his shoulder.

'Did you get out for a pint?' Pursell asked as he and Keerins went in the opposite direction.

'For a walk,' Keerins said stiffly.

'I could do with a pint,' Pursell grumbled. 'That fucker's given me a headache. Blinking and chattering away like a demented duck. I think I prefer him when he's doing the staring at the wall number.'

Keerins sighed. 'There's nothing in his car? On him?'

'Not a thing. That's why he's so fucking voluble.'

'No mention of Callan?'

Pursell shook his head. 'I didn't mention him either. But he knows who we're after.'

'So what do you think?' He looked at Pursell as they stopped outside his office.

'Hold him for the forty-eight hours,' the sergeant replied. 'Until the search is finished, anyway.'

'Is there any point?'

'Sure. Keep him out of circulation. Keep Callan on the run. And put the rest of the bastards off their stroke.'

That made sense, Keerins thought, but he said, 'We could let him go and follow him. See if he makes contact again.'

Pursell gave him a scathing look. 'Blinker's not going to lead us anywhere. Except to the nearest tourist office to lodge a complaint. Like he says.'

A phone rang inside and Keerins hurried in to catch it. He listened for a moment and thanked the caller and hung up. Pursell stood in the doorway, waiting.

'The address Callan gave in Cork doesn't exist,' he said.

'Wonders will never cease,' Pursell snorted sarcastically. 'Come on. There's nothing more we can do here.'

They went to a large lounge where a two man band were perched on a small podium. One strummed a guitar and sang and the other played a keyboard: a drum machine beat out a mechanical rhythm. Keerins thought about Archie. Go back and see him again, he told himself, get him to find out why Blinker was meeting Callan. That was the most profitable thing to do.

'You ever been here before?' Pursell asked above the music as they watched the barman top up two pints of Guinness. 'In Galway?'

'I played a couple of matches here. Against Galwegians.'

'Rugby,' Pursell nodded knowledgeably.

Keerins tried to remember if his team had won or lost but all that came back to him were wintry afternoons covered in a drenching mist that turned the pitch to slithery muck and the chances of clean running play to nil.

'A thug's game played by gentlemen,' Pursell added.

'I haven't played for a while,' Keerins said. 'Never got beyond the B team.'

'Forwards or backs?'

'Backs. A winger.' Keerins wondered idly why Pursell was in such an uncharacteristically sociable mood. Even his attitude to Blinker seemed relatively benign. Maybe he just liked being out of Dublin. On the subsistence allowance.

'Always a fast man on your feet,' Pursell laughed.

Keerins glanced at him to see if he was being sarcastic. Pursell winked back and raised his glass to him.

'I think I'll go back first thing in the morning,' Keerins said after a while. 'You can hang on and oversee the search.' Recruits were being bussed in at dawn along with soldiers and a spotter plane to sweep through the Maamturk Mountains where Callan had disappeared.

'OK.' Pursell sounded pleased. 'There's not much chance of cornering him out there,' he added to mask any trace of excessive enthusiasm.

'He won't get too far on foot.'

'He's a smart bastard,' Pursell suggested. 'And those mountains are crawling with hikers and climbers and campers this time of year.' The helicopter had already confirmed that in the short time it had been able to operate before dusk it had sighted more than a dozen people in the apparently empty mountains, but no trace of Callan. 'I don't know what they see in the place.'

'It's pretty spectacular.'

'I was brought up near mountains,' Pursell said. 'All I see are rocks and useless land and poverty.'

The singer announced a special request for Georgina and Carmel, the belles of Belfast city, and a group on the far side of the lounge raised a cheer. The band broke into a vigorous version of 'I'll Tell Me Ma' with the boisterous help of the girls' companions.

'It's interesting that Blinker was the one to turn up,' Keerins said, hoping to use Pursell's mellow mood to sound out his opinion. 'He's a long way from his patch.'

'He pops up all over the place,' Pursell offered in a tone of superior experience. 'A regular little general.'

Keerins stared at the bottles lines up behind the bar and thought about Callan. Until today, he had just been an object—a name, a picture, a file—but he had assumed a more palpable presence since his return was confirmed and they had come so close to catching him.

Why had he gotten involved with the IRA in the first place, he wondered. People like Blinker you could understand. He was from West Belfast, his father interned in the 1940s, no prospects but unemployment: he'd been born into revolt. It must have been as natural to him as breathing, particularly in the emotionally charged early days of the troubles when everything had seemed simpler.

But Callan was different: he didn't fit the predictable profile. His family had no republican background and he hadn't been short of opportunities. He'd been sent to college. And thrown it all up. Keerins shook his head. He didn't understand people like that: maybe they had it too easy, maybe that was their problem.

He resented them, too, he realised. If I'd had it handed to me on a plate, he thought, instead of having to work and get a degree the hard way. He had been unusual on the corporation estate where he grew up, an only child in a neighbourhood of large families. Unusual, too, in his determined ambition to get out of there. And to do it legally. Maybe that was the difference between himself and people like Callan. A matter of temperament.

'I wonder why Callan's come back,' he said aloud.

'Who cares?' Pursell shrugged. 'The main thing is that he's back. And we've blown his cover, closed off the exits. It's only a matter of time.'

'He's got to be up to something. Blinker wouldn't have been there unless they were planning something.'

'Those fuckers are always planning something. Anyway,' Pursell added with a harsh laugh, 'they sometimes think that if they've been out of sight that they've been out of our minds too.'

I don't buy that, Keerins thought but said nothing. You can't forget a forty-year sentence. There's no way Callan could forget that. Nobody could.

Callan took his finger off the hot cigarette lighter and folded the map in the dark. He flicked the lighter again and held it to a cigarette and then got up from the corner where he had been kneeling and went back to the chair he had positioned near the window. He smoked with a hand cupped over the glowing tip.

The plan was simple. He had to get out of the natural box created by the four roads around the mountains where any follow-up search would be concentrated. Heading south to the shores of Galway Bay seemed the best bet.

The night had swallowed the contours of the land, transforming everything into a mass of unrelenting black. The lights of a few, scattered houses winked like distant stars and he watched the headlights of cars far off on the main road flare up into the darkness. The silence was broken only by the occasional creaks of the empty cottage. It was so quiet he could hear his own breathing.

For the first time since the trap had been sprung he allowed his mind to roam over everything that had happened. Somebody had shopped him. Set him up with the rifle to give him no chance of bluffing his way out of the trap. If it wasn't for the gun, he'd have talked his way through that checkpoint. That much was blindingly obvious. But who had done it and, more importantly, why?

He blew smoke at the small window and felt his stomach grumble with hunger. He pushed the button to light up the figures on his watch and realised he hadn't eaten since the lunch with his mother and Brendan. Twelve hours ago. An age ago.

More like ten years ago, he thought, his mind grappling with the bewildering speed of the transformation from feeling safe to being hunted. Half a day and he was back where he had been after shooting Maher. Only worse off: he couldn't rely on the army, on anyone, to help now. He really was on his own.

He suddenly remembered the time, the only time, he had let his cover slip in Boston. A casual work acquaintance, a Vietnam veteran who boasted that he was off to become a mercenary, dismissed Northern Ireland as a Mickey Mouse war, no more deserving of the title than a quiet night at a Shriners' convention. Callan had demurred,

61

one thing led to another and he ended up shouting at the veteran that he knew nothing about a state of permanent war, all he had done was a short tour in Nam and then flown home to the safety of his country to bullshit about it in bars. While there were fighters in Ireland who could never go home, for whom it could never end short of victory.

I was right, he sighed. I should have known I could never come back.

He tossed the cigarette end into the open fireplace and rummaged through the backpack for the darkest clothes he had. He changed quickly and loaded the magazine into the Kalashnikov and checked the safety catch. He left the cottage by the back door beside the window he had broken to get in.

He stood for a moment in the shadow of the huddled building, breathing in the cool air and looking around. The night seemed brighter outside and the sky was dusted with a myriad of stars twinkling like diamonds under an unseen light. Then he set off down the slope with the rifle balanced easily in one hand and his eyes averted from the distant car lights to keep his night vision.

He felt oddly at ease and confident, as if he had finally come through a long, debilitating illness.

'Good night. Thank you. And safe home,' Archie slurred into the microphone and a couple of drinkers glowered at him as though they had not been aware of the Rambling Boyos' presence for the previous two hours. The lights flashed off and on again and the short-sleeved barmen fanned out among the tables, aggressively gathering the empties. Nobody moved.

'What a shower,' Archie muttered to himself as he bent down to lay his guitar in its case.

'Coming round to my place for a jar?' the drummer asked.

Archie shook his head. 'The mot's waiting for me.'

The drummer gave a suggestive cackle and a voice behind them said, 'Good gig, boys.'

'Mr Amber,' Archie shot upright and round in one jerking movement. He stared in surprise at the smoothly suited talent scout. 'Jesus, I didn't know you were going to be here.'

'I didn't want you to know, did I?' Amber gave him a mocking smile. He was in his early thirties and spoke with the long vowels of some English region. He looked lean and fit in a dapper way and had a slightly crooked mouth that gave him a sneering look. He looked to Archie like a serious businessman. 'Didn't want to put you off your performance.'

'It was all right, was it?'

The manager of the pub came over to them, said a curt thanks and held out a brown envelope. The drummer grabbed it while Archie's attention was still focused on Amber. Archie shot him a distracted glance.

'I've got a pint lined up for you,' Amber said. 'Lager, isn't it?'

Archie raised his eyes to the two other members of the group behind Amber's back and followed him over to a corner seat. Amber sat on the plastic upholstered bench and Archie squatted on a stool across the table. The barmen were beginning to raise their voices at the customers.

'We haven't got the demo ready yet,' Archie said.

'Cheers.' Amber raised his pint of Guinness and Archie followed his example. Amber replaced his drink, unhurried.

'There's no rush,' he said. 'I wasn't expecting it until next week. And, after tonight, I'm less concerned about it.'

'Yeah?' Archie asked eagerly.

'It's still important, of course. The company'll have to have it. But I'll be able to give them a stronger recommendation now.' He nodded solemnly. 'That was a good show.'

Archie let out a silent whoop which almost bounced his body off the stool. 'You mean we'll get a contract?'

'It's not up to me at the end of the day. But I'll be recommending it. Strongly.'

'Fuck me,' Archie said triumphantly. 'That's great. Really fucking great.'

Amber smiled at him like a benign aunt willing to excuse the lapse of taste as an excess of youthful enthusiasm. He held on to his glass as a scavenging barman swept by their corner with an automatic 'finish up now, gents'.

Archie swallowed a long draught and held his pint in mid-air. 'What sort of deal?' He took a sly sip. 'How much, like?'

Amber spread his hands helplessly. 'I can't say, mate. That's up to you and the record company. Matter for negotiation. I don't get involved in any of that.'

Archie nodded soberly.

'A word of advice, though,' Amber added. 'You should see about getting a good manager. Someone who knows the scene.'

Archie nodded again. Jesus, he thought, wait till the lads hear this. He drained his pint quickly, eager to go and spread the news. Into the big time. 'Thanks, Mr Amber,' he said. 'We really appreciate it.'

Amber nodded but made no move to finish his drink. 'There's something you might be able to help me with,' he said casually.

'Sure,' Archie said expansively. 'Anything.'

'I want to find somebody.' He locked Archie's artless eyes into his stare. 'Fergus Callan.'

Archie froze into total immobility. Then he pulled his eyes away and looked frantically around the emptying pub and reached for his glass in a sudden splurge of movement. He had it to his mouth before he realised it was empty.

'There's money in it,' Amber said.

'I don't know him.' Archie tried to keep his voice from rising with horror at what he was hearing. He steadied the glass back on the table, trying to calm himself. Get the fuck out of here, he ordered himself. But he was too bewildered to move. 'Never heard of him.'

'A thousand quid,' Amber said. 'Cash.'

'I don't know what the fuck you're talking about.'

'You know.'

'I don't know this guy,' Archie whined. 'Swear to God.'

Amber looked at him sadly. 'You know him,' he said calmly. 'Or of him. You shopped him to the Irish police.'

Jesus fucking Christ, Archie thought. Sweat broke out on his back and cooled instantly. His stomach tightened into a churning knot. Most of the lights went out in the pub. He wanted to puke.

Amber watched him impassively.

'Listen,' Archie pleaded in another attempt to exorcise his fear. 'You've got it all wrong. I don't know what you're talking about. I swear to Christ.'

Amber leaned forward and rested his arms on the table. 'Let me lay it out simply for you,' he said slowly. 'I want to find Callan. To talk to him. That's all. No rough stuff. I will pay handsomely for your help. Five thousand in cash. And, if you want, help to set you up somewhere else.'

Archie's mind spun round like a roulette wheel, the ball bouncing on random numbers. At least he's not a Provo. Thank Christ. Five thousand. What had Keerins said about selling information? Fuck this. The RUC. I don't want any of this. Get out of here now.

'The other possibility,' Amber added slowly, 'is that we drop your name on the Falls Road. As a garda informer.'

Archie stared at him like a rabbit transfixed by a light.

'Know what I mean?' Amber sat back and opened his hands in an offering. He shrugged inquisitively.

A barman appeared at their table and grabbed the glasses. 'Ah come on now, lads,' he said. 'Have you no homes to go to?' They didn't pay him any attention.

'Who are you anyway?' Archie croaked. The ball had finally stopped. 'A Brit spy.' He shook his head in amazement. 'Jesus.'

Amber said nothing.

'Do you realise the risk you're taking here?' Archie asked, encouraged by Amber's silence. He looked around as if there might be IRA gunmen lurking in the shadows. 'There's an awful lot of Provos around here.'

'Spare me.' Amber gave a short, crooked laugh.

'I'm serious.'

'So am I, mate.' Amber leaned forward on to the table again. 'The choice is yours. Five thousand or the word's out on the Falls tomorrow morning.'

Archie shivered and closed his eyes for a moment but the darkness couldn't settle his thoughts. 'You're too late,' he said. 'The guards have got him.'

'They missed him.' Amber paused to let the significance of his next word sink in. 'Again.'

Oh, Christ, the fucker knew everything. 'Then I don't know where he is,' Archie admitted bleakly.

'But you can find out.'

'I don't know. It depends.'

'On what?'

'On what I hear.'

'You'll try to hear. Listen very carefully. Won't you?'

Archie nodded glumly, admitting defeat.

'Half the money when you give me the nod. And half after I've talked to Callan.' Amber stood up and put his hand on Archie's shoulder. 'And don't do anything silly. My people know all about you.

If I turn up with a bag over my head they'll drop the word.
Automatically.'

Archie followed him meekly to the door and they waited for the
manager to let them out. 'Your mates are waiting for you,' Amber said
on the footpath.

Archie glanced at the dirty Hiace van and the headlights flashed in
his eyes. 'That was all bullshit about the recording contract, wasn't it?'

'All this whingeing paddy music sounds the same to me,' Amber
shrugged. 'But you find Callan and I'll see what we can do. As an
added bonus. Drop a word in a few ears.'

Archie went towards the van, his feet dragging like weights, trying
to get his thoughts together. Run. Everything told him to run, get the
hell out of the country. And quick. Either way he was dead. Don't help
Amber and he was dead; help him and he was probably dead. But five
thousand quid would make it easier to get away.

The piano player took one look at his skeletal face as he sat in on
the passenger side and said, 'No dice.'

'Well?' the drummer demanded.

'He'll see what he can do,' Archie repeated. 'Drop a word in a few
ears.'

The other two looked at each other. 'What more can anyone do?'
the drummer asked the piano player. 'Sounds fair enough to me.' He
pulled another bottle of Guinness out of the six-pack and levered the
top off and handed it to Archie. 'What the fuck's the matter with you?
It's not the end of the world.'

'Me?' Archie lifted the bottle to his mouth and emptied half of it.
'Nothing.' He stared across the dark car park to where the street lights
lit the road with a sickly yellow. 'I'm over the fucking moon.'

Seven

The dawn came up pink and clean and the landscape was as still as a painting. The mountains were far behind, propped up by their long dark shadows, and the land rippled down in a series of humps and hollows to the glassy bay. Grey stone walls marked out small fields, pocked by unmovable rocks, and the low white houses were becoming more frequent.

Callan was on a narrow, winding road when his ears caught the faint purr of an engine. He looked around for somewhere to hide and saw an open shed sinking into the boggy land beside the road. He quickened his pace and got under its thatched cover. A dog began to bark in a nearby house.

He stood back from the opening and listened between the barks. The engine grew louder, coming from the east, and turned into the drone of a light aircraft. It passed close by and faded again but did not disappear altogether. The dog gave up its barking.

The shed was built of thick stone walls and a flat cart, resting on its shafts, took up most of the space. Faded fertiliser bags were strewn about and a harness and rusty implements hung from the walls. Callan sat on the edge of the cart, between the shafts, and yawned as he stared out at the calm countryside.

A grey donkey rested its head like a rock on a stone wall in the next field and watched him with infinite patience. He lay back cautiously on the cart, testing its equilibrium, and then put the rifle by his right arm and covered it with the backpack. He closed his eyes and drifted into an uneasy sleep.

He awoke suddenly and reached for the gun. Its cold, reassuring metal was still there and he scanned the scenery quickly. The donkey was gone but everything else was unchanged.

He stood up and stretched, wondering if he had had that nightmare again, the one that had unsettled him on the plane. I must have, he decided uncertainly: otherwise, why would it have come back to me now? He thought about it for a moment, its mixture of the real and the unreal. The Winchester was a gun he had used a few times for longer range shots but the situation was unreal. He had never been in a situation like that, would never have fired from such an obvious point as the brow of a hill.

He shrugged it away irritably: in spite of its images it had nothing to do with the present situation. It was a product of Boston, a manifestation of the aimlessness of his life there. The onset of the male menopause, Sharon had diagnosed, half jokingly, one night when it had roused him in a confused panic. The end of immortality, she had said seriously; helplessness in the face of death. That's what it means. He had laughed and told her not to be so Californian about everything.

But afterwards when she was asleep and he'd huddled close to her warm body, he had decided that maybe she was right. It had seemed ridiculous that he should be more scared of death in this happy bed than when it had been a real and immediate possibility in the treacherous hills of Armagh. But at least you could fight it there, he'd thought; it was a game where the penalty for a mistake could be fatal. But here you could do nothing but wait for it. And that's all I'd been doing. Stuck in dead-end jobs; constantly hiding from reality; no other purpose to life; nothing ahead but more of the same pointless existence; no way out.

Except for Sharon, of course. He had kissed the back of her neck lightly and stroked the curve of her shoulder with a finger. Even that wasn't enough in itself. It still left him with a precarious half-life, which seemed to go on diminishing itself with an ever-increasing momentum.

The memory stirred his yearning for her but he shook it away quickly. That was the sort of sentimentality that had got him into this corner. There was no room for it any more. Not if he was going to make it back to her.

The countryside was beginning to stir. A light breeze had come up and swept tentatively over the fields and eddied around the shed. Far off, the spotter plane moved silently around the mountains like a rigid bird.

Callan took a rusted plastering knife from the wall and picked with its point at the maple-leaf flag on his backpack. He took his time undoing the stitching and waited until it was after eight-thirty before he left the shed.

He continued down the narrow road towards the bay and found a rutted lane leading to a small cove. The sea moved with an undulating swell and the tide tumbled in in small white breakers, feeling at the powdery sand. There was nobody to be seen and he walked along the sloping shelf of rounded stones to the jagged rocks at one side.

He climbed into a secluded cleft and settled down with his back against a rock. The sun shone warmly on his face and he closed his eyes and listened to the soothing surf and dozed lightly for a long time. Then he moved stiffly and went down the rocks until he found a tiny pool and splashed its ice-cold water on his face.

He made his way up to the coast road and headed east. He had gone less than a mile when he rounded another bend and saw two teenage girls ahead of him. One was sitting on a low stone wall, the other stood patiently by the road. Two brightly coloured backpacks rested by the wall.

He was almost upon them when he heard a chugging car coming from behind and the girl by the road stuck out her thumb. A battered Toyota passed him and slowed. He quickened his pace as the girls gathered their bags and caught up with them.

'Can I come too?' he asked.

One of the girls gave him an expressive shrug and said something quickly in French to her companion.

Callan opened the front passenger door and looked in at the red-faced driver. He wore a bedraggled jacket and an open-necked shirt and had a soft hat slanted on the back of his head.

'Where're you going?' he asked.

'Galway.' Callan looked at the French girls and they both nodded.

'You're in luck,' the man said.

Callan got in the front and angled the backpack against the dashboard, feeling the rigid weapon through the fabric.

'That's a terrible load to be carrying in this weather,' the man laughed as he let out the clutch and the car moved off. 'Where're you from?'

'I'm from California,' Callan said and turned sideways to look into the back. 'I don't know about these ladies.'

'Lyon,' one of them said.

'You're not together, then,' the driver raised his eyes to Callan and reached for a packet of Major on the dashboard. Callan took the offered cigarette and the man proffered the open box over his shoulder. The girls shook their heads.

'No, we met back there.'

The man opened a box of matches with his hands together over the wheel and tried to strike one. The car bounced over another bump and he missed the box and cursed. He succeeded on the second try and bent sideways to hold out the burning match to Callan. The car veered across the road and took a bend on the wrong side.

'Light your own,' Callan said quickly.

'I have relations in Boston,' the man said, passing him the matches. Callan took the box, wondering if the man was telling him he recognised his accent. 'And what brings you here?'

'It's different.'

'Yeah,' the man gave a hacking laugh, 'it's that, all right. So different everyone wants to get out of it. Most of the place is in America already and the rest's waiting to go.'

'But you're still here?'

'I'm too set in my ways. I've two brothers and two sisters over there. Two in Boston and two in New York. A score of cousins, nieces, nephews. Most of the wife's family's over there. And if we'd had any children they'd be there too.' He shook his head. 'All doing well but they're all illegals. Can't come home for holidays, Christmas, funerals or anything.'

Callan caught passing glimpses of the sparkling sea through the casual walls as the road tried to follow the pitted edges of the bay. I know how they feel, he thought. I've got two passports and can't use either one. The Cleary one is certainly compromised and the Canadian one probably is too. I shouldn't have used both. But that was hindsight: it was too late now.

'So tell me about California,' the man said, leaning his right elbow out the open window as though he was settling down for a bar chat. 'What's it like?'

'Weird,' Callan said, thinking of Sharon and seeing her mischievous smile. 'They've got too much of everything. So much they don't know what to do with it.'

'Sounds like a good complaint.'

'Maybe everyone in Connemara should swop places with everyone in California,' Callan smiled. It would have been nice to have been able to bring her here, he decided. But that could never be. 'Solve both their problems.'

The man laughed and asked the girls where they had been and where they were going. Callan looked at the shop fronts as they drove

70

through Spiddal and thought how nice and uncomplicated it would be to be a genuine tourist. After the village the road curved round a grey beach and went past the solid block of an Irish college. Children poured out of its doors on their lunch break and reminded him he hadn't eaten for twenty-four hours.

Modern bungalows drifted past in a continuous ribbon of incongruous suburbia as they neared Galway and he thought about what he needed to do. Bale out before they got too close to the city, for a start. There were only two roads leading in from Connemara and road-blocks were likely. It'd be safer to walk.

'Somebody told me there's a nice beach along here,' he prompted the driver, trying to remember the approach to the city. 'Before you get to Galway.'

'Yeah,' the man said. 'Silver strand. At Barna. Grand spot.'

'Is it far from Galway?'

'A couple of miles.

'Can you drop me there?'

Callan turned and walked slowly back along the edge of the land towards the lego-like diving tower at the end of the promenade. On his left, the fairways of the golf course rolled in a smooth carpet towards the flapping flags on the greens. Four men wearing checks and caps waited impatiently on a nearby tee for another group to get clear. On his other side, the tide ebbed reluctantly from the loose stones, rolling away with the lingering promise of its return.

He saw Eoghan appear at the wall beside the tower and climb over stiffly and come towards him. Callan kept his eyes fixed beyond him, on the wall and the tower. Two boys were fishing with hand lines from the base of the tower, spinning the baits in a tight circle before letting them fly out to sea. There was no sign of anyone following him.

'It's all right,' Eoghan said as they met and shook hands solemnly. 'I've posted a couple of lookouts.'

'You heard what happened?' Callan asked without relaxing his vigilance. He didn't trust Eoghan totally; he couldn't afford to trust anyone totally any more.

'There's a problem?' Eoghan said, inviting an explanation without committing himself. His eyes behind his glasses were the colour of the wet stones left by the receding tide, shining slightly with a glint of anticipation. He had on the same used navy-blue suit he had worn at their last meeting and his grey face was grim with purpose.

'Somebody set me up,' Callan said.

Eoghan listened carefully to what had happened and asked him one or two questions and then fell into a pursed silence. 'Let's sit down,' he said after a moment.

They moved down the shifting stones and perched side by side on a large rock, facing the bay like an elderly father and adult son. Callan felt suddenly vulnerable, imagining a line of gardai sweeping steadily across the unseen golf course behind him. But he had to trust Eoghan a little: he needed him. Besides, he reassured himself, he wouldn't shop me like that.

'The first thing I want to say,' Eoghan began, as if he had prepared a formal speech, 'is that I had, and have, no knowledge of any plan to set you up. Needless to say, if I was aware of any such plan, I would not have revealed your presence to anyone. No matter what you said to me at our last meeting.' He paused. 'Understood?'

Callan nodded at the stones beneath his feet. If he was going to shop me, he was thinking, he'd never do it in a way that would point the finger at himself.

'The second point is that obviously I am not aware of everything that goes on any more. I have been shoved on to the sideline, as I told you.' Eoghan sighed as if the admission was as bad as the fact of his dismissal. 'But I still have some friends in the army, people who are not altogether enamoured with the way things are going but are not prepared to cause a split. Which, I agree, would be, ah, inadvisable.

'So I passed on your request for a meeting to an appropriate contact. But I took the liberty of not telling him why you wanted to meet. I merely said you were back, had contacted me for old time's sake and wanted to talk to somebody in a command position.'

Callan heard the undercurrent of authority in his measured tone as he watched the two boys whirl their baits and toss them out in a competition to see who could cast the furthest. He tried to detect their splashes but they were lost to him in the heaving water.

'Now,' Eoghan said. 'The question is, why? Why would anyone want to do this to you after all this time?'

He waited for an answer and Calian said, 'I have no idea.'

'There has to be a reason.'

'Not that I know of.'

'You're certain? Absolutely positive?'

Callan nodded. This was pointless. There was no reason. And, even if there was in somebody else's mind, he didn't want to know about it. He didn't care. He only wanted to get away again.

'Could it have something to do with the Maher business?'

He relishes the prospect of a conspiracy, Callan realised. He's dying to get involved. 'Hardly,' he said.

'But you can't overlook that possibility.' Eoghan wagged a finger at him.

'I don't see any connection,' Callan said patiently. 'And I don't think that's of any great relevance. All I want is to . . .'

'No relevance,' Eoghan interrupted with astonishment. 'How can you say that? That was a very significant event. In the light of subsequent developments as well as in its own right.'

'Maybe,' Callan said defensively. 'But it's of no great importance to me right now. What I need is some help. To get out of the country.'

'Cause and effect.' Eoghan looked at him with the sadness of a teacher disappointed by a favoured student. 'You have to study the cause and effect to understand anything.'

Callan sighed inwardly. He had never had much time for the conspiracy merchants, the people who revelled in the endless picking and sifting of information into elaborate theories. In his experience, it was usually a waste of time; they nearly always got it wrong. Although that never deterred them, only increased their relish for the next conspiracy.

'You have been set up twice,' Eoghan was saying. 'Once to shoot Maher and again now. And this time the plan was to have you arrested and jailed. Presumably for shooting Maher.' He paused. 'Can't you see the connection?'

It had a neat symmetry to it, Callan admitted to himself. Like all good conspiracy theories, it sounded perfectly obvious when it was put that way. 'But why?' he asked.

Eoghan didn't answer. 'You know I conducted an inquiry into the Maher affair?' he asked rhetorically. 'Personally.'

Callan nodded. He had heard that some time later, some time after his initial determination to find out what had happened had given way to disinterest.

'You were used,' Eoghan said, picking his words with a politician's care, 'by some of our impatient and less scrupulous comrades from the Six Counties. What it boiled down to was a crude attempt to overthrow the army council. It didn't succeed, of course. Not at that time.'

Callan had heard that, too, but it hadn't eased his personal predicament or made him feel any better about the comrades who had used him. He was still the one who had pulled the trigger and was left with the consequences. Contacted at the last minute, given no time to think about it. An RUC detective was coming across the border, he was told, expecting to meet an informer. He was to snipe him.

It was a murky, wet November morning, everything sopping with damp. The car windows clouded with condensation as he was driven to the site, shown where the RUC man was supposed to rendezvous and quickly picked his position. He waited under a dripping tree for the car to arrive and then silently willed the man to get out. The man had sat in his car for a while and then stepped out and Callan was aware only of a dark anoraked figure with a tweed hat. He shot him once, quickly. In the head.

Later, in his safe house, he heard the radio news and realised with a numbing shock that he had shot a garda inspector. And the nagging doubts that had been in the back of his mind as he was hustled to the scene had come to the fore. It wasn't a job for a sniper. It was a close-up job: drive up to him like the person he was expecting; do it at close range; make certain. But it was too late by then: it didn't make a hell of a lot of difference that he had been conned about the target's identity. Nor did it make any difference that he had been the unwitting pawn in a plot to pressurise the leadership. He had been used, all right.

'That's all history,' Callan shrugged. 'I don't see how it can have any bearing on what's happening now.'

'I thought you might be aware of some other factors,' Eoghan admitted with a faint air of disappointment.

'I'm not.'

They fell silent. The sun shone and the waves broke and seeped among the stones and withdrew. A man with a rolled towel under his arm walked along the base of the tower and peered uncertainly at the sea and disappeared round the other side.

Eoghan seemed to have been deflated by the absence of anything to keep his theory buoyant. Callan wondered if his interest was spurred by something more than concern with his fate. Part of some plot connected, perhaps, with Eoghan's fall from power. Maybe I'm being used again, he thought. To get back at the people who had finally toppled him. But that's not my concern.

'I need a clean passport,' he said.

'I'll see what I can do,' Eoghan nodded.

'And a secure house,' Callan added, hoping that the landlady of the guesthouse where he had left his backpack wasn't the inquisitive type. She had seemed vague and uninterested, a middle-aged woman with two yapping poodles, but you never knew.

'Anywhere in particular?'

'Dublin, maybe,' Callan shrugged.

Eoghan took a small diary from his pocket, wrote an address on a page and tore it out. 'That's secure.' He handed it over. 'Tell them I sent you.'

Callan thanked him and was about to move when Eoghan said casually there were one or two other things he had learned. 'You remember Blinker?' he asked.

Callan remembered a short, chubby man bouncing with delight behind the wheel of a getaway car, alternatively yelling, what a fucking shot, and giggling, you see how the fucker jumped? Callan had felt the gloating, the unmistakably personal triumph, in his voice at the death of the policeman and it made him uneasy. It was not as personal a war to him as it was to some of the Northerners: he understood, but never quite shared, their highly personalised euphoria at every blow struck against an individual enemy. Jesus, Blinker had breathed at him with reverence, what a shot. Shut the fuck up, Callan had said.

'He was the one sent to meet you,' Eoghan said.

'What does he do now?' Callan inquired, as if he was asking routinely about an old school acquaintance.

'Headquarters staff.'

'I take it he's not one of your contacts?'

'You take it correctly,' Eoghan said stiffly. Then he shifted on the rock and added slowly: 'The other thing is that Willy is back home.'

Callan turned to him sharply and their eyes locked in a mutual questioning. Eoghan gave a barely perceptible shrug. 'Perhaps he can fill in some of the gaps for us,' he suggested.

So it was all a set-up, Callan thought, right from the word go. His mind ran quickly over everything that had happened since the phone call from Peggy. I should have known, he thought, when they produced the passport for me. Without any recriminations or delay; just happened to have one that they wanted someone to take out of the country to clear the name from the immigration records. I'd have seen it if I hadn't been so anxious to come back anyway.

'Where do I find him?'

'He's got a place down the town,' Eoghan said with the satisfaction of a deliverer of bad news. 'Off Nun's Island.' He looked away across the stretch of the bay, knowing that he was being drawn into something as shifting and as inexorable as the restless ocean. A helpless piece of flotsam twisting on the tide.

The hall door swung in easily under his hand and Callan stepped quickly across the threshold, straight off the street. The house was gloomy after the sunlight and the air was heavy with the trapped heat of the departing day. He knocked once on the first door.

Willy pulled it open and sank back in his wheelchair as if he was stepping backwards with surprise. 'Fergus!' he exclaimed. 'What're you doing here?'

Callan brushed past him and looked around the sparsely furnished room. There was a narrow bed along one wall, a television in a corner, a coffee table and a light armchair in front of the empty fireplace. An archway led off into a small kitchen and dining area.

Willy angled his wheelchair back and forth with quick, practised movements to close the door. His head seemed too large for his body and was topped with receding gingerish hair. Pain and concentration had lined and dulled his face prematurely.

'You tell me.' Callan swung back and levelled the cold anger, that had built up since his conversation with Eoghan, at him.

'Tell you what?' Willy demanded, automatically matching his aggression.

'What I'm doing here?'

'How the fuck would I know.' Willy threw his hands in the air and went to wheel his chair forward but Callan blocked his path.

'What you mean,' Callan glared down at Willy's upturned face, 'is why am I here when I should have been caught in the trap you set for me.'

'What?' Willy let out a startled laugh. 'I don't know what you're talking about.'

'You know.' Callan leaned forward and put his hands on the arms of the chair and began to push it steadily backwards. 'You arranged to get me back. Pretended to disappear. Had Peggy call me. To walk me into your nice little trap.'

The chair bumped against the net-curtained window and Callan leaned closer to his hostile face. 'Why?' he demanded.

Willy gave him a glare of contempt as if his helplessness was his strength.

'Why?' Callan repeated. 'You working for the cops now? Sold out?'

'Sold out,' Willy spat out angrily. 'Jesus. Listen to who's talking.'

'What's that supposed to mean?'

'What the fuck d'you think it means? You're the one who abandoned the struggle for an easy life in America.'

Callan shook his head in disbelief and straightened up. 'You seem to have a very short memory,' he said. 'Is that why you did it? That's the reason?'

'I didn't do anything to you,' Willy said flatly. 'Except . . .'

'Yes,' Callan nodded bitterly. 'Say it. Except save my life. Which is why you knew I'd come back when you called.'

'I didn't want you to come back.'

'Don't bullshit me,' Callan said and recited his evidence again, numbering off each item with a raised finger. 'You told Peggy to call me if you disappeared. Then you disappear. She calls. I come back. Almost get caught. You re-appear when it's supposed to be safe.' He paused. 'And then you try to tell me you know nothing.'

'Peggy,' Willy sighed with exasperation. 'She treats me like a helpless fucking invalid.'

Which is what you are, Callan thought angrily, but he said: 'She only did what you wanted her to do.'

Willy said nothing and they glared at each other across the gathering gloom. Callan broke the silent stare to glance out the window over Willy's head. The shadows were stretching out into the square but the low sun still glistened off the parked cars at its centre.

He realised he didn't feel anything at Willy's betrayal, just the same anger at the knowledge that other people were playing some obscure game with his life. The anger that now had him trying to intimidate a cripple. He sank into the armchair and lit a cigarette, wondering what he had expected. An instant explanation? Cosy reminiscences about the old days? This man wasn't the Willy he had known; he didn't even look like him any more.

'Why?' he repeated quietly, after a while. 'Because you really think I've an easy life in America?'

Willy appeared to shake his head but Callan wasn't sure. All he could see was Willy's huddled shape against the outside light.

'If that's what you think, you're very wrong,' Callan sighed cigarette smoke. 'I'm still on the run. Permanently.'

'That's not what I hear,' Willy said. 'I hear you've settled down very nicely. Shacked up with a shapely blonde and all.'

Callan cursed silently. Someone had been keeping a close eye on him. And he had thought he had become practically invisible.

'But then,' Willy added with a harsh laugh, 'you always had a way with the women. I never knew whether you were really fighting for Ireland or just out to impress whatever piece of skirt you were chasing.'

Envy, Callan decided: he's bitter with the world and with me and what looks from here like a wonderful life. But, at least, he was talking. 'What's going on, Willy?' he pleaded.

Willy said nothing.

'You owe it to me,' Callan persisted. 'To tell me that at least.'

'Because you saved my life too,' Willy snapped. 'Thanks very fucking much. Look at it. It's a great life you saved me. It might've been better if you hadn't.'

'What happened happened. A long time ago . . .'

'Not for me it isn't.'

'I know, I know,' Callan conceded. 'Something similar happened to me. And I'm still living with it every day too. But there was nothing either of us could do about it then. And there's nothing we can do about it now. Except put up with it.'

Willy gave a derisive snort as if Callan was a well-meaning social worker.

'You're still involved in the movement?'

'Oh yes,' Willy said. 'Handing out leaflets. Selling An Phoblacht on street corners. Really big stuff. As long as someone remembers to take me along.'

Callan tossed his cigarette end into the fireplace and wondered if Willy was deliberately exaggerating his plight, seeking sympathy instead of providing explanations. It's so much easier to be a victim in this goddam country, he thought. You can wallow in it, blame everyone and everything else. Use it to justify anything.

Still, he felt a twinge of sympathy for him. For the old Willy. He didn't recognise this person any more: there was none of the boisterous energy, the dedication and anarchic humour of the old Willy in this sullen and bitter presence. The man he had once known was as dead as if they had carried his corpse back over the border that night. Maybe he was right. Maybe it would have been better if he had died then.

Callan stood up and looked out the window. The sun had gone down and the street lights come on but they made no impression yet on the slowly dwindling twilight. He looked down at Willy's vague features, flattened by the gloom. He shrugged and held out his hand.

'It wasn't meant to be a trap,' Willy said. 'It was intended to bring you back for a few days.'

Callan let his hand fall to his side and waited.

'Somebody wanted to talk to you. That's all.'

'Who? About what?'

'I don't know. I was ordered to arrange it.'

'How did you know where to find me?'

'I was given the number.'

Callan closed his eyes for a moment and saw himself floating on the tide again. Drifting helplessly into deeper waters. It was not just a simple question of getting back to Boston any more. He'd have to sort out whatever it was that was going on first. Otherwise, it wouldn't go away.

'They could've talked to me in Boston,' he said.

Willy shrugged. 'I wasn't told anything. All I do is sell fucking newspapers.'

'Blinker?' Callan asked. 'Was he the one?'

'No. I don't know.'

Callan waited.

'Why don't you ask your wife,' Willy said with a crooked smile.

'Maire?'

Willy nodded. 'If she'll talk to you.'

'It was her?'

'No.' Willy shook her head. 'But she should know. She's an important person these days. On the army council now.'

Eight

'Mammy!' The boy's voice rose in a panicked shriek. 'Mammy!'

Maire leapt out of bed without thinking and the pounding on the front door broke into her consciousness as she went into the boy's bedroom and hugged him and told him it was all right. The pounding continued and she went back into her bedroom and grabbed a full-length dressing gown.

She pulled it on as she went down the stairs. The sunshine spread brightly around the bulky shadows outside the glass-panelled door and lit up the small hall. She threw the door open and three armed men pushed her back against the wall and raced into the downstairs rooms.

'Very fetching.' Sergeant Pursell looked her up and down from the doorstep. Her dark hair dangled lankily down to her shoulders and her face was pale and unfocused from broken sleep. He had a smirk on his face and a Smith and Wesson revolver in his hand.

'Have you got a warrant?' she demanded automatically.

'Of course.' He stepped in.

'Show me.'

'Why? You've seen one before. They're all the same.'

The three other detectives crowded back into the hall and Pursell took her by the arm and led her to the bottom of the stairs. She shook her arm free and he prodded his gun into her back. 'Up,' he said. 'Show us your etchings.'

One of the detectives sniggered and another covered the upstairs landing with his Uzi sub-machine-gun as she led the procession upstairs.

'Mammy,' the boy's voice came down, tentatively.

'It's all right,' she answered. 'I'm coming.'

Pursell guided her to the main bedroom and followed her in. One of the detectives tossed the duvet on to the floor and felt the double mattress and the other opened a built-in wardrobe and poked the muzzle of his Uzi among the hanging clothes.

Maire suddenly realised that Pursell was no longer behind her. She hurried from the room and collided with a detective who was coming out of the third bedroom.

'What'd your dad bring you from America?' Pursell was asking the boy as she burst into the room.

The boy was sitting up in the bed with his hands grasping the duvet up to his mouth. His round eyes were staring at the revolver hanging from Pursell's hand and he was shaking. Maire stepped in front of Pursell and pushed at his chest.

'Out,' she said.

Pursell stood his ground. 'I was only asking a civil question.' He looked over her shoulder at the boy. 'Did he bring you a toy gun or anything?'

'Fuck you,' she breathed, thumping his chest with her fist. 'Get out of here.'

The boy began to sob. She turned away quickly and sat on his bed and cradled his head on her breasts. She closed her eyes and rested her chin on his hair and rocked him gently with soothing sounds.

Pursell looked on, unmoved, and then dropped heavily to his knees and checked under the bed. He got up again and glanced around the room at a large poster of Michael Jackson in a forked lightning pose and a small mirror with a green Gaelic script saying, *Tiocfaidh ár Lá.* There was a huddle of toys on the floor and he glared down at their alien shapes. None of them looked new.

'You bastard.' Maire was looking over her shoulder at him with a mixture of hatred and hurt. She was still cradling the boy and had his ear covered with her hand. 'You didn't have to do that.'

'Do what?'

'He's terrified of guns.'

Pursell's face crumpled into a humourless smile and he broke into a slow, rumbling laugh. 'Well, well,' he said. 'Isn't that something?'

She turned away and Pursell shook his head pensively. 'And what do you think he sees when he looks in that mirror?' he asked. 'Our day will come. Through the barrel of a gun.' He let out another derisive laugh.

Maire ignored him and he stepped out of the room. A detective was dangling from the trapdoor into the attic, his legs searching for the flimsy railing on the landing. He found it and jumped down quickly and shook his head to Pursell.

Pursell heard the other man moving about downstairs and he went into Maire's bedroom where the third detective was going through the drawers of a bedside table. He held up a foil of contraceptive pills and raised his eyes. Pursell took them and went back to the boy's bedroom.

'Where's Fergus?' he demanded.

Maire said nothing and he flipped the foil against his nails until she looked at him.

'Getting ready for his return, are you?'

She gave him a withering glare and turned away again and hugged the boy tighter.

'You don't expect me to believe you haven't seen him,' Pursell went on. 'He's been to see everyone else. Like a regular returned Yank.'

She ignored him and he watched the tableau of a distraught mother and child, tempted to haul her in for questioning. It would be a waste of time, he knew, but it would assuage his frustration, if only momentarily. The longer he thought about it, the more pointless it seemed.

He tossed the pills on to the boy's bed and went out.

Inspector Keerins held the phone impatiently and heard the door slam and a mumble of voices and then the clanging of the other receiver as Archie knocked it against something metallic.

'I want to see you,' he said. 'Tonight.'

'No,' Archie replied quickly, as if any hesitation would weaken his resolve. 'Not possible.'

'Usual time and place.'

'No. It's not on. I can't help you any more.'

'What do you mean?'

'I can't help you any more,' Archie repeated. 'I've quit.'

'Why? What's happened?'

'Nothing. Do what you like but I don't want any more of this shit.'

Archie hung up and Keerins replaced the phone slowly and slipped back disconsolately in his chair. This was just what he didn't need right now. Callan had disappeared without trace, the raids on his known associates and a selection of suspected safe houses had produced nothing. Everyone was waiting for him to come up with a new lead and, without Archie, he had nothing. Not even a prospect of any- thing.

Something must have happened, he decided. Archie was scared. Maybe his contact had turned sour on him. Or worse. Maybe the

82

Provos had uncovered the contact. In which case he'd find out soon enough who it had been. His body would turn up somewhere.

Pursell looked up from the reports he was reading and caught Keerins's eye. 'These fuckers really are priceless,' he said wearily. 'His mammy's shocked at any suggestion that her Fergus would harm a fly. And that bitch Maire who's orphaned more children than all of us have sired gets upset when I let her precious little boy catch sight of a gun. I bet you the little git's in the Fianna already, being trained as a so-called freedom fighter. Jesus.' He shook his head in bewilderment. 'I'll never understand how they do it? How the fuck they square this double think?'

Keerins shrugged, his mind on his own difficulties. It wasn't enough to be able to say that they now knew for certain Callan was back in the country. Not when the harsh reality was that he had let him get away twice. Nobody had actually said that to him but his new-boy sensitivity imagined the sniggers behind his back. If he wasn't careful he'd end up with some god-awful nickname. Getaway George.

'Anything of any use at all in that stuff?' he asked.

Pursell lifted up the sheaf of reports from the raids. 'Not a morsel.' He let the papers drop back on to his desk. 'Nobody's seen hide nor hair of him. He doesn't exist, if you'd believe them. Fergus who?'

'Is there anyone we missed out on?'

Pursell shook his head decisively and Keerins's extension rang. He answered with his name and listened for a moment. 'Summons from the Super,' he said, getting to his feet. 'What the hell am I going to tell him?'

'Tell him they all love their children.' Pursell smirked with the satisfaction of his lack of official responsibility.

'Thanks,' Keerins muttered drily. He went down the corridor, trying to formulate an optimistic report for his superior and wondering if he should tell him about Archie. No, he decided, not until he got to the bottom of it first. The little fucker couldn't be allowed to walk out on him just like that.

The superintendent pointed to a chair beside his desk and Keerins sat down. 'Any more thoughts on what you like to call the mole?' he asked as he opened the file Keerins had already sent to him.

Keerins shook his head involuntarily. He wasn't expecting this and hadn't done anything further about it since he had compiled the list of people who knew about the Callan operation at Shannon.

The superintendent scanned the list. 'A lot of names here,' he said.

'Yes,' Keerins admitted, taking it as a rebuke. 'I'm afraid I probably mentioned it to too many people.'

'There is no room for idle chat here. We operate on a strict need-to-know basis.'

Keerins shifted uneasily. Me and my big mouth, he thought, trying to show off and make a mark. But he had already learned that lesson: tell nobody anything from now on. Which would be all right until they discovered he had nothing to tell them anyway.

The superintendent picked another sheet of paper from his desk. 'There was a meeting of the Anglo-Irish conference in Belfast yesterday,' he said, studying the paper. 'At which the other side said that the Callan extradition warrant was merely a formality, clearing up paperwork. They accept that Callan has to be tried here for capital murder.'

Keerins waited, wondering why he was being told this, what was his need to know.

The superintendent put down the paper and faced him. 'Someone also let slip casually over coffee that Callan had escaped the net in Connemara.'

'Ah,' Keerins sighed knowingly. So there was a mole. Archie wouldn't have known about it that quickly.

'Our masters are not happy about the extent of their knowledge.' The superintendent nodded. 'They want to know how this came about.'

Keerins racked his brain. 'It was a pretty big operation,' he said. 'With the follow-up search and all. There were a lot of people involved.'

'You can exclude the locals and the recruits.' The superintendent handed him back his list. 'Cross-check those names.'

Keerins ran his eye down the list. 'Most of them definitely knew,' he said helplessly. 'Probably all of them could have known.'

The superintendent watched him pensively and Keerins felt inadequate and searched the list again to avoid his eyes. It was hopeless, he thought. The whole place knew about it.

'What do your instincts tell you?' the superintendent asked.

Instincts, Keerins looked up incredulously. Surely he didn't believe in instincts?

'Anything you know or have heard unofficially which would point you towards anyone in particular?' the superintendent added.

Keerins shook his head quickly, vaguely uneasy at the implications of what he was hearing. 'I'm too new,' he said. 'I hardly know most of the people here.'

'Precisely. You might notice something the rest of us would miss.'

Keerins shook his head.

'Keep your eyes and ears open.' The superintendent turned back to his desk. 'This cannot be allowed to drag on.'

He wants me to spy on my colleagues, Keerins decided as he got up. Which means that he probably has somebody else spying on me, that I am suspect too. He felt a sense of shock as though someone had suggested something sordid. Yes, of course he was right: the mole couldn't be allowed to go on operating. But still.

'Callan?' The superintendent looked up as he reached the door.

'Nothing definite yet,' Keerins replied. 'The raids produced nothing. The airports and ports have been circulated with pictures and one name he's already used and three other possibles.'

The superintendent nodded as though it was a minor matter.

Archie sat at one end of the cheap couch, mesmerised by the meshing dark images of sinister alleys on an MTV rock video. His head beat to the thumping music and he sucked on a cigarette like it was the remnant of the joint he had just abandoned.

He slowly became aware that Sue hadn't come back and he dragged his attention away from the television and tried to hear if the baby was still crying. But the music dominated his heightened hearing and he shrugged and reached down beside the couch for the bottle of Guinness. His hand couldn't find it and he leaned over the arm to see where it was. He straightened up with it and there were two men smiling down at him.

One breathed in deeply and raised his eyes upwards. The other tut-tutted and said, 'Smoking the profits again, Archie.'

'What?' Archie said.

'You'll never get into the big time if you keep on smoking the merchandise yourself,' the man said.

Archie looked at him without comprehension. Sue was standing behind them, her face taut with tension, saying something. The infant was squalling, puce-faced, in her arms. The music blared from the television and the screen was filled with bright, overlapping figures. Archie didn't know what was going on.

One of the men picked the end of the joint out of the ashtray and held it in front of Archie's eyes. 'This is a bust,' he said slowly. 'Drugs squad.'

'Ah, Jesus, lads,' Archie said, looking from one to the other.

The other detective stepped over to the television and slid down the sound. 'Don't the neighbours ever complain? he asked rhetorically.

'Look what you've done,' Sue whined in the sudden silence, 'bursting in here in the middle of the night. She's going to have a seizure or something.'

She swung round in a desperate circle as the baby caught its breath and then resumed its strangled howling. Archie looked on as if everything was happening outside a plate-glass window.

'Come on.' A detective took the Guinness bottle from his hand and grabbed his elbow. He hauled him easily to his feet.

'Where're you taking him?' Sue shouted above the baby.

'Never mind,' one of the men said. 'Just be grateful we're not going to take the place apart.'

'Go on,' she screamed and pushed the baby at him. 'Take her too and charge her. Why don't you? Go on, you heap of shit.'

The man holding Archie pushed past her and his colleague followed them out the door of the flat and along the open balcony, muttering curses to himself. 'I think I'm going to be sick,' Archie said but they didn't pay any attention.

They hustled him down the narrow concrete stairs, down six short flights, in a hurry to get out of there. Most of the lights were out and the stairs stank of urine. At the bottom, they half ran him to the second of two cars in the courtyard between the flats and one detective pulled open the passenger door.

'He's stoned,' he said to Keerins as the other detective pushed Archie into the seat.

'Thanks,' Keerins said.

'Get the fuck out of here.' The man slammed the door. They ran to their own car and a bottle splattered on the concrete behind one of them. He looked up at the dark balconies but didn't stop.

Their car moved off as soon as they were in and an empty beer can bounced on the bonnet of Keerins's car. He accelerated towards the archway as if his life depended on it.

He shot out of the flats and braked hard to pause at the street. Archie lurched forwards and Keerins grabbed him with a restraining hand and let him loll back into his seat. 'I'm going to be sick,' he moaned.

'Hold on,' Keerins shouted and swung the car on to the street. The drugs squad men had disappeared and he sped towards the city centre.

Archie groaned and leaned his head between his legs. 'Open the window,' Keerins shouted at him and slowed the car. Archie fumbled feebly with the handle and Keerins stopped the car by a line of steel-shuttered shops. He leant across and pulled the passenger door open.

Archie swung his head out and threw up into the gutter with a long drawn out, stomach-emptying splash. Keerins looked away at the sickly sodium street lights and waited for him to finish. The warm smell of the vomit and Archie's spluttered retching made him feel nauseous. Wonderful, he thought.

A patrol car came down the empty street and slowed and its driver and observer watched them for a moment and then cruised by. Archie hauled himself up in the seat and swept his bare arm across his mouth. He seemed to have revived and Keerins drove off slowly.

'Right,' he said grimly. 'Talk.'

'Where're we going?'

'That depends. On what you've got to say for yourself.'

'You're taking me in. OK,' Archie shrugged and lit a cigarette. 'I can't help you any more.'

'Why not?'

'Because my nerves can't take it.'

'Balls.'

'Look at me,' Archie pleaded. 'I'm a fucking nervous wreck.'

Keerins glanced at his peaky face and snorted. He didn't believe that for a moment; Archie wasn't going to get any sympathy from him. Not when so much was depending on him.

'Honest to God,' Archie said. 'I can't take it. You know what those fuckers are like. Blow you away without blinking.'

'So what's new?' Keerins retorted. 'You knew that from the start. When you volunteered to get this information for me. And it was you suggested it in the first place. Not me, remember.'

Archie did not answer and Keerins let the silence drag out as he drove slowly up Burgh Quay. The city centre was like a dozing assembly-line worker, its traffic lights and flashing advertisements running unheeded through their automatic routines. A newspaper delivery van swung out of the lane beside the Irish Press and roared past them through the green lights at O'Connell Bridge. Keerins stopped the car abruptly as the lights turned orange.

'What's happened?' he demanded. 'What's making you so nervous all of a sudden?'

'Nothing.' Archie shifted uneasily. 'I found the fucker for you twice. That's enough.'

'Don't give me that,' Keerins said irritably.

Archie considered, for a fraction of a second, telling him the truth but that would only complicate things even more. Might even get him killed. 'It's not worth it,' he said.

'What do you mean?'

'Well, what do I get out of it?' Archie tossed his cigarette end out the window and the sense of grievance seemed to revive him further. 'Nothing but my nerves shot to pieces. And every chance of having my head shot off as well. I must've been out of my fucking mind to get involved at all.'

'What you've got is your freedom,' Keerins reminded him. 'And my guarantee we'll look after you if you're really worried about your safety.'

Which was worth less than sweet fuck all, Archie told himself. He knew that now; he had certainly found that out. The only way out was to get Amber what he wanted, take the money and run. Nobody would see his heels for the dust.

The lights changed and Keerins drove across the junction. 'Money?' he asked. 'Is that what you want?'

'I want out,' Archie said with feeling.

Fuck it, Keerins thought bitterly. He didn't believe anything Archie had said. It wasn't nerves that made him twitchy; he'd been born twitching. Something must have happened. But he couldn't see any way of prising it out of him at the moment.

'OK,' Keerins said. 'One last time. Go back to your contact and find out what's going on. And then we're quits. That'll be it.'

'No way,' Archie said. 'I'm not going back to him any more. Not after you let Callan get away again. Suppose he thinks I haven't been tipping you off like I was supposed to.'

'Haven't you seen him since?' Keerins turned right, across the Liffey, and drove past the dark bulk of the Four Courts.

'No. And I don't want to.'

A thought struck Keerins. 'How d'you know we didn't get Callan?'

'What d'you mean?' Archie parried, alarm bells ringing in his mind.

'Who told you we didn't get Callan?'

'It's obvious,' Archie said with an attempt at rising impatience. 'Your picture would've been in the paper if you had.'

'You were talking to him.' Keerins nodded to himself. 'Your source.'

Archie said nothing and looked at the lit door of the Bridewell garda station as the car stopped outside.

'Last chance,' Keerins nodded towards the door. He took the keys from the ignition and hung the ring on the top of his index finger and swivelled it in Archie's line of sight. 'What'd he say?'

'Nothing you'd want to hear,' Archie sighed. Fuck him, he thought. Let them lock me up and nothing's my problem any more. Except that that bastard Amber would decide I was avoiding him and drop the word to the Provos.

'What?'

'He said you fuckers couldn't catch the flu in the middle of an epidemic.'

They stared at each other for a moment and then Keerins told him to get out and followed him into the station. He guided Archie past the public office and into a corridor as one of the drugs squad detectives came down a stairway. Someone was shouting in a slurred voice from the cells away to the right.

'He's all yours,' Keerins said.

'Oh, good.' The detective rubbed his hands and took Archie by the arm and led him towards the cells. Archie didn't look back.

Keerins continued on to the detective unit where the second man from the drugs squad was sitting on the edge of a table reading the first edition of the Irish Independent.

'Charge him,' Keerins said. 'But make sure he gets bail. I want him back on the streets tomorrow. When I've had time to organise a tail.'

'No problem,' the detective said.

'Thanks,' Keerins said. 'I owe you one.'

He went back the way he had come and got into his car. The lingering smell of vomit mixed with stale tobacco seemed to be a suitable odour for the way he felt. Playing dirty was the order of the day, he thought viciously. Archie was going to produce a lot more intelligence. By fair means or foul.

Nine

The hum of the city, heavy with the unaccustomed heat, carried through the open window but the bedroom was still cool. A bright shaft of sunshine came down from on high and spread its glare, but none of its warmth, around the room. Callan lay propped against the headboard of the narrow bed, fully clothed. He glanced with little interest at an evening-paper story about another possible cure for AIDS and he turned the page to a political report. Most of the names were recognisable but the context of their abusive controversy was as obscure as a clouded mirror.

He felt relaxed, lulled by the steady rituals of the house and the dull throb of the city. The waiting was soothingly familiar, paradoxical proof that he was back in action. Which was oddly reassuring.

Crossing the country by train he had wondered about the anger which had made him barge in impetuously on Willy, destroying any chance of a fruitful meeting. It wasn't directed particularly at Willy, he realised as the thickly hedged fields went by. Nor at whoever had set the trap for him. Nor even at the predicament in which they had landed him. It was a reaction to the fact that someone was trying to drag him back into what was past. Which was strange, given that he had chosen to come back to the past. But nostalgia was selective: it required the awkward parts of the past to stay in their place.

He had turned up in Dublin at the address Eoghan had given him and found an elderly couple, a retired civil servant and his wife. They took him in without question, hovering solicitously while keeping their distance, as though they feared he would disappear if they questioned him about anything. Like a long lost son. They didn't ask his name and he didn't tell them.

There was a polite knock on the door and he folded the paper and swung his legs off the bed. The elderly woman edged in sideways with a tray and said, 'I thought you might like a cup of coffee.'

'You should have called.' He stood up as she put the tray on the narrow desk. 'I would have come down.'

'Milk?' she fussed. 'I can't remember if you take milk in your coffee.'

He shook his head. 'Black is fine.'

'And no sugar.' She handed him a cup and saucer and offered him a plate of chocolate biscuits. He took one out of politeness, idly thinking he'd become too fat to move if he stayed here very long. She had instantly rejected his suggestions that he would go out to eat and fed him three meals a day with mid-morning and mid-afternoon coffee.

'There's no sign of the weather breaking,' she said. 'The forecast said it'll continue through the weekend at least.'

He stepped over to the edge of the sunshine and looked out at the long, rolled lawn behind the house. It was carefully edged with flower beds and led down to a patch of vegetables. A line of evergreen trees at the back wall screened the next row of houses.

'We had a letter from Aileen this morning,' the woman said.

'How's she getting on?' Aileen was one of their talking points, the couple's only daughter. He had heard all about her academic achievements and her boyfriend and her mother's hopes and fears for her.

'She's got a proper job now, she says.' The woman sounded dubious. 'In public relations.'

'That sounds good,' he offered. A social-science graduate, Aileen's textbooks were still lined up on the desk against the wall. She and her boyfriend had recently emigrated to Australia.

Callan finished the coffee in silence and she took the cup. 'Harry said to tell you you're welcome to take the car again,' she said. 'If you need it.'

'Thank you.' Harry had talked about the situation, confining himself to what he presumed Callan would want to hear, a denunciation of the latest sectarian killing by loyalists. He had offered the use of his car which Callan borrowed to scout the cul- de-sac where Maire lived. He had driven slowly by her house, noting everything he could without stopping, particularly the number of the small red Renault outside. 'He's very kind.'

'He had to go into town to get something but he'll be back for lunch.' She picked up the tray. 'The car will be free after that.'

He thanked her again and she left and he lay back down on Aileen's bed with his hands behind his head. Everything would be fine as long as he took it easy, moved with caution. He had no doubt that he would get back to Boston.

Four boys shouldered one another through the door of the shop and burst on to the pavement and reformed into a shifting huddle. Callan tipped the cigarette ash out of the car window and watched them, wondering what an eleven-year-old looked like. They unwrapped their ice pops and he studied their faces and saw nothing and everything. Any one of them could be Shay.

His unseen son had always been vague, an undefined presence at the edge of his consciousness. Just a name. It was all he knew about him; he had no idea what he looked like. He realised now that he couldn't even tell if the boys strolling away, schoolbags dragging heavily, were the right age. They crossed the road towards the cul-de-sac and his interest heightened, shaded with apprehension. What if he really was one of them?

The boys stopped on a patch of green at the corner and one climbed on to the lump of granite bearing the road name and defied the others to dislodge him. Callan watched until they tired of the game and drifted away, past the mouth of the cul-de-sac. Shay hadn't been among them after all.

The afternoon stretched out and the suburb shifted lazily on the side of a hill. People drifted to and from the line of local shops: cars went down the hill and groaned up from the valley: a butcher stood idly by his sun-shaded window. The huddles of houses faded away on the slopes of the distant hills which ran away inland, smudged blue by the heat haze, in a series of aloof humps.

Callan lapsed into a drowsy wait, no way of knowing whether he was wasting his time, half hoping that he was. Maire and the boy were not part of the past that he had intended to revisit. But he had no choice now. He was desultorily debating buying something to read when the red Renault came to the mouth of the cul-de-sac. It paused and the sun flared off its windscreen and then the car swung into the other road and accelerated down the hill.

Callan gunned the engine, his reluctance replaced by automatic action, and the butcher looked round as he roared out of the cramped parking space. He sped down the hill, part of his mind unsure whether he had really seen the car or had dozed off for a moment and imagined it. Another part of his mind watched for other pursuers: Maire was a marked woman, certain to be under surveillance at least part of the time.

There was no sign of Maire or any pursuit car but then he rounded a bend and the Renault was stopped at a traffic light, its right indicator flashing feebly. Callan flicked down the sun visor and coasted slowly to a halt behind the red car, as if he was sneaking up silently. He checked his rear-view mirror, nervous of being caught between Maire and the gardai, but there was nothing behind him.

A slice of her cheek and the corner of one eye were reflected in her wing mirror. She seemed to be looking straight ahead and he found he was breathing shallowly through his open mouth. Cars raced through the intersection and he wondered if it was really Maire; she had changed her hairstyle, let it grow, since he had seen her last. But that had been a long, long time ago.

The lights changed and she followed the green arrow across to the left-hand side of the dual carriageway. She's going down town, he thought as he let the gap between them open up. A small van pulled in between them and he speeded up behind its cover.

He was so close to the van that he almost missed her change of direction. She turned into a slip lane to the left at an intersection and he swung sharply into it too and slowed quickly. A large sign for Dunnes Stores caught his eye as he turned off the main road and the Renault was halted at a T-junction, indicating right. Is she going shopping, he wondered with amazement. Whatever he had expected, it hadn't been that. He never associated Maire with the mundane matters of daily life.

She was turning into the shopping centre as he went through the T-junction. He took his time and cruised along the car park until he found a space on the right where he could see the area where she had driven. He turned off the engine.

Maire was striding in front of the grey building towards the entrance, a matronly figure, large-framed and slightly heavy-hipped; looking like a typical suburban housewife. Her black hair was swept back over her ears, making the contours of her face seem more pointed than they were. She was wearing a belted, striped summer dress, buttoned down the middle, and a bag swung from her shoulder.

She had never been beautiful but she had a quality of strength behind her deceptively wistful face that caused people to look again. Her figure had filled out but she was still instantly recognisable and Callan saw the young woman he had once loved. Or thought he had.

Or told himself that was what he was seeing. He watched her with a confused detachment.

They had met in the movement and he was attracted by that wistful quality he could see in her now, her air of being slightly lost and vulnerable. He was already well established in the tight world of republican activists and she, five years younger, was moving into the front line of the struggle. Their relationship developed quickly and intensely in the fevered atmosphere where everything was secondary to the next operation and victory was still this year's goal.

She had looked up to him and he had drawn on her family's experiences to fuel his own loftier but vaguer motivations. Her eldest brother had been killed while she was still a schoolgirl, shot in the back by the British army while running from a post office in which he had, amateurishly, left a bomb.

Within a year she was pregnant and they married for the sake of her parents and it was only with hindsight he knew that, by then, it was too late. They were already moving apart, pushed by the personality differences that had been overwhelmed by their initial passion and by different perceptions of the war that had drawn them together. She had outgrown him quickly, become impatient with his natural caution while she herself turned into a formidable fighter who dared to do what others baulked at. He found her growing ruthlessness and fierce determination unsettling, suspecting that it was driven mainly by revenge. She put his unease down to a lack of commitment.

The last time he had seen her he had woken early in the terraced house in Monaghan where they were making a half-hearted pretence at leading a family life and she was pulling on her jeans. He asked her what was up and she said, 'I'll be late,' and he rolled back to sleep. She did not return and two days later he heard she had been arrested across the border, at her parents' house.

He had blamed it on her recklessness, the recklessness he had warned her about continually. But he never knew whether she had left him or not. He suspected she had: why else would she have been so foolish as to go there? It had not troubled him greatly either way: he had felt an unsuppressible sense of relief. Tinged with guilt.

Callan got out of the car and looked around, conscious that he was now doing something equally reckless. There was nothing to arouse suspicion and he made his way into the building and down a short corridor to where the shopping centre divided into two. He glanced

95

into both sections and then wandered among the racks of clothes in the department store. There were few customers there and he crossed to the supermarket and took a basket.

Maire was standing by a cold cabinet, looking at packaged trays of meat. Callan watched her for a moment and then retraced his steps and toured the other aisles. It was no Safeways, he thought idly: it seemed small and dingy and the shelves carried little choice, in meagre quantities. Two girls were restocking from a trolley, one pasting labels on to tins of fruit with a clicking pricing gun. A scattering of shoppers wandered around, their attention tunnelled on the shelves. Most of the checkouts were closed and the tinny piped music accentuated the emptiness.

She was holding a plastic-wrapped piece of beef as if she doubted its stated weight when he came up beside her and said, 'Hello, Maire'.

She looked from the meat to him and they stared at each other in silence for a moment. Up close, her face was beginning to show lines but her grey eyes were as distant and dreamy as the first time he had met her.

'You're looking well,' he offered, not knowing what to say.

A hint of an enigmatic smile crossed her face. 'You haven't changed,' she said.

'You don't seem surprised.'

'I heard you were back.' She shook her head, a gesture that seemed to be more than a simple negative. She was still holding the meat in her hand. 'It would have been hard not to.'

Her Northern accent was undiluted and resonated with the remembered mixture of confidence and amusement and a hard- edged tone of betrayal. She seemed totally confident and at ease, perhaps even politely pleased to see him. As though he were a casual school friend whom she had not met for years. It occurred to him that she might have given more thought to their meeting than he had.

'How've you been?' He did not want to get into a personal discussion but it seemed somehow necessary to go through the ritual.

'Getting by.' She dropped the meat into her trolley and turned away.

Callan glanced around casually but the few shoppers within sight were not paying them any attention. He left his empty basket on the floor by the cabinet and walked along with her. A large cabbage sprawled on the bottom of her trolley among some other vegetables and fruit.

'How's Shay?'

'Fine.'

'What class is he in? Still in primary school?'

'Going into his last year.' She picked up a packet of tightly bound sausages from another cabinet as they went by.

'What does he look like?' he heard himself ask and immediately wondered why. The schoolboys, he decided; the realisation that he knew nothing whatever about the boy.

The question seemed to shake her out of her casual politeness as well. She stopped abruptly and swung round to face him. 'Why?' she demanded.

'Just curious.'

'Is that what brought you back?'

'No.' He shook his head quickly, surprised. 'But I'd like to see him. As I am here.'

'No,' she said sharply. She pushed the trolley ahead and turned away to roam the shelves with her eyes.

'Why not?' he inquired, curious now as well about her reaction.

'Because he thinks you're dead.'

Callan shrugged to himself: it wasn't a major issue. Not to him. You can't miss what you've never known, he thought. Brendan's suspicions about his claim to the farm came back to him. Why did everybody assume he wanted to get back into their lives, he wondered, even disrupt them. It was the last thing on his mind. But the thought made him feel even more like an outsider than usual.

'And that's the way you stay,' Maire added, looking him in the eye. 'As far as he's concerned.'

'OK.' Callan opened his hands in a gesture of surrender, tempted to ask how he was supposed to have died. For Ireland? 'I was only curious.'

They proceeded in silence into another aisle. She gave all her attention to her shopping and seemed to be almost oblivious to his continuing presence. The piped music tinkled and Callan had the odd feeling that he wasn't really there at all. The setting created an air of unreality which brought back their last days together and he could see again the stand-off positions they had adopted and feel the enervating emptiness that had hung around them like a debilitating fog. It stirred something within him but, at the same time, it was like looking at somebody else's experiences.

'Why don't we go some place to talk?' he suggested.

'What do we have to say?'

Nothing, he told himself. It had all been said before, in deeds rather than in words. But he felt a need to put it into words, to provide, belatedly, the formalities that had never been stated. 'I'm sorry,' he offered. 'About the way things ended up.'

'It was all for the best,' she suggested lightly, selecting a packet of biscuits from a long array. She had recovered her poise and his presence was almost a matter of mild interest to her once again. 'Although I could have done without the four years in Armagh.'

He nodded, taking what she said as a confirmation that she had indeed walked out on him. A long-buried suspicion that she was behind the Maher set-up floated unbidden to the surface. He dismissed it irritably: it was ridiculous to think he had been singled out because he hadn't stood by her while she was in prison. But there had been people ready to let him hear their views on that, voiced in snide asides and hooded looks at his other women.

He glanced around impatiently: there was no point shuffling over history. None of that mattered and he was exposing himself more and more the longer he stayed here with her. 'I need your help,' he said, taking hold of the trolley as she selected a tin of spaghetti hoops.

'What's your problem?' She gave him a quizzical look.

'I need to know what's going on. And to get out again.'

'The same old Fergus.' She gave him a fleeting smile. 'Still on the run. Trying to get away from something.'

She has been thinking about our meeting, he decided. About me. Which means she knows what's going on. And she can help me if she chooses.

'Tell me all about it,' she added soothingly.

'Don't you know?' He pushed the trolley and they dawdled along.

'Tell me anyway.' She kept an eye on the shelves.

He sighed and told her quickly what had happened, assuming she wanted to hear his version because of whatever was happening. Or, perhaps, to underline his role as supplicant. 'What I've got to know,' he concluded, 'is why Willy was ordered to get me back? Why I'm being set-up?'

'Willy's not the man he used to be,' she suggested as though that explained something.

'None of us are,' he grunted.

'True,' she shot back. 'But he's erratic. Unreliable.'

'That doesn't answer my questions,' he insisted. 'Why was he used to bring me back?'

'I don't know.' She looked at him evenly. 'Why do you think I would?'

'Because you're on the army council,' he said impatiently.

'Did Willy tell you that? You wouldn't want to pay much attention to him. He doesn't count.'

She moved away and left him staring at the jumble of groceries in the trolley and wondering what she was up to. Maybe it had been an unrealistic presumption to expect her help. Why should she? She certainly didn't owe him anything. On the other hand, why shouldn't she? She didn't seem particularly hostile either. Callan heaved the trolley round a corner facing the checkouts and followed her zigzag path back down the store.

'Why are you sparring with me?' he inquired.

She looked surprised at his directness. 'I'm not. I've told you. I don't know what's happening.'

'But you knew I was back.'

'Everyone I meet tells me,' she said. 'Even the guards woke me up yesterday to tell me.'

'You knew I was coming.'

'You might as well have announced it on the radio.' She paused to consider two bottles of dilutable orange, rejected both and moved on.

'You're trying to make your story to Shay come true,' he said bitterly, trying to provoke some other reaction. 'You want me dead. Or locked up. Is that it?'

Maire stopped and gave him a tired look. 'I don't want you around,' she said slowly. 'Dead or alive. In jail or out. What happened between us is over and done with. Long ago. I don't have any feelings about it one way or the other. I'd like you to disappear again. That's all.'

'That's what I'm trying to do. But I need help.'

'Talk to Blinker,' she said.

'He's behind it, is he?'

She gave him a curt nod and moved away. Then she stopped and faced him again. 'I honestly don't know what it's all about. All I've heard is idle gossip. I was left out of it officially. In deference to my feelings apparently. Because, in case you've forgotten, we're still officially married.' She gave a humourless laugh. 'The feelings I don't have.'

'But you have some idea. Some hint.'

'I'm only the wife,' she smiled to let him know she wasn't serious. 'The last to know.'

Callan studied her closely, deciding that she had changed more than he had thought. She had never played verbal games like this when he had known her: she was much too serious and direct. An action woman with no time for these kind of games. Which had been one of the factors that had once united them. But prison or age or being a member of the army council had changed that, he decided. He preferred her the way he remembered her.

'OK,' he said. 'Where do I find Blinker?'

She thought for a moment and then gave him the name of a pub. 'Tomorrow night,' she added.

He shook his head. 'I can't wait till then.'

Maire shrugged. 'Try there tonight. I'll see if I can get a message to him.'

Callan thanked her and she added: 'Don't expect him to greet you with open arms.'

Callan shrugged. He and Blinker had never gotten on well.

'You were the cause of him being interrogated for forty-eight hours,' she added. 'And he doesn't take kindly to being questioned. By anybody.'

'That wasn't exactly my idea,' Callan retorted with heavy sarcasm. 'I'd like to know whose it was just as much as him.'

'I'm only telling you.'

They lapsed into silence, both lost in their thoughts. There's nothing more here for me, he decided. This is a part of the past that is gone irretrievably. He held out his hand formally and Maire shook it.

'Take care,' he said, feeling that this was the farewell that they had never had.

'You too.' She nodded politely.

He turned and walked away, vaguely uneasy. That hadn't worked out the way he had expected. She was a changed person, someone he didn't know any more.

Maire went back to the shelves. She didn't watch him go.

Ten

The phone warbled in the hall and Keerins, lounging in front of the television, waited for Deirdre to answer. Its bleating continued and he hauled himself out of the armchair.

'I'm not in,' Deirdre called from upstairs. 'OK.'

'Be ready in ten minutes,' she added.

'Carol's not here yet,' he said.

He lifted the phone and a voice identified himself as Paul from the surveillance detail. 'Our friend's made contact,' he said.

'With whom?' Keerins felt his pulse quicken. They were getting somewhere at last.

'Not sure yet,' Paul said. 'He's gone into a flat in Ballsbridge.'

Ballsbridge, Keerins thought. That had to be well outside of Archie's normal circuit. This must be it.

'Still trying to identify the resident,' Paul added. 'Got somebody in the building now.'

'Is our friend still inside?'

'Been in there ten minutes. You said to call you as soon as anything developed.'

'Yes. Thanks.'

'You coming over?'

Keerins hesitated and then said 'yes' and jotted the address on the pad by the phone. 'Keep away from the front of the building,' Paul said. 'I'm in a van round the corner.'

Keerins took a deep breath and went upstairs to the bedroom where Deirdre was sitting in front of the dressing table. 'Something's come up,' he said over her shoulder to the mirror. She stopped with her eye liner poised. 'I've got to go into town.'

Her face settled into a hard line and she put the eye liner down. 'Now?'

He nodded and said, 'Sorry.'

'And what am I supposed to do?' she demanded, looking lopsided with one of her angry eyes made up. 'I haven't been out of the house all week. You've hardly been here all week.'

'It's the Callan case.'

'What's so bloody important about him anyway?'

'You know very well,' he said, growing impatient. 'I've got to go.'

'What about Carol?' she asked as he turned away. 'What am I supposed to tell her?'

'Explain what's happened,' he replied from the door. 'Ask her if she can babysit tomorrow night.'

He went down the stairs in a hurry and heard her bang a door as he left the house. Shit, he thought, irritated equally by her lack of understanding and his fear that Archie might have gone by the time he got there.

He drove fast and made it to Ballsbridge in less than half an hour and slowed down on a tree-lined road of high old red-brick buildings. A small van was parked under a heavy tree near a T-junction where the houses ended and the pavement was lined by the high walls of the gardens of the next street. The sun peered over the houses at the far side of the junction and spread up the street.

Keerins cruised to a halt behind the van and went over to the passenger side. The van was marked Dublin Gas and Paul turned out to be the stubby one that he remembered from his briefing, the one who had reminded him of Blinker. A drooping moustache made his round face looked doleful and he had longish hair and wore a one-piece boiler suit. A walkie talkie rested silently on his lap and a radio under the dashboard spat out one-sided staccato messages.

'He's still in there?' Keerins asked as he sat in.

Paul jerked his thumb across the street towards the blind side of a building which rose behind the granite wall.

'Anything yet on who he's meeting?'

'John Amber.'

'Amber?' Keerins asked. 'Who's he?'

'Nothing known,' Paul shrugged and reached over to turn the radio down to a mumble. 'Ran him through the computer but no record, nothing. He's got an English accent, businessman of some sort, drives a light-green Granada. That's all we've got.'

'Sounds like an alias,' Keerins said, thinking aloud and wishing that he was better informed about the current IRA leadership. He made a mental note to bone up on them again when he had a spare hour.

'Could be,' Paul agreed. 'Have to wait till we catch sight of him. Snap his picture from one of the houses over there.'

The sun edged down behind the houses, leaving fiery shreds trailing up the sky. A bird twittered in the tree above them and an occasional car hummed past, scarcely ruffling the sedate surface of the evening. They listened to the mumbled messages from the radio and waited.

'What's he been doing all day?' Keerins inquired.

'Scurrying all over town,' Paul said. 'In and out of pubs and shops. Went down Henry Street like a frightened chicken tossed into a crowd. In a hell of a hurry. Dodging in and out of department stores.'

'Did he know he was being followed?' Keerins asked anxiously.

'No way,' Paul said with a hint of pride. 'We kept well back, didn't give him a chance. Like you said. Lost him for a bit in the stores.' He paused. 'He a Provo?'

'Sort of. A messenger really.'

'Doing a bit of shop lifting on the side?'

'Was he?'

'Could've been.' Paul shrugged. 'Just wondered why he went into nearly every store on the street.'

'It wouldn't surprise me,' Keerins sighed. Wouldn't surprise me at all, he thought. Archie was the kind of character who'd always be involved in any number of shady deals, never getting any of them right.

The walkie talkie hummed into life and a dispassionate woman's voice said, 'Coming out.' Paul picked it up and waited: the channel was still open. 'Two of them,' the voice said slowly. 'Standing by Granada . . . perfect picture . . . other one getting in . . . target walking out. . . going towards you . . .'

'Fuck,' Keerins said. 'He'll recognise me.'

'Get in the back,' Paul ordered, as the voice said: 'Turning the corner . . .'

Keerins clambered awkwardly, head first, between the seats and pulled himself with his hands into the empty back. 'Read the reg number,' Paul said into the walkie talkie and pulled a clipboard from the parcel shelf and propped it on the steering wheel. 'Belfast reg,' he muttered as the radio delivered the number. He turned over a sheaf of flimsy forms and noted the number and went on pretending to write something.

'Here he comes,' he said under his breath. 'Still in a hurry.'

'Oh God,' Keerins groaned from the back. 'He'll recognise my fucking car.'

'Passing,' Paul said slowly. 'Other side of the road. OK. What do you want us to do?'

Keerins angled himself round and looked sideways out the back window and Archie came into his vision. He had both hands jammed into the pockets of a short denim jacket and he was swaggering fast up the opposite footpath, like a teenager who'd just made it with the girl of his dreams. He didn't look to the right or left.

'Which of them do we take?' Paul said urgently.

Keerins let out a sigh of relief: he hadn't seen the car. 'Stick with Archie,' he said, struggling back into the front. 'I'll take the other one.'

'Are you sure?' Paul sounded doubtful. 'Wily fucker, if he is a Provo.'

'I'll be careful,' Keerins said impatiently. 'Where is he now?'

Paul repeated the question into the walkie talkie and the woman's voice replied, 'Waiting at the entrance.'

'See,' Paul said to Keerins. 'Waiting for you to step out. Wily fucker, all right.'

Keerins turned and tried to look out the back window to see where Archie had got to. He couldn't see anything. 'We can't just sit here,' he exclaimed nervously. 'You'll lose Archie as well.'

'Got him covered,' Paul flashed him a satisfied smile. 'Another unit up the road.'

Keerins felt his face colour with embarrassment and hoped it wasn't noticeable. 'Can't you take both of them then?' he asked.

Paul shook his head slowly. 'Rather not. Too risky. Need a lot of manpower to do one properly.'

'I've got to see this other man,' Keerins said desperately.

Everything depended on getting to him and getting his information directly. He had to have a look at him and find out who he was. At the very least.

'You're the boss. Your operation. But don't blame us if it goes sour.'

'OK,' Keerins said impatiently. 'Is he still there?'

'Yeah.' Paul nodded. 'Take off like a bat out of hell in a minute. Hope to Christ he doesn't come this way. Or that's it.'

'What should I do?' Keerins pleaded.

'Get in your car. Wait for my signal and get after him. But slowly. Sedately. He'll probably double back, do a loop or something. Don't do anything sudden. Follow him into any cul-de-sacs. Or anything like that. You might get lucky,' he added pointedly.

Keerins got out of the van and ran to his Mazda and reversed until he could see round the van to the other street. All the things that could go wrong ran through his mind as he waited, tight with tension. If he comes this way, we've really had it all right: he'd disappear and that'd be that. I'll never be able to keep up with the Granada if we get into a chase. But, if it became a chase, the game'd be up anyway.

The brake lights on the van glowed and he took off without thinking, seeing Paul's finger pointing right as he shot by. He braked at the junction and reminded himself to take it easy as he turned right and the road was empty. He really must have taken off like a bat out of hell, he thought.

Keerins sped down to the junction with Pembroke Road and stopped and looked in both directions. To his left, a line of cars waited at the traffic lights at the end of Baggot Street: to his right, another line of cars approached but he couldn't see anything going away from him. He looked back at the halted cars. There was no sign of a green Granada. Fuck. He'd lost him already.

He imagined the surveillance unit's walkie talkie cackling with laughter as he sat there, undecided and deflated. Then a green Granada swung out of a narrow road off to his left and came down Pembroke Road towards him. Keerins let out a whoop of delight and flicked on his right indicator. He looked up and down the road and caught a passing glimpse of the Granada and its driver as it went by.

You sneaky fucker, Keerins muttered as he turned into Pembroke Road and followed slowly, letting the Granada increase the distance between them. Thought you were being smart.

The Granada turned right on the green light at the top of Lansdowne Road and Keerins held his breath. But the lights flicked to orange when he was still too far away and he eased out over the stop line. The Granada's tail disappeared round a parked bus and into the forecourt of Jury's Hotel and he sighed with relief. All was not lost.

Keerins followed cautiously when the lights changed. A tour bus was drawn up by the entrance, releasing a line of elderly Americans into the hotel. He cruised between a line of parked cars, alert, and turned into a second row and Amber was almost beside him, locking the Granada's door, close enough for him to reach out and touch.

Keerins looked away quickly, filing away a description: five foot eight or so, slim build, thirtyish, fair hair. He had on a well-cut white suit over a broadly striped shirt and Keerins caught a glimpse of a pale tie. Then he was past and he watched him in the rear-view mirror until he turned into another row.

A car was leaving a corner spot by the perimeter wall and Keerins made way for it to drive off and reversed into the space. He could see the roof of the Granada but the tour bus blocked the distant entrance. Amber had gone.

He sat for a while, visualising Amber and fixing his description firmly in his mind's eye. There was something about him that wasn't quite right. The suit perhaps: it sat on him a little oddly as if he was not accustomed to dressing like that. Which would figure, he thought. He was masquerading as a businessman; the flat and the car pointed to that, too. Could be a fund raiser. Maybe meeting some American contacts.

Caution advised him not to go into the hotel. The bus moved away and a steady stream of cars moved in and out of the hotel grounds. The dusk began to filter slowly down like a quietly falling ash breaking up the daylight and the electric lights began to glow. Curiosity and the waiting finally got to him and he decided to go in. There was nothing to be gained from sitting here.

He noted the name of the garage on the back window of the Granada as he walked to the building. The high-ceilinged lobby was almost empty but the bar beyond it was crowded, a moodily lit jumble of plants and corners and levels. He couldn't see in properly and he wandered by its open entrance and looked into the brightly lit Coffee Dock next door. Amber was sitting up at the counter, his back to the door. The high seats on either side of him were occupied by two men: they all faced straight ahead with the rigidity of people who were alone.

Keerins went on to a bank of phones in a deserted lobby and put in two coins and punched out the headquarters number.

'Anything for me?' he asked when he got the right extension.

'That car,' the detective at the other end said, 'was hired in Belfast five days ago. By a John Amber.'

'Anything on him?'

'No.'

Keerins looked around but there was nobody within earshot and he reeled off his description of Amber. 'Can you check that out?'

'Jesus,' the detective groaned. 'That sounds like half the male population.'

'I thought that's what computers were for,' Keerins retorted icily. 'Check it against the leadership first. He's got to be one of the main ones.'

'OK,' the detective sighed. 'Anything else?'

Yes, Keerins thought, trying to work out the implications of the fact that Amber had hired the car in Belfast so recently. It could mean he didn't live at the flat, that it had only been used for the meeting with Archie. Which meant that he needed help to tail him from here. Unless the Amber who hired the car was not this Amber.

'Any word from the other unit?'

'Their man's having a jar.'

'Ask them to join me in Jury's. Front car park,' he said.

Keerins strolled by the Coffee Dock again and Amber was at the cash desk, picking a mint from a bowl. Keerins cursed silently: he'd have to try and do it on his own. He kept going, taking his time, and sauntered out of the building and headed across the car park, conscious of Amber's presence behind him. He got to his car and dug into his pockets for his keys and glanced casually back the way he had come.

There was no sign of Amber and he thought for a moment that he either hadn't left the hotel or he was already in the Granada. Then he saw him out of the corner of his eye walking along by the front of the low building. Keerins went back to the car door and when he looked again Amber was walking along the side of the building towards the car park behind it. Fuck, he thought, he's switching cars. He'll go out the back gate.

Amber disappeared round the back of the hotel and Keerins made up his mind quickly. He slammed the car door, not waiting to lock it, and set off briskly after him. He went along by the glass wall, half expecting Amber to come driving past in a different car any moment. Inside the glass, people were standing about with glasses of wine in their hands and a waitress carried a tray of canapés. He got to the end and hesitated and then looked round the corner.

He stepped back immediately, as shocked as if somebody had punched him in the stomach.

Amber was in the passenger side of a dusty cream Opel, his sideface visible as he spoke to the driver. The car was pointed towards a hedge and Keerins couldn't see the driver but he didn't need to. He recognised the car. It was Pursell's.

Keerins took a deep breath and steadied himself against the wall. His mind was in a whirl. What was going on here? Pursell was meeting Archie's contact. Archie's contact was one of Pursell's sources. They had known all the time, he decided. And they had let him carry on like a harmless fool.

Anger propelled him round the corner. It was all a plot. No wonder Pursell seemed so happy. The patronising fucker.

Amber saw him coming and said something to Pursell. Then Keerins was beside the driver's door and Pursell was winding down his window. He searched Keerins's face with a helpless, despairing intensity.

'Well, well,' Keerins snarled sarcastically. 'Fancy meeting you here.'

Pursell said nothing. His heavy face was pale and tight with a kind of animal wariness. He exuded none of his usual know-all certainty.

Keerins bent down and leaned his elbows on the window ledge and looked across at Amber. Amber was studying Pursell intently.

'Aren't you going to introduce me?' Keerins demanded.

Pursell cleared his throat and said, 'John Amber, George Keerins.' He didn't look at either of them.

'Pleased to meet you, mate.' Amber stuck his hand across in front of Pursell's face and Keerins shook it perfunctorily. 'I really admire you lads. You're doing a great job.'

Doing a great job? Keerins stared at Amber, taking in his crooked smile and his accent. What did he mean? Up close, he looked like an English version of Archie, maybe fractionally more successful. Something wasn't quite right here.

'Look,' Pursell said, opening his door. 'This isn't what you're thinking.'

Keerins stepped back, his certainty shaken. He didn't know what he was thinking. Something was definitely wrong. Pursell stood up and Amber got out of the passenger side and came casually round the back of the car. The way he moved suddenly made Keerins apprehensive and he glanced beyond him. The car park was deserted in the half-light and a cloud of steam came from a pipe at the functional back of the hotel. Amber stopped near the back of the car, blocking his way out, and Pursell stood by the open door. Christ, Keerins thought wildly, feeling that he was being surrounded. He looked desperately at Pursell.

'John has offered us some help,' Pursell said. 'To get Callan.'

Keerins looked from him to Amber.

'Yeah.' Amber nodded, ingratiatingly. 'Absolutely. Anything I can do. All on the same side, aren't we? Up against a common enemy.'

Jesus Christ, Keerins thought and looked back at Pursell. It was all becoming clear but he still couldn't believe it. The man he thought was a Provo was a British agent. And so, unbelievably, was his own colleague. Pursell was the mole.

'That extradition thing was a mistake,' Amber said with an air of bosom pals explaining a minor misunderstanding. 'An over-zealous RUC man. Who's had his balls in the wringer over it.'

Keerins was only half-listening, his attention on Pursell who was still watching him with the wariness of a cornered animal. I should arrest them, part of his brain told him. But he was still too stunned to do anything. 1

'Our only interest is in having Callan locked up,' Amber was saying. 'Down here or up there doesn't matter. You have a prior claim. We know that. What matters is putting the terrorists out of circulation. And we'll give you all the help we can.'

Pursell waved a pleading hand at Amber as if he was trying to quieten an irritating child. 'Let me talk to George,' he said.

'Sure,' Amber said and turned away.

'Hold on,' Keerins snapped. Amber stopped and Keerins wished he could have five minutes to think all this through. His assumptions had all been overturned so suddenly, all certainty removed. So many unanswered questions revolved through his mind that he couldn't fix on a decision. His natural instinct was, as always, to play it by the book; arrest them for breaches of the Official Secrets Act. But he wasn't sure he could effect an arrest and he wasn't sure that that was the thing to do. This was a security issue, not a criminal one.

'John's got a line on Callan,' Pursell offered quickly into the silence.

'What?' Keerins demanded from Amber.

'Nothing absolutely definite yet,' Amber said. 'But I'm working on a scrap of information. As soon as it checks out you'll have it. Like I told you, my only interest is to help you get him.'

Archie, Keerins thought. Another fucking betrayer. But the fact that he knew of Amber's dealing with Archie made him feel a little better. At least, he was one small step ahead of all of them.

'He might have it tonight,' Pursell said with a touch of desperation. 'Within twenty-four hours at most. Right?' He looked to Amber for confirmation.

'At most.' Amber nodded. 'No question. It looks good.'

'Share it now,' Keerins demanded.

Amber gave him a sly smile. 'Come on, mate. You know how these things work. I guarantee you'll get it the minute it checks out.'

'Twenty-four hours,' Pursell interrupted. 'That's all we're asking for.'

'Maximum.' Amber nodded.

Keerins glanced from one to the other, tempted as much by a feeling of power over both of them as by the prospect of Amber leading him to Callan. He did want Callan too, of course, and Amber seemed to have succeeded where he had failed with Archie. It would be some sort of justice to have Archie lead him to Callan through Amber.

But he couldn't see what Amber's interest in Callan was. He didn't believe his offers of disinterested help for a moment. But Amber hardly wanted to whisk Callan back across the border. Why bother? Maybe it was just the usual inability of the Brits to keep their fingers out of everything.

'OK,' he said to Amber, giving in to the temptations. 'Where will I find you?'

Amber glanced at Pursell who bowed his head and he told Keerins the address of the flat where he had met Archie. Keerins nodded, satisfied.

'Cheers,' Amber grinned. 'Be in touch.'

They watched him disappear into the gloom and Pursell said with a sigh, 'What're you going to do?'

'I should arrest you,' Keerins shot back. He felt a contemptuous superiority over Pursell. How could he have become an informer for such a sleazy character? 'Who is he, anyway? Who does he work for?'

'MI6.' Pursell shrugged. His normal physical presence seemed to have given way to a helpless, hang-dog willingness to please.

'I thought they were all upper-class types,' Keerins said.

'Don't be fooled by appearances,' Pursell said. 'He's a good operator.'

Keerins snorted with the benefit of his own knowledge. Amber couldn't be all that good when he himself, a relatively raw beginner, had been able to tail him here. 'How long have you been doing this?' he demanded. 'Working for the Brits?'

'It's not like that,' Pursell retorted quickly. 'It's a trade-off. Sharing information. It's happening all the time. Officially.'

'But not like this,' Keerins waved at their surroundings.

'What's the difference?' Pursell demanded with some of his old certainty. 'It's like he said. We're on the same side.'

'The difference,' Keerins said coldly, determined to reassert his dominance, 'is that you're spying for a foreign government whose dirty tricks have . . .'

'Oh for fuck's sake,' Pursell blurted impatiently. 'We're both trying to contain fuckers who don't give a shit who they kill, who believe that they have the right to do whatever they want so they can get whatever they want.'

'Yes, but we're policemen. We've got to contain them within the law. We're not part of a dirty tricks outfit like your friend.'

'That's grand for schoolchildren,' Pursell snapped back. 'For fucking civics classes.'

They fell silent as an expensively dressed man and woman came down the line of parked cars, the woman's heels clicking unsteadily on the tarmac. The night had crept down around them almost unnoticed but a faint light still lingered in the sky. The couple went to a nearby car and the man glanced curiously at them.

'I'm sick to death of pussy-footing with those animals,' Pursell sighed when the couple had driven off. 'Day in, day out. Getting nowhere. And all the time they're laughing in our fucking faces.'

'You should reconsider your position,' Keerins suggested pompously. 'As a policeman.'

'You saw that bastard Blinker the other night,' Pursell continued. 'Laughing his fucking head off at us. Because he knows there's nothing we can do. We can't touch him because his fucking rights are so sacred. And the people he kills have no rights because it's a war. OK, if they want a fucking war, we should give it to them.'

'They're just dragging you down to their level.' Keerins shook his head vigorously. 'If you win like that you've lost.'

'And if you don't win you've lost anyway,' Pursell retorted.

Keerins sighed. This was all a diversion from his real problem; what to do about Pursell. He should report it to the superintendent, get the credit for unmasking the mole. But he wouldn't be any nearer to catching Callan which would still be his problem. And his only lead on him was whatever Amber had got out of Archie.

'You could go to jail,' he said harshly.

'No.' Pursell shook his head. 'I'm not important enough to have an Anglo-Irish crisis over it. I'll just lose my job and my pension.'

He was probably right, Keerins thought. Like much of what he said about the IRA was right too. This business wasn't like ordinary crime where you just nabbed offenders when you caught them and locked them up. This was about leverage, trading things off against each other, being on top of the situation. Being in control.

Pursell sat into his car and looked up at him. 'You're going to report it, then?'

'I don't know,' Keerins shrugged. But he did know. He wasn't going to do anything for the moment. Except maintain his new-found leverage over Pursell. And give Amber twenty-four hours to produce Callan.

For the first time since his promotion into security he felt the satisfaction of being in control of something.

Eleven

'Mr Callan.'

The sound of his name came from behind with the suddenness of the sharp slap of a shot and Callan's whole body tensed with the shock. He kept going, half-expecting the explosive thud of a bullet in his exposed back.

He was out for a walk and there was no hint of danger ahead. The broad footpath stretched away further than the eye could see and was empty. Heavy trees shaded the road from the mid-morning sun and several cars rolled smoothly by. He kept walking, trying to think quickly, knowing that the slight falter in his step had already betrayed him.

Don't run, he ordered himself. Keep going or turn into the driveway of one of the houses. But I'll be cornered then. The safe house was a hundred yards away but that was out anyway. Bluff it out. That's the only chance. You're a tourist. The Canadian passport is in the inside pocket. Or should be.

He resisted the temptation to check and suddenly saw the 'B & B' sign of a guesthouse on the other side of the road. He turned to cross and waited at the kerb, using the traffic as an excuse to look back along the road. There were no police cars, no dawdling vehicles coming up behind.

'Mr Callan,' the voice said behind his shoulder. 'I only want a word.'

Callan placed the accent as English and his brain raced with the possibilities of what that might mean. He turned doubtfully as though he wasn't sure the voice was addressing him and saw a slightly-built man about his own age wearing an off-white suit over a black shirt. He looked like a Hollywood hood.

Callan glanced past the man and there was no one in sight. 'Sorry.' He focused on the man, suddenly buoyed with hope and relief that it mightn't be bad as he had feared. 'You're talking with me?'

Amber gave him a slow smile and shook his head. 'It's all right, Fergus,' he said, raising his hands to show they were empty. 'Just want to have a word with you.'

'You've got me confused with someone else,' Callan said, slightly impatiently. He waited for a car to pass and then crossed the road. Amber went with him.

'You've got a big problem, mate,' he said with the insinuating air of a backstreet car mechanic. 'And I've got a proposition for you. To solve your problem.'

Callan ignored him.

'Your cover is blown,' Amber continued conversationally. 'The local boys in blue are closing in. They want you badly, very badly. You're facing a very long stretch inside. If they want to take you alive, that is. Your old comrades don't give a shit what happens to you. They're not tripping over themselves to help.' Amber shook his head as if the enumeration of Callan's difficulties was too depressing even for him to contemplate.

'I don't know what you're talking about.' Callan stopped at the gate to the guesthouse. 'I'm a visitor . . .'

'Yes, yes,' Amber smiled dismissively and sidled between him and the gate. 'You haven't got a chance on your own. Not a chance. And you know it. If I could find you the plods can't be that far behind. Right?'

'Excuse me,' Callan said, reaching round him to unlatch the gate as though his patience was finally wearing thin with this strange local custom of accosting visitors in the streets.

Amber stayed in his way, blocking the entrance. 'So, what's the deal?' he asked, like a man determined to play both parts of the conversation himself. 'Simple. My people are prepared to get you out, back to America. In return for a little help, of course. But all you've got to do is cross the border which, as you'll remember, is as secure as a fucking sieve. So, what do you think?'

'I think you've mistaken me for somebody else.' Callan stared at him blankly. I don't believe this guy, he was thinking. He's unreal. 'And if you'll excuse me, please.'

'I know what you think.' Amber smiled and switched his tone a shade to that of a second-hand car salesman. 'You're thinking, what's the deal, where are the guarantees? Right? The deal is simple. You hang around the fringes of the organisation in New York or Boston or wherever and pass on anything interesting.'

Amber raised a hand to silence any arguments although none came from Callan. 'Nothing risky. Frequent the right pubs. Keep your ears open. That's all.'

Callan gave an exasperated sigh and pointed at the building. 'Will you please let me into my guesthouse?'

'The guarantees? We know you're out of it, kept your nose clean for a long time. So we're prepared to let bygones be bygones. You with your eyes and ears open in the right place would make us happier than you locked up till kingdom come in Portlaoise. Call it mutual self-help.'

Amber beamed at him and Callan kept his face blank. 'Is this some kind of practical joke?' he asked. I don't believe this, he told himself again.

Amber produced a small card from his breast pocket and held it up between two fingers. 'My number.' He shoved it into Callan's pocket. 'But like all the best offers, there's a time limit. Six o'clock tomorrow evening. The phone won't answer after that.'

Amber stepped aside and Callan pushed open the gate and gave him a bemused look as he went by. He walked down the garden path to the door, his back chilled by the cold sweat soaking his shirt, and rang the bell. He shivered slightly.

A hand-printed sign just inside the door advertised a benefit for prisoners' families the next night and Callan cursed under his breath. This was where Maire had suggested he should go. She might as well have sent him to the Sinn Fein offices. His choices seemed to be narrowing all the time, exposing him to greater and greater risks. He pushed open the inner door.

The pub was long and narrow but spread out at the back into a low-ceilinged square marked out with low tables and stools. The bar ran along one side of the narrow part and a stage area was lined out by loudspeakers at the back. Three scruffy-looking men were playing an energetic Irish tune to a scant audience. The music made no impact on the atmosphere: gloom hung down from the shaded lights and refracted off the brown walls.

Callan squinted around, his eyes still attuned to the lingering light outside, but he did not recognise anybody. He took a seat at the bar where he could watch the entrance and the door at the back marked toilets which had a dim exit sign overhead. He ordered a pint of

Guinness and lit a cigarette. You're smoking too much, he told himself. But that was not surprising.

Everything had changed. He was no longer a nostalgic tripper to the past; he was well and truly trapped in the middle of it. Boston had receded to the point where he couldn't remember when he had last thought about Sharon. A day? Two days? It didn't sound long but it felt like for ever. The change had been building up gradually since his escape in Connemara but had speeded up with the shattering reality of the British agent's appearance.

Callan still didn't know what to make of him. He looked and sounded like a spiv but he overdid it, like an actor who couldn't altogether contain his relish with his own performance. He wasn't what he pretended to be, Callan decided. Maybe he wasn't even a Brit agent. Maybe he was one of the lads. But why? To test him in some way, perhaps.

His glass was almost empty and he sipped at it, to slow himself down. The group was groaning its way through 'Four Green Fields', trying to compensate with excessive sentimentality for their musical shortcomings. A drunk at the bar sang along with them.

The proposal was just the sort of crazy scheme the Brits would try, Callan thought. Worked out by people who devoted all their energies to avoiding the obvious. He shrugged mentally. He couldn't make sense out of any of it. What really mattered, the only thing that mattered, was that he had been found. That someone had been able to simply walk up behind him when he believed he was secure.

That fact had played on his mind all day as he had tried to disappear again. He had wasted time examining rooms in the guesthouse and spun the landlady a story about needing three rooms for the following week. When he left, he had headed away from his safe house, taken a bus into the city centre, doubled back and forward several times before returning to a pub in the same suburb.

He phoned the safe house and asked Harry to bring his bag to the pub immediately. He was across the road in a chipper when Harry drove up to the pub. 'Trouble?' Harry asked anxiously: he looked flustered. 'You're OK,' Callan assured him. 'Look after yourself,' Harry said as Callan took his backpack.

It could have been them, Callan thought as he clambered on to another bus. Or Eoghan. They were the only people who knew where he was. Harry was doubtful as an informer: he didn't know who Callan was. It was inconceivable that Eoghan was a traitor. Unless the Englishman was not a Brit agent but a player in some Provo plot.

Or he could have been picked up on the streets. Followed from this pub last night after he had looked in to see if Blinker was around. He was not sure he had checked for a tail but he had been tired and relaxed. Not as alert or cautious as he should have been.

He gave up on the permutations and concentrated on making sure he wasn't being followed. He crossed the city again, slowly and carefully, and checked into a small bed and breakfast place on the south side.

Callan finished his pint and considered another one. He knew he shouldn't, that he should get out of here, that this place was dangerous. As if to underline his nervousness, the group burst into 'A Nation Once Again' and half the customers joined in with gusto. His eyes swept across those who didn't, seeking danger, while the song roused old embers like a draught of warm air on the calculating part of his brain.

Fuck it, he thought, resigning himself to the mood of the pub, now flickering with patriotism, and trying to catch the barman's eye. It was almost closing time and it had been a long, tense day. The day that it had been borne in upon him forcefully that he no longer controlled his own destiny. That the hunter had become the hunted. There was nothing to do but wait for Blinker.

'Forgotten the words, have you?' a man said in a low voice as he slipped up to the bar beside him. He was young and had a Dublin accent and a fresh freckled face which gave Callan an open smile. 'D'you want another pint?'

Callan shook his head. He hadn't seen him earlier and hadn't noticed him come in. You've lost your touch, he told himself.

'Let's go then,' the man said.

Callan followed him obediently towards the back of the pub, weaving through the maze of small tables as the song came to an end and a ragged cheer ran around.

'Good night. Thank you. And safe home,' Archie sang out from the stage as they went through the door marked toilets. 'Thank Christ that's over,' the policeman tailing Archie muttered under his breath to his woman colleague and checked his watch. Their task was to watch Archie's contacts. They paid no attention to the two men going into the gents.

The man led Callan down a bare concrete corridor, out into a high-walled yard and through a wicket gate into a lane which led to a street at the back of the block. He nodded at a large car and they sat in.

'You were being very casual back there,' he said cheerily as he drove off. 'But it was all right. I had you covered.'

And what were you going to do if the cops walked in, Callan wondered irritably. Produce an M60? 'All day?' he asked aloud, forcing some innocent awe into his voice.

'No. From the minute you walked in.'

That's better, Callan thought. But the man was right. He had made the oldest mistake in the book; allowed himself to wallow in the boredom of inaction.

They followed the one-way system half-way round the block and headed south. There were small knots of people outside some of the darkened pubs and the traffic moved steadily.

'How does the old home town look?' the man inquired. 'After all those years?'

'The same,' Callan grunted, not bothering to tell him that it was not his home town. Maire was right, he thought: he might as well have advertised his return on the radio. Everybody seemed to know everything about him.

They swung round Kelly's Corner and went down the South Circular Road until the red-brick houses lost their basements and edged closer to the road. The driver turned into a side road and parked and they walked back to a house near the corner.

It was divided into two flats, one on each floor, and they climbed the bare stairs to the door on top. The man opened it with a key and showed Callan into the front room. The heavy curtains were pulled tight and a bright light hung from the ceiling. The only furniture was a jaded couch, two matching armchairs and a scratched table against a wall. There were no decorations.

Blinker was sitting on the couch with his back to the door and another man was in an armchair. They were eating thick chips and a rigid wedge of battered fish from brown paper bags.

Blinker turned to look over the back of the couch and his eyes flicked a question to the driver who flushed slightly and stepped in front of Callan with an embarrassed shrug. Blinker turned back to his chips and Callan stared impassively at the back of his head while the driver frisked him. The other man gave no indication that he was aware of Callan's arrival.

'OK,' the driver said.

'What about ye.' Blinker turned back to them as though they had just arrived and dismissed the driver with a nod. 'You haven't changed a bit.'

'Thanks for the welcome home,' Callan said tetchily. Blinker hadn't changed much either although he looked heavy rather than chubby now and his face was more lined. He still had the faint air of a bemused schoolboy faced with an incomprehensible maths problem. The other man was younger and thick set. Callan did not recognise him.

'Come and sit down,' Blinker shrugged. 'The last time we were supposed to meet cost me two days in the company of the peelers.'

'And nearly cost me forty fucking years.'

'Aye. But you didn't show.'

'I was there.' Callan sat down. 'And only got out by the skin of my teeth.'

'So you say.' Blinker chewed cautiously on the edge of the fish and then held out the bag, blotched with grease, to Callan. 'Have a chip.'

Callan shook his head impatiently. 'What are you trying to say?'

Blinker dug a couple of chips out of the bottom of the bag and put them into his mouth. 'I don't know.' His round face broke into a wide smile. 'I don't fucking know.'

He scrunched the bag into a ball, tossed it into the litter in the narrow fireplace and rubbed his hands across his grey sweatshirt. The other man was eating one chip at a time, his eyes focused across the tattered hearth rug at Callan. Callan didn't notice him any more, aware of his role. It was all staged: an interrogation session.

'Why did you contact Eoghan?' Blinker inquired.

'Because I didn't know you'd been promoted,' Callan said sarcastically.

'But why him? A has-been?'

'Because I was in his area and I didn't remember anyone else there.'

'What about Willy?'

'Willy was supposed to be missing. Remember?' Callan snorted.

Blinker gave him a sheepish grin but Callan didn't believe him for a moment. He was only sparring, wasting time perhaps: whatever the point of all this, they hadn't got anywhere near it yet.

'Perhaps you'll tell me why I'm here,' Callan suggested. 'And we can all get down to what's on our minds.'

'Never one for the small talk, were you?' Blinker shifted his bulk sideways and raised his feet on to the couch to lie sideways. He propped his head on his hand and they stared at each other in silence.

Blinker was Maire's age and had always been friendly with her. Which was a factor in their mutual antipathy although it went deeper than that, into their opposing personalities and backgrounds. Blinker had been urban and a natural manipulator who arrogantly assumed his superiority in the movement because he was from Belfast and working class. Callan had been rural and direct, despising the talkers and the politicians.

Nothing had changed much, Callan thought. Although I'm not the person I used to be.

'So what do you think of the situation?' Blinker asked.

'What situation?'

'The war.'

'It's not going well.'

Blinker looked faintly surprised. 'Why not?'

'You've been making a lot of mistakes.'

'You think so?'

'That's the way it looks.'

'That sounds like Brit propaganda.'

'I only know what I read in the papers.' 2

'You think we're being beaten?'

'I don't know. It doesn't look like you're winning.' Callan shrugged. 'But you didn't get me back here to ask my opinions.'

Blinker frowned. 'So you don't believe in it any more?'

Yes and no, Callan thought. You didn't stop believing or you'd deny everything you once did. 'I don't think about it much,' he said.

'You've changed sides.'

'No.' He could see where this was going now.

'But you think we should give up?'

'That's up to you. Or,' he added pointedly, 'to the volunteers who do the fighting.'

121

Blinker ignored the provocation. 'You just opted out,' he nodded, determined to reduce Callan's attitude into a single phrase.

'You seem to forget why I've been where I've been,' Callan retorted. 'It wasn't my choice.'

The silent man rolled his paper bag into a ball and tossed it towards the fireplace without taking his eyes off Callan. It missed and bounced on to the rug.

'It was your choice to keep your distance. After we got you to safety in America.' Blinker made it sound like an accusation, a sad reflection on ingratitude.

Callan nodded. The line of questioning was transparent but it didn't worry him. He was not intimidated by Blinker: he remembered him as one of those who was happier in a back-up role, who didn't really have the stomach for pulling the trigger himself. Besides, his suspicions were unfounded.

'What would you have done?' he asked. 'Dropped in the shit by your own comrades. And facing deportation and forty years if you were caught.'

'That's the way you look at it? That we set you up?'

'There's no other way to look at it.'

'But you still came back?'

'Yes.'

'Why?'

This was becoming like some kind of medieval witch hunt, Callan thought. He was damned for staying away and damned for coming back. 'You know fucking well why.'

'I was a bit surprised actually.'

Callan gave a short laugh. 'Why? Because one of your schemes actually worked?'

Blinker gave him a fleeting smile. 'Because you're supposed to be so worried about forty years in jail.'

'I wasn't expecting to be set up.'

'You like Boston, do you?'

'Do I have a choice?'

'You seem to have a nice arrangement there.'

'Meaning what?'

Blinker shrugged and tossed out the name of an Irish pub in Boston. 'When were you there last?'

'Last week.' It seemed like an age since he had gone there to arrange his return after the call from Willy's sister.

'And you met Gerry?'

Callan nodded.

'And he got you a passport?'

Callan nodded again.

'And before that? When were you there?'

'I don't remember.'

'Try.'

Callan thought back. He had only been there a couple of times in all his years in Boston. As part of his decision to distance himself from the Irish community, lower the risks.

'You were there before Christmas,' Blinker interrupted.

Callan remembered the Irish music mixing incongruously with the Christmas decorations, the bar packed with newly arrived and mostly illegal immigrants, seething with heartfelt homesickness. Which was why he had gone there, too. That was when his first thoughts of returning had been insinuating themselves into a possibility.

'And you saw Gerry there then,' Blinker said. It wasn't a question.

Gerry had been part of a small group which formed a still centre among the raucous revellers. In his early sixties and in Boston for forty years, he wore a fainne in his lapel and still lived in an Ireland of his mind. He had always reminded Callan of a slightly seedy schoolteacher from his childhood.

'I had a few words with him,' Callan said. 'Hello, happy Christmas. That sort of meaningful conversation.'

'Who was with him?'

Callan tried to visualise the scene and shrugged. 'I don't remember. I don't think I knew any of them.'

'And who was with you?'

'Nobody.'

'Your girlfriend? Was she there?'

'No.'

'You were on your own,' Blinker said, as if that fact was significant. 'What were you doing there?'

'Having a drink,' Callan snorted.

'But you don't normally drink there. Why did you go that night?'

'I was feeling homesick,' Callan said.

Blinker stared at him, his eyelids fluttering as though they reflected his incredulity. Callan held his gaze, defying him to contradict him. Neither said anything for a long moment.

'Why don't you tell me what this is all about?' Callan suggested.

Blinker glanced at the other man and then turned back to Callan and sighed. 'We lost a shipment at the start of the year,' he said. 'A container put together in Boston. The Free Staters were waiting when it got to Dublin.'

'Jesus Christ,' Callan exploded. 'You've brought me back just to ask me about that. Something I've never even heard of.'

'You must have heard about it,' Blinker said mildly.

'For fuck's sake. You didn't have to get me back for that.'

'It was in all the papers.'

'I didn't see it. I never heard about it. I know nothing about it.' Callan shifted in his chair with anger. 'I don't fucking believe this.'

Blinker said nothing.

'You could have asked me in Boston.' Callan glared at him. 'Instead of walking me into the mess I'm in now.'

'Let's look at this calmly,' Blinker suggested, holding up his free hand. 'You turn up in that pub when the final arrangements are being made. The shipment is moved and staked out here. We lose two men and all the gear. Then,' Blinker pointed a finger at Callan, 'you respond to a cock and bull story about your old comrade and come back to Ireland, which you'd have us believe is the last thing you want. We set up a meeting and the cops are everywhere, coming out of the fucking rocks.' He paused. 'What would you make of those facts?'

Callan shook his head with irritation and disbelief. He considered getting up and walking out. This was all too bizarre for words. 'Where do you want me to start?' he demanded.

Blinker waited impassively.

'First, this is the first I've heard about this shipment. Maybe I didn't read the papers that day. I don't know. Second, I came back for my own reasons. I wanted to see my family. Third, I was set-up when I went to meet you. They were after me, not you. As is perfectly fucking obvious.'

'Maybe you were expecting to meet somebody else.'

'I didn't know who I was meeting. I had no idea.' Callan leaned forward. 'But I'll tell you one thing. If they'd got me, you wouldn't be here now either. Because whoever set us up left me with a

Kalashnikov. Which would have got you seven years if you'd been found within shouting distance of it.'

'Maybe that was the plan.'

'Then it was the plan of whoever tried to set me up. Your messenger gave me that gun.' Callan slumped back in his chair. 'I didn't ask for it. And I was given no choice but to take it.'

Blinker's face screwed up into a puzzled frown.

'Check with the young lad who gave me details of the rendezvous,' Callan added. 'He'll tell you how happy I was with the arrangement.'

'Who have you seen since you came back?'

'Your messenger, Eoghan, Willy, Maire.'

'Anyone else?'

Callan shrugged. 'Willy's sister. My mother, brother. People I've stayed with in Dublin.'

'Who are they?'

'They don't know anything. Not even who I am.'

'Anyone else?'

Callan shook his head.

'You see my problem?' Blinker sighed. 'Not many people knew about that shipment. The people who put it together. A handful here.'

'I'm not a fucking tout,' Callan said, secure in his certainty, angry that he could be even considered to be under suspicion. 'You seem to have a very short fucking memory. I did my bit. More than my bit. And it wasn't my idea to be sidelined, to run away. That was your friends' doing. Not mine.'

'Look at it objectively.'

'I am looking at it objectively.'

Blinker shook his head impatiently. 'You've opted out. You feel hard done by. You've got a cosy arrangement in America. And you'd like to keep it that way.' He paused. 'All reasons why you might do a deal. With the FBI or someone.'

Callan thought about all the pressures of the last ten years; the strain of always looking over his shoulder; the guarding against any incautious word or act; the lies and the endless deviousness; the unrelenting worry that was so much a part of his being that he no longer knew what it was like to live without it. He felt betrayed all over again.

He said: 'That doesn't hold up. If I were working for the FBI I'd be hanging around Gerry and the others every fucking day, wouldn't I?'

Blinker yawned and rubbed his eyes with the base of his thumbs. 'We'll call it a day,' he said and swung his legs off the couch. He nodded to the other man who stood up and left. 'You sleep here. We're a bit tight for space.'

Callan lit a cigarette, aware that it was an order and not an offer. The fuckers, he thought bitterly. They had put his whole future in jeopardy for nothing, constructing a conspiracy theory on little more than the twisted belief that he might be guilty if he was still free. And the coincidence that he had once gone to the right place at the right time. They hadn't given a shit about the possible consequences for him if he was innocent. Which meant that he couldn't rely on them for any help now.

The other man returned with an uncovered pillow and a blanket and tossed them on to the couch and left again. Blinker stood up and stretched himself, raising his sweatshirt to reveal a flabby stretch of stomach. He crossed to the door and opened it and turned back.

'We'll talk some more tomorrow,' he said. 'About your meeting with Amber.'

'Who?'

'The Brit spy you neglected to mention.' He flicked off the light and he was a dark silhouette in the doorway. 'The one you had a meeting with this morning.'

Twelve

Inspector Keerins paused to take a deep breath and calm his sense of anticipation. He had to play this coolly; he couldn't afford to expose any hint of the excitement which had taken him over from an early hour. To do so would look unprofessional and, worse, could land him in deep trouble. He was playing a potentially dangerous game but the consequences of it going wrong were not something he cared to think about. He opened the door and went in.

The superintendent swivelled his chair round from the window and raised an inquisitive eyebrow. He looked like he had simply summoned Keerins out of a sense of duty and didn't expect to hear anything interesting.

'Nothing concrete to report,' Keerins obliged him. 'There are a couple of straws in the wind I'm checking out but nothing definite yet.'

'On which?' the superintendent inquired. 'Callan or the informer?'

'Both, actually.' Keerins hoped he wasn't going to ask for details. He was committed now and there was no going back. 'But I'm afraid they're still very vague.'

'Has he flown?'

'Oh, no. All the indications point to him still being in the country.'

The superintendent rested his elbows on the desk and Keerins felt his nervousness rise under his studied stare. What if he knew? What if he had had somebody else watching Pursell and himself? He was perfectly capable of doing that.

'How do you find this work?' the superintendent asked.

'Very interesting.' Keerins tried to smother his paranoia and look innocent but eager. I'd make a lousy criminal, he thought. Even Deirdre had been able to see through him, asking anxiously what had happened when he returned from finding Pursell with Amber. She clearly did not believe his assurance that it was nothing much and had gone into a huff over his unaccustomed reticence.

The superintendent grunted and suggested that it was like shovelling mercury with a fork; very little got to where it was supposed to go. Keerins laughed politely. It was typical of life that the

Super should appear willing for the first time to have a heart-to-heart talk at the one point when he didn't want it.

'I'm still learning,' he offered. 'Getting to grips with it.'

'What you have to remember,' the superintendent said, 'is that it is just the same as other police work. We are dealing with a well-organised conspiracy instead of the usual ragbag of petty thieves and the like.'

He knows, Keerins thought with alarm.

'Our methods have to take account of that,' the superintendent went on. 'Otherwise, it is the same. We investigate crimes, gather evidence, send it to the DPP and so on. We are not judges.'

Keerins nodded solemnly.

'What I am saying,' the superintendent summed up, 'is that you should not look on this job as being different from any other police work. Don't be intimidated by it. And you'll get to grips with it in time.'

Keerins thanked him and left. What the fuck was all that about, he wondered nervously on his way back to his own office. A warning? A prepared speech for raw recruits? A criticism? You'll get to grips with it in time. Whatever it was, it was a bit much coming from the Super who was known to be so devious it was a miracle he didn't have a twisted spine.

He shrugged it off as he arrived in his office and caught Pursell's worried glance, apprehension widening his bloodshot eyes. Pursell's face was a sickly grey and he looked like he had replaced sleep with the cause of a near terminal hang- over. Keerins ignored him, feeling again the satisfaction of his new-found control over him, and busied himself at his desk. So much for the Super's patronising spiel, he thought. I have got to grips with this business already.

When he looked up eventually, Pursell was still watching him. 'What did he say?' he asked, his voice matching his gravelly pallor.

Keerins leaned back in his chair and took his time replying. 'He gave me a lecture. About the duties of policemen.'

Pursell swallowed.

'But I honoured our deal,' Keerins added. 'I said nothing.'

Pursell nodded and muttered thanks.

'Don't thank me,' Keerins snapped, suddenly irritated by his abject demeanour. He had half expected Pursell to be aggressive, to defend himself by attacking as he had the night before. He had been ready to slap him down but all the fight seemed to have gone out of him. 'Just pray that your friend comes up with the goods. By tonight.'

They lapsed into silence.

'This morning's raids produced nothing,' Pursell said. 'A total blank.'

'What about Archie? What's he up to?'

'Still in bed.'

'So it's all up to your friend,' Keerins noted. I can't spend the whole day sitting around here, he thought impatiently, watching Pursell squirm and waiting for Amber to make contact. I've got to do something. 'Tell the surveillance unit to alert me when Archie moves,' he ordered.

It'd be no harm to take out a little insurance. Just in case.

Archie walked jauntily past the short queues waiting for buses against the river wall on Eden Quay. A worried inspector haggled with a driver over the right time and a bus roared its engine. The sun was shining on the shabby buildings and a light breeze carried a trace of salt water in from the sea. Archie didn't notice that, his senses filled with incipient nostalgia for all around him; the exhaust fumes, the rancid scent of the river's sludge, the frenzied buses, the illuminated advertisements outshone by the sun, the resigned bus queues.

I'm going to miss this place, he thought. Dirty old town.

The words of a jumble of other songs ran through his mind but he knew he had no choice. He had taken the queen's shilling. Amber had made his down payment and the rest was due today. Which meant he had to get out tonight. As soon as he'd got the other two and a half grand.

He turned the corner on to O'Connell Bridge and a limousine festooned with wedding streamers went by. Archie caught a glimpse of a white bride in the back, her headdress askew as she climbed on top of her new husband. He sniggered aloud and thought of Sue. He hadn't told her he wouldn't be back. It was a pity but that was the way. Pity about the band, too; just when they'd got a few more gigs.

But I'll be back, he promised himself. A couple of years.

He crossed at the traffic lights to the Aston Quay corner and, at the last moment, saw Keerins waiting on the footpath. Archie tried to dodge round him but Keerins stepped in front of him. People bunching up for the lights to change watched their silent dance with curiosity.

Then Keerins took hold of Archie's arm and suggested they have a cup of coffee.

'I don't want a cup of coffee,' Archie moaned but he let himself be led into a small sandwich bar. Keerins kept a firm grip on him while he ordered two coffees, paid and settled the cups on a tray with one hand. The two women behind the counter raised their eyebrows to each other.

'Well,' Keerins said as they took a seat at a plastic table, 'you're looking very happy with yourself.'

Archie sank his face into a sullen sulk.

'Finally struck it rich, have you?'

Archie tried to keep his eyes on the coffee but they jerked all around the bar. I'll be jumping bail too, he suddenly remembered. That had slipped his mind. But that was a minor problem compared to what faced him if he stayed. His IRA contact wouldn't have to think for long to work out what had happened once Amber had plugged Callan.

'Made a big sale, have you?'

'I'm not talking to you.' Archie mustered some righteous indignation. 'The deal's off. You broke it.'

Keerins nodded in agreement. 'But I'm not interested in Callan any more. Something bigger has come up. Something much more serious.' He paused for a sip of coffee and lowered his voice. 'A question of spying. Treason.'

Archie moved so violently his chair scraped off the floor.

Keerins watched with satisfaction as he squirmed. 'I think we talked about this before,' he suggested conversationally. 'In relation to the RUC. But it now looks even more serious. It seems that the British are involved.'

'I don't know anything about it,' Archie said indignantly. 'And even if I did, which I don't, I couldn't help you again. Not after what you did to me.'

'You mean what you did to me,' Keerins suggested icily.

Archie shook his head violently. 'What you did to me. I found this Callan character for you. At great personal risk to myself. And you let him get away. And then you broke the deal and had me charged anyway. It wasn't my fucking fault you didn't get him.'

Keerins felt his hackles rise. The little fuck would worm his way out of anything.

'The deal's off,' Archie repeated. 'I don't care if I get five years in the Joy. It'd be a lot less than the risks I ran for you.'

'What I'm talking about,' Keerins calmed himself, 'is a new agreement. Forget what's happened. We start again. You tell me what you know about British spies operating in Dublin and I'll have the drug charges dropped.'

'I know nothing.'

'And I might be able to throw in some money. As an added bonus.'

Archie shook his head.

Keerins drank some coffee and debated whether to push him further. There was nothing to lose. 'His name is John Amber,' he prompted.

'I don't give a fuck if his name's Mickey Mouse.'

'Have you come across him?'

'Who? Mickey Mouse?'

'Amber.'

'Never heard of him.' Archie shook his head. 'I can't help you.'

Keerins tried to stare him into submission but holding his eyes was like trying to catch a frantic fly beating itself against a large window pane. 'You're lying.' He shrugged and went back to his coffee.

Crowds swarmed by the window and the squeal of stopping traffic came through the open door. A small fan behind the counter didn't dilute the heavy heat around them. All the other customers were alone, eating with an unrelaxed dedication, in a hurry.

'I don't think you realise the trouble you're in,' Keerins tried again. 'You're in very deep water, Archie. You're facing a lot more than five years in jail. Life, at least.'

Too fucking right, Archie thought. Death.

'You're playing with ruthless people. Who don't hesitate to drop you in the shit.'

Archie flirted with the idea of giving him the address he had given Amber. Get him off his back. All he needed was a few more hours. Collect the money and then run like fuck. But he had worked himself around to believing his own indignation.

'You've got it all wrong,' Archie said. 'All I know is that you dropped me in the shit. And I'm facing a few years in the Joy. At worst.'

Keerins finished his coffee. 'You've been warned,' he said. 'Your last chance.'

'Can I go?' Archie looked directly at him with the sudden relief of a chastised child about to be released. Keerins nodded. 'Thanks for the coffee.' He hadn't touched it.

Archie went out the door, squaring his narrow shoulders, and disappeared to the right. Bye bye, he said happily to himself. And good fucking riddance.

A moment later Keerins saw him pass back in the opposite direction, borne along by the tide of pedestrians.

Keerins splashed water on to his face and let his head hang over the washbasin, watching the drips fall. The waiting was getting to him, unsettling his mind and making his stomach queasy. He tried to think things through, diverting himself with what he would do with Archie afterwards. Amber would have to be let off, told to get out. And, no doubt, be replaced by someone else.

But Archie was a different matter. He could pressure him with the photographs and details of his meeting with Amber. Really come the heavy and force him to reveal his IRA source. And then he could set himself up with a permanent army council contact. If he was lucky and played it right.

He dried his face and hands and went back to the office. Pursell was still at his desk, his face closer to its normal red. Keerins suspected he'd had a couple of drinks to get his colour up again. He'd become less abject but still treated Keerins with caution, as if he was slightly unstable.

Pursell shook his head at Keerins's unasked question. 'Your wife called,' he said. 'That's all.'

Keerins looked out the window, watching a steady stream of cars leaving the depot on their way home. Suppose Amber had just fucked off, he thought. Then he really was up shit creek. He hadn't a single lead on Callan and no idea where to find one. Unless he moved in on Archie again. And, realistically, that wasn't much of a prospect.

'How long have you known him?' He turned to Pursell.

'Few months.'

'And has he ever held out on you before?'

Pursell shook his head.

'And before that?'

'Before that what?'

'Were you dealing with someone else?'

132

'No,' Pursell flushed with anger. 'I'm not a fucking spy. It was like I told you. A trade-off of information.'

'Only with Amber?'

'Yes.'

'And he delivered the goods? Or was it all one-way traffic?'

'He delivered whatever he said he would.'

'So you trust him?'

Pursell shrugged.

Keerins went back to the window and saw the superintendent marching upright across the parade ground towards his car. You'd think he owns the place, Keerins thought as his patronising tone rang in his memory. You'll get to grips with it in time.

He picked up a phone and dialled home.

'I called to see if you'd be home for tea,' Deirdre said.

'I told you I wouldn't,' Keerins said irritably.

'I just thought I'd check. In case your plans had changed.'

The phone on Pursell's desk rang and he swept it up swiftly.

'I don't think so,' Keerins said vaguely. His attention had switched to Pursell who was listening with a frown.

'Is that yes or no?' Deirdre demanded.

'No,' Keerins said. That leaves us in a very awkward position, Pursell was saying. 'I don't know.'

'Well, which is it?' Deirdre asked. Pursell raised his eyes to Keerins and shook his head mournfully. You've got to share what you've got now, Pursell pleaded into the phone.

Keerins muttered a curse. 'I'm still waiting for an answer,' Deirdre said with a harsh edge to her voice. 'It's a simple question.'

'I can't talk now.' Keerins dropped his phone and stepped quickly round the desk towards Pursell. He was too late. Pursell had let the receiver go limp in his hand. He put it back on its cradle slowly.

'He needs more time,' Pursell said. 'He hasn't got what he's expecting yet.'

'What'd he say?'

'He said the information he's waiting for hasn't come through yet.' Pursell looked grey again. 'He was very apologetic. Said to tell you he's very sorry. But he'll definitely have it tomorrow.'

'Fuck that,' Keerins exploded. 'What's his number?'

Pursell leafed through a small notebook and called out a number. Keerins dialled, thinking that this was Archie's doing: he was stringing

Amber along the same way he had strung him along. The phone rang out.

Keerins shoved his hands into his pockets and slumped against the desk, all the doubts that he had pushed aside coming to the fore. Pursell watched him warily.

It should have been obvious that Amber would try something like this, Keerins told himself. His interest in Callan, whatever it is, does not coincide with ours. All that nice-sounding stuff about being on the same side and only being interested in helping us was so much bullshit. And I fell for it, because I wanted it to be true; because I wanted to get Callan so badly.

'He's probably telling the truth,' Pursell suggested sympathetically, as if the problem belonged to Keerins alone. 'You know how it is. Things never work out exactly like they're supposed to.'

'You think we should trust him?'

Pursell nodded as though he could not quite bring himself to put his agreement into words. 'I mean,' he added tentatively after a moment. 'I can't see any reason not to. Why should he fuck us about? When you come right down to it? What's in it for him? We have to give him the benefit of the doubt.'

Do we have a choice, Keerins wondered, feeling tainted and cornered. I should have played it straight, handed Pursell in, taken the kudos for uncovering him and Amber. But it was too late now. He was as compromised by Amber as Pursell. Almost. He closed his eyes and rocked his body to and fro as if he was soothing himself.

'What do we do?' Pursell asked anxiously after a while, implying that they were in this together, co-conspirators relying upon each other.

Keerins eyes flashed open and he stared at him for a moment. 'You persuaded me to give him twenty-four hours,' he declared, setting the record straight, making Pursell realise that he was still in a subservient position. 'Now you tell me to trust him. What do you think I should do?'

'Wait,' Pursell said quietly, humbled. 'Give him another chance. One more.'

Keerins nodded non-committally. 'You go on home.'

Pursell seemed reluctant to move but then cleared his desk and locked the drawer. He rose slowly and went to the door. 'It'll work out all right.' He turned back as he left. 'This is just a temporary hitch.'

Keerins shrugged himself upright and sat down at his desk. He picked up an internal phone and dialled a number and ordered a tap on Amber's phone.

'Got a warrant?' the voice at the other end asked sweetly.

'I'll get the paperwork over to you tomorrow,' Keerins replied with impatience, hoping to sound authoritative. 'But it's important to get the tap on immediately.'

He sat in the empty office for a long time, thinking. The phone tap was a risk: Pursell might well end up on the tapes but that was his problem. He had to do something other than wait impotently.

The main thing now, he decided, was to keep his nerve.

Thirteen

The dawn came early and seeped around the edges of the heavy curtains, replacing the murk of the street lights with a gradually lightening grey. The industrious chirping of the birds outside was the only sound in the creaking stillness of the house.

Callan lay on the couch, his hands on the armrest beneath his head. Sleep hadn't come and he made no effort to induce it. He hadn't tried the door or the window either to see if they were locked or guarded. He was a prisoner and he accepted the fact passively.

He thought of all the dawns he had seen. Those at the beginning of love affairs which all seemed to have been summer dawns coming up while the night was still young and there was still so much to talk about and know. And those before action when the thought that this might be the last one hung untouched at the back of the mind like a superstitious protection against it coming true. Like this one.

Callan wondered again why he hadn't told Blinker about Amber or whatever his name was. He didn't know. He hadn't consciously decided not to. He had simply excised him from his mind. Amber's approach hadn't seemed real somehow, even though it had scared the shit out of him when it happened. He had been too concerned with his own objectives in coming here to have realised that they might have another agenda waiting. It had been a big mistake.

The sun was well up and forcing its way round the room when the door opened and Blinker came in. He sniffed with distaste at the stale air and then smirked knowingly. 'Smoking is bad for you,' he said and handed Callan a cracked mug.

Callan sat up and sipped at the lukewarm instant coffee. Blinker crossed to the curtains and drew them back a few inches and leaned through the gap to lower the top half of the window a little. The daylight took over the room and raised the sounds of passing cars. A passer-by whistled and the brakes shrieked on a stopping bus.

'Sleep well?' Blinker inquired as he sank into one of the armchairs.

'Perfectly.' Callan looked at him impassively.

'Good. What's the crack? You've got an explanation for me?'

Callan nodded and drank some coffee and grimaced at the foul edge of its taste. Blinker waited.

'He's not a Brit spy,' Callan said. 'He's one of yours.'

'What?'

'An agent provocateur.'

'What the fuck are you talking about?'

'You sent him, to test your theory. See how I'd respond to his offer. And if I fell for it you'd have your proof.'

Blinker frowned and Callan decided his confusion was genuine: Amber really was a British agent. 'But he overdid it,' he added. 'Overplayed his hand.'

'Bullshit,' Blinker snorted. 'You know fucking well who he is and what he is.'

Callan nodded. 'You confirmed it last night when you came up with exactly the same bullshit. It was very neat. But it didn't work. Because I am not an informer.'

'Nice try,' Blinker laughed. 'But you'll have to do better.'

'Look at it objectively.' Two can play this game, Callan thought vindictively. 'You get me back to Ireland because you think I might have turned into a tout. You tip off the guards that I'm here, forcing me into a corner. Then you have someone approach me pretending to be a Brit to tempt me with an offer of help. If I respond, you have your proof. If I don't it doesn't prove anything. I can't win.'

'How long did it take you to work all this out? You must have been awake all night.'

'How else did he know where to find me? How could a single Brit agent do it? It could only have come through the movement.'

'But I didn't know where you were.' Blinker entered into the mental exercise in spite of himself.

'Then how do you know I met this guy?'

'Someone saw you,' Blinker said with a sudden air of distraction. Callan could see that he had at last provoked some doubts, that Blinker was sorting in his mind a new set of possibilities, re-examining who knew what and who said what when.

'And how do you know his name is Amber?' Callan demanded and noted the flash in his eye that showed that Blinker was going through the same process. 'He didn't give me a name.'

Blinker sat back in his chair and closed his eyes. Callan finished his coffee and lit a cigarette. The day already felt old and weary; the sunshine might as well have been coming from a holiday brochure.

Blinker stirred eventually and opened his eyes. 'Interesting,' he grunted. 'But for one thing. I know for a fact that Amber's not one of us.'

'And I know for a fact,' Callan snapped back, 'that I'm not one of them. I'm not an informer.'

'OK.' Blinker sighed, a punctuation mark rather than an agreement. 'Let's go through it from your point of view. From the start. From the time you got the call.'

Callan stood back a little from the window and looked out through the rectangular slit between the curtains. The glass was clouded with grime and he could see the roof and chimney stack of the house across the road. Overhead, the sky was an incredibly soft blue.

He had persuaded Blinker that he wasn't the person he was looking for. At least he thought he had. He had gone through everything that had happened, outlining the sequence of events as they had unfolded. It had occurred to him that the informer was the person who had tipped off the guards about the rendezvous. Which meant that it was someone on this side of the Atlantic. But he hadn't mentioned that to Blinker. That was his problem. It wasn't Callan's concern.

Blinker bustled back into the room with a decisive air. He held out the card that Amber had given Callan: it was blank except for a hand-printed telephone number.

'I don't want it,' Callan said.

'We want you to take him out.' Blinker still proffered the card.

Callan gave a half laugh of surprise and shook his head.

'It's a sure way of clearing your name.'

'Fuck off,' Callan said.

'Why not?' Blinker demanded, as if he had made a perfectly reasonable request. 'You haven't discovered religion, have you? Been born again or something?'

'I've retired. I'm not on active service any more. I don't take orders.'

'Look on it as a request,' Blinker suggested. 'From your old comrades.'

Callan stared out at the sky and didn't answer. Blinker tapped the card against the fingers of his other hand as if he was beating out time. 'You want help, don't you?' he said. 'To get back to your retirement home.'

Callan turned his attention to him and nodded. Blinker shrugged.

'I'll call him,' Callan offered. 'Arrange a meeting. And you can take it from there.'

'You'll turn up?'

'No,' Callan said. 'You can turn up. Do it yourself.'

'You're supposed to be a trigger man.'

'I seem to remember,' Callan glared at him, 'that you always found a reason not to be the one who pulled the trigger.'

'And I remember,' Blinker sneered, his eyes flashing with anger, 'you don't like doing it up close. You prefer to snipe them. Keep your distance.'

Nobody loves a sniper, Callan thought. An instructor had said that to him a long time ago. Not even your own side, the man had warned him.

The door opened and the man who had driven Callan to the house came in with a large brown bag and put it down on the table. 'Food's up,' he said.

The smell of vinegar and grease made Callan realise how hungry he was. 'What is it?' Blinker demanded irritably, putting Amber's card back in his pocket. 'More fish and chips?'

The driver nodded.

'I'll start growing fins if I eat any more fucking fish,' Blinker groaned as he accepted his portion. 'Bring us a cup of tea, will you?'

The driver left and they ate in silence. It's like a time warp, Callan thought. The coming and going. The restless manoeuvring. The anonymous rooms. The edgy anticipation. The waiting. Even the fish and chips. History had reclaimed him.

'I know,' Blinker said in a conciliatory tone, starting their conversation afresh, 'that we're not each other's favourite people. But leave that aside.' He chewed thoughtfully on a thick chip. 'Think of the opportunity we've got here. We've got a Brit spy. Operating in the Free State, which is a bonus. And we can take him out. You can take him out. No problem.'

'You can do it,' Callan replied. 'I told you I'll make the call, arrange it.'

Blinker shook his head slowly. 'He's a trained killer. Anyone else turns up at the meeting and Christ knows what'll happen. They might get blown away. But you can do it. He'll be expecting you.'

139

Callan nodded sardonically. 'That's right. And I don't know what he's got planned for me, do I? Suppose I get blown away. That's all right, is it?'

Blinker considered the possibility for a moment. "'No,' he said. 'Why should he do that? He could have done that yesterday. And he can't kidnap you and bundle you across the border from here. No,' he repeated, 'I think he's on the level. It's a typical Brit move to try and get you back to Boston. And bleed you dry.'

'He could hand me over to the guards.'

'He could have done that yesterday, too.'

Callan screwed up the paper bag and tossed it on to the mound in the fireplace. He faced Blinker and said: 'The last time I shot at someone who wasn't in an enemy uniform he turned out not to be who I was told he was.'

'He was a legitimate target in the circumstances.'

'But it wasn't necessary to lie to me.'

'I agree.' Blinker nodded vigorously. 'And I don't know why they did. Probably thought it better that you didn't know.'

'And now you're asking me to do the same again. I don't know who this guy is.'

'Of course you do,' Blinker's voice rose. 'He's told you, for fuck's sake. What more do you need?'

What I need, Callan thought, is to get the fuck out of here.

'You think he'd hesitate,' Blinker added, 'if he was told to kill you. Remember Gibraltar. You wouldn't be here now if that was in their interests. But it is in our interests to get him. This is a one-in-a-million opportunity. I don't have to spell that out for you, do I?'

'And if I do it,' Callan inquired, 'what then?'

'We get you out again. Like we did last time.'

'The same way?'

'Don't worry about the details. We'll do it OK.'

'And if I don't?'

Blinker shrugged.

'What does that mean?' Callan demanded.

'There are some people who think you're a liability,' Blinker said. 'Your presence has caused a lot of hassle. A lot of people have been hauled in, a lot of safe houses raided. We've had to put a stop on various moves until things calm down.'

'Help me get out now and you solve that problem.'

Blinker shook his head.

Callan sat down on the couch and blew a stream of smoke at the overhead light. Blinker watched him for a moment and then looked at his watch. 'We don't have a lot of time. If we're to set it up right. Give you a back-up and all.' He paused. 'Will you do it?'

Callan nodded at the inevitable. He was a legitimate target.

'Good on you.' Blinker clapped him on the shoulder. 'I never had any doubts about you. And, for your information, it wasn't my idea to bring you back.'

He went out the door in a hurry.

Archie started talking before the coins had settled into the phone box and broke off in mid-sentence as Amber said hello. 'Listen, what's going on?' Archie repeated. 'Where've you been? I was trying to get you all night last night.'

'Business,' Amber said casually. 'I was having a listen to some other groups. Very interesting.'

'Yeah, well, what's happening?'

'Everything is fine. On course.'

'What about our deal?' Archie whined, his voice rising as if he had been spurned. 'When do I get the rest?'

'It's all coming together nicely. Don't worry. We're nearly there.'

'Have you found him? Your man?'

'We're nearly there, I said.' Amber sounded almost amused. 'A few bits and pieces to tidy up. That's all. Small print sort of thing.'

'So when do I get it?'

'Soon. Very soon.'

'I can't hang on any longer,' Archie pleaded. 'I'm being hassled by the cops. About you. They even mentioned your name. Wanted me to tell them all about you.'

'Who did?' Amber demanded quickly.

'The cops did. They seem to know . . .'

'Yes, but who?' Amber interrupted. 'Which one?'

'Mr Keerins,' Archie said impatiently as if that was an irrelevance. 'I can't hold out any longer. I've got to get the fuck out of here.'

'OK, OK,' Amber said. 'Come by this evening.'

'You'll have it then?' Archie asked with a mixture of doubt and relief.

'Yes,' Amber said. 'At eight.'

'Right,' Archie said, pleased with himself. That had shaken him up. 'See you then.'

He stepped out of the phone box and into the throng of afternoon shoppers in Henry Street. He didn't pay any attention to his surroundings any more.

The rush hour traffic had tightened up on its way to the suburbs as they drove towards the city centre. Callan sat beside the driver and Blinker was in the back. They did not speak.

They slowed to a crawl in the circle of cars jammed around St Stephens Green. Callan watched the crowds on the jostling footpaths, mini-skirted women with large shopping bags, young men with briefcases, their jackets hooked over their shoulders. All released from work and shopping, in a hurry to be elsewhere. Their purposeful movement and the throb of idling engines seemed to raise the heat of the sunshine. His mind was empty.

'Fuck it,' Blinker muttered, a release of tension. It was five-thirty-one. 'We're running out of time. Try and find a place to park.'

The driver hung his hand from his window in a plea to change lanes and moved over to the right when someone held back. Crawling round the Grafton Street corner, they were finally in the right-hand lane. It was five-thirty-nine.

'Anywhere here,' Blinker ordered.

As if in response to his command a parked car signalled and they let it out and swept into its spot. Blinker had his door open before they had stopped. 'Come on,' he said impatiently to Callan.

Callan followed him up the wide footpath overhung by the park's perimeter trees to a cluster of phone boxes. 'You've got it all straight?' Blinker asked as he picked up the receiver from the box on the edge. Callan nodded. Blinker put two coins in the chute and punched the number from Amber's card. He handed the receiver to Callan.

It answered almost immediately and Callan waited a moment for the box to swallow the coins. 'I'm interested in your proposition,' he said.

'Good,' Amber replied.

'But I want to talk about the details.'

'What details?' Callan thought he heard a hint of suspicion in Amber's voice but the noise of the passing traffic made it difficult to tell. Blinker's ear was up against the back of the receiver and Callan could smell his sweat. 'I've told you what to do,' Amber added. 'Cross over and report to the first people you meet. That's all there's to it. They'll be expecting you.'

'That's not on,' Callan said. 'I've got to have a definite arrangement.'

Amber said nothing.

'And I need some cash,' Callan added into the silence.

'That'll be waiting for you.'

'No. I need it now.'

'What for?'

'You can look on it as a gesture of good faith.'

'I'll see about that,' Amber said.

'It's got to be today. This evening.'

'That's not possible.'

'Right,' Callan said. 'Forget it.'

Blinker shoved his elbow into Callan's ribs and mouthed something in front of his face. Callan ignored him.

'Hang on, mate,' Amber said. 'We'll talk about it.'

'Not on the phone.'

'OK, OK. Nine o'clock in the Burlington Hotel. The underground car park.'

'No,' Callan said and paused as if he was thinking. 'Sandymount strand. The second car park on the way out from town. At six-thirty.'

'No way,' Amber protested. 'I can't make it that quick.'

'Seven o'clock,' Callan said. 'That's it.'

He replaced the receiver.

'Fuck's sake,' Blinker exploded. A woman at another phone gave them a startled look as they stepped away. Blinker stopped in front of Callan. 'You trying to be fucking smart or what?'

'He'll be there,' Callan said calmly. Blinker was only an irritant; he was thinking about Amber. He had sounded different, less phoney, more professional.

Blinker shook his head. 'You did that deliberately. Tried to blow it.'

'How else could I have done it?' Callan demanded. He walked round Blinker and strode off towards the car. Was Amber just being cautious too, he wondered. Or had he wanted to plan an ambush as well?

'He better be there,' Blinker threatened as he caught up with him.

'He will. I didn't give him any choice.'

'He better be,' Blinker repeated. 'For your sake.'

They got back into the car. 'Ringsend,' Blinker snapped at the driver as if he was deaf.

Inspector Keerins could now see the broken-down juggernaut that had narrowed Bachelor's Walk into two lanes and caused the tailback. He cursed and wished he had taken an official car: it could have helped him through the tail end of the rush hour but it would have involved bringing someone with him. And he didn't want anyone with him.

The tension in the office had built up steadily during the day. Amber hadn't called. Pursell looked sicker by the hour. Keerins became more and more agitated. The only relief had been the superintendent's absence: he'd been locked in conference all day.

'It's not like him not to call.' Pursell shook his head as if he was genuinely amazed.

Keerins grunted in disgust.

'He did call last night,' Pursell reminded him. 'Like he said he would.'

The traffic crawled forward until he was halted again, alongside the obstruction. The cab was tilted forward and a couple of men were standing by, waiting for something or someone.

'I'll call him,' Pursell had offered in desperation later as they sat idly in a prickly fume of unspoken recriminations.

'No,' Keerins ordered, without explanation.

'We can't just sit here. Doing nothing.'

'What do you suggest?' Keerins snapped.

Pursell threw his hands up hopelessly.

'You can start writing your confession, if you want,' Keerins suggested.

At least that had shut him up, Keerins thought as he finally drove by the juggernaut. Even though it was a pretty empty threat by now. Pursell knew that too, he suspected, but he wasn't sure enough yet to say it.

He turned on to O'Connell Bridge at the lights and the traffic thinned out.

'Where're you going?' Pursell had blurted when Keerins, unable to wait any longer, had made decisively for the door. 'Out.'

It was a long shot, he told himself as he went up Kildare Street. But that's all that was left now. Long shots or long waits for calls that never came. Movement, any movement, was better than that.

He turned round by the Shelbourne Hotel and headed for Baggot Street, suppressing the faint hopes that still clung stubbornly to the edges of his mind. I should have put a tail on him, he told himself. But he hadn't wanted anyone else to discover Amber's true identity. Being too fucking smart again.

He reached Amber's road in Ballsbridge and drew up outside the house they had staked out. Keerins stepped out of his car 4 and gave a sigh of resignation. The car park before the flats was half full but Amber's car was not there. He's done a bunk, he told himself. All I want to do is to confirm that. So that I know where I stand.

He went up to the door.

They were parked in a street of single-storey terraced houses in Ringsend, waiting. A group of small boys kicked a ball between chalk goalposts on the red-brick wall that marked the dead end. Two elderly women chatted at a door. Blinker had a walkie talkie on his knee, half-covered by his hand. Callan looked towards the playing children but didn't see them: he was concentrating on remembering everything he had ever learned. The driver had his hands looped over the steering wheel and seemed to have lost his previous night's chattiness.

The only sound was the cries of the children. It was eight minutes before seven.

'All clear,' the walkie talkie said.

'Right,' Blinker bustled into action, handing the walkie talkie to the driver and pointing at the glove compartment for Callan. 'The short's in there. Get into place.'

Callan swung round in the seat. 'Who was that?'

'The scout.' Blinker opened his door.

'And where are you going?' Callan demanded. 'Bailing out again?'

'You just do what you're supposed to be good at,' Blinker retorted. 'And do it right.'

'Hold on,' Callan said. 'Where do I find you afterwards?'

'He'll take you back.' Blinker nodded at the driver.

'The same place?'

'He knows what to do. You look after your part.'

'Where do I find you? If anything goes wrong.'

Blinker sighed as if he was dealing with a nervous, elderly relative and gave him a phone number. Callan repeated it after him.

Blinker stepped out and the driver started the engine and did a quick three-point turn. 'Fuck,' he said to himself about nothing in particular. Callan saw Blinker strolling back towards the city centre as they edged out of the cul-de-sac.

They turned in the opposite direction and drove to where the road touched the edge of the bay and then ran along its contour. The tide was far out, baring a huge expanse of muck-grey sand. Off to the left, the twin stacks of the Pigeon House power station tapered up to the sky, bound with red aircraft warnings like sticks of seaside candy. Dark smoke spread in a horizontal line from one chimney.

Callan pushed the button on the glove compartment and took out the cloth package. Inside was a 9-millimetre Heckler and Koch semi-automatic. He withdrew the magazine and thumbed out the rounds to count them. There were only five. He replaced them and checked the action and clicked the magazine back into place.

The driver glanced at him and there was a sheen of perspiration on his freckled forehead. Callan felt the knot of tension in his own stomach and breathed deeply.

They pulled off the road into the first car park and idled into a space. The driver killed the engine and looked at his watch. The walkie talkie rested on his lap. Callan gave him an inquiring look.

'Seven,' the driver said hoarsely and cleared his throat.

Callan put the cloth back into the glove compartment. He held the gun between his knees, flexing his hand to get the feel of the grip and the trigger.

'Right on time,' the walkie talkie said. 'Green Granada. All clear.'

Callan opened the door and shoved the gun under his jacket and into his waistband at the base of his spine in one movement. The driver said something into the radio but it was lost in the slam of the door.

He stepped up to the broad path above the beach and walked steadily towards the Martello Tower. There was a scattering of people out strolling and sitting on benches. A few small figures were way out on the sand and a man was practising with a golf club. An aircraft came in low beyond the invisible tideline. A light-blue haze hung over the sea, enclosing the smudge of the approaching car ferry and a cluster of white sails off Dun Laoghaire. As if they were an impressionist painting.

146

The sun was behind him and Callan felt the fresh breeze off the sea. He was acutely aware of everything; the open seascape, the fringe of bushes along the car park, the people, the cars rushing along the half-hidden road, an advertising hoarding with a sketch of Mount Rushmore.

It's very exposed, he thought, wondering suspiciously why Blinker had chosen this spot. It was far from ideal: too open, too many people, too many places where surprises could come from. But Blinker hadn't explained why here, hadn't explained anything. Treated him as a hired gun. He didn't think about what he was going to do. Only how he was going to do it.

He passed the tower, walking steadily, the beach on his left, a narrow stretch of grass on his right. He took in the thick concrete walls forming a large open box on the sand and its faded graffiti about the IRA. On the other side of the road a long, low block of flats overlooked everything, increasing his sense of exposure.

Then he saw the car park and the green Granada angled out behind a clump of bushes.

He stopped on the path, masked from the car by the bushes, and turned to look out to sea for a moment. He completed the circle and noted everything behind him. An elderly couple was coming by the tower. There was no one nearby. He went down into the car park.

There were six other cars there, the nearest ones empty as far as he could see. At the far end, a long-haired youth wearing a leather jacket with the name of a courier firm sat on a heavy motorbike. He had a radio clipped to his chest and a black helmet rested on the petrol tank. The scout, he thought. But he couldn't assume that: they had told him nothing.

Amber was sitting in his car and their eyes locked as Callan approached. Amber inclined his head towards the passenger seat. Callan shook his head. They were still ten paces apart.

Amber lowered his window. His hands were out of sight.

'Let's take a walk,' Callan said, his body tense, ready to leap and roll.

Amber shrugged his shoulders and opened the door slowly. Callan shifted to signal his nervousness.

'Relax,' Amber smiled slightly, revealing his empty hands as the door swung wide. He stepped out and closed the door behind him. He was wearing a light-grey suit.

They walked together, hands hanging by their sides.

'The money,' Callan asked. 'Did you bring it?'

'I can let you have a hundred.'

'That's not enough. need a thousand at least.' They stepped up to the path and Callan scanned both directions, quickly. There were some figures far off to the right. The elderly couple to the left were coming closer.

'You didn't give me time. And you won't need it once you cross the border. We'll cover all expenses.'

Amber paused and Callan edged him towards the boulders slanting down to the beach. Amber grimaced down at the dirty grey sand.

'What guarantees do I have?' Callan demanded as they picked their steps down. He had to keep him talking, get him out behind the concrete walls. He'd be able to take his time from there. Afterwards.

'Well,' Amber began as they stepped on to a strip of powdery sand, 'you have to trust me to an extent. You can see . . .'

They both heard the footsteps behind and turned at the same time, looks glaring off each other with mutual fear. The biker was above them, his head closed in a full visored helmet, a gun in his hands. They both moved. The biker fired.

Amber staggered backwards with a grunt, his hands flailing up helplessly. The second bullet thudded into his head, the third sank into his chest. He fell. Callan froze, his hand on the butt of the pistol. The biker lowered the gun and raised it again in his two-fisted hold. He fired twice more and turned and walked away.

Callan bounded up the rocks after him. The elderly couple watched, their mouths limp with horror, the woman clutching the man's jacket. Callan leapt between the bushes into the car park as the motorbike roared away. It swerved round a car coming into the park and took off along the footpath.

'What is it?' a man said beside Callan. He didn't know where the man had come from, hadn't realised he had stopped.

'Call an ambulance,' Callan shouted and spurted into action. He ran for the entrance. The man went with him.

'What happened?' he gasped.

'Shooting,' Callan said as they went out on to the footpath. 'You try the houses. Get an ambulance. I'll try the filling station.'

Callan ran down the path towards a petrol sign and back towards his waiting car. If it was still there. The fuckers, he thought. They've set me up again. The man hesitated and then stepped into the road, waving his arms at the traffic, and ran towards the houses opposite.

Callan passed the garage and began to slow down. He went round a bend and slowed to a quick walk, his chest heaving, perspiration coursing from every pore. A passing cyclist looked at him curiously and he avoided her eyes.

The driver had turned the car to face the exit and Callan pulled open the door and sank in.

'Jesus,' the driver said, aghast at his appearance. 'What.. .'

'Move,' Callan ordered.

The car shot forward and Callan leaned back against the head rest and closed his eyes. I'm too old for this, he thought. He could see and hear it all again. The curve of the courier's visor reflecting the painting of the bay like a dark fish-eye lens. The gun jerking in his hands. The crack of the impartial bullets overlaying the instant thud of their arrival. Amber's groan. His face deformed into a lopsided twist. His suit darkening.

In the old days I'd have shot that fucker, he thought. And I didn't even get the gun out.

The weapon was still crushing into the small of his back and then the wail of a thin siren opened his eyes. An unmarked car was weaving towards them, headlights on, a beacon flashing on the edge of its roof.

'Oh fuck,' the driver groaned.

'Steady,' Callan dragged the word out and the police car went by in a blur.

They crashed a light just turned red and took a sharp right. The car lurched sideways but straightened up and they sped by a group of brightly painted tall houses. Callan rubbed his sleeve over his forehead and tried to get his bearings.

'Where are we?' he asked.

'Heading for the toll bridge.' The driver was intent on the wide road ahead.

'What toll bridge?' Callan felt confused. He didn't know of any toll bridge.

The question upset the driver's concentration for a moment. 'What d'you mean? To the north side, of course.'

'Slow down,' Callan ordered, grappling with a host of mental uncertainties. 'Where are we going?'

'Raheny.'

'Why not back to the other house?'

'Because I was told to take you to Raheny.'

'Why?'

'I don't fucking know.' The driver swung impatiently on to a roundabout and took the exit for the toll bridge.

Callan tried to think straight but all he could see was the biker's featureless head and the pointing gun. All he could feel was the terrible instant of freezing shock before Amber fell. The moment when he thought the biker was Amber's hit man. When he thought he was the target.

The car went straight to the automatic toll and the driver tossed the coins he had been holding all the time into the basket. The barrier rose after what seemed like a long time and they went through.

'Go back up the quays,' Callan said as they crossed the bridge. 'To the city.'

The driver shook his head and paused at the roundabout to let a car by.

'Do it,' Callan said and pulled the gun from his back with his left hand.

'Jesus Christ, Fergus.' The driver swallowed as the muzzle jammed into his ribs. 'What the fuck's got into you?'

He turned up the quays. Callan withdrew the gun but kept it pointed across his body at the driver.

'What was supposed to happen back there?' he barked.

'I don't know,' the driver flicked a nervous glance at him. 'You were to execute a British spy.'

'Who was the scout?'

'I don't know. I wasn't told.'

'Tall, thin, long hair. Dressed like a motorbike courier.'

The driver shook his head. 'You know Blinker. He told me nothing. Where to leave you. Where to take you after. That's all.'

The river was an uncharacteristic blue, fired by the sun. They passed a row of dangling cranes and a series of blank stone warehouses. The road was empty. The driver had slowed down.

'What happened?' the driver asked.

'The scout did it,' Callan said. 'Was that the plan?'

'No. I don't know. I thought you were to do it.'

'You were talking to him on the radio. What did he say?'

150

'Nothing.' The driver paused and licked his lips. 'I let him know you were on your way. And I heard nothing more for a long time. Then he gave a shout, a sort of yahoo.'

That figured, Callan thought. A fucking cowboy.

'That was all,' the driver added. 'Then you came back.'

They were approaching the first of the city bridges and the driver asked him where he was to go.

'South,' Callan ordered. He didn't know what to do. His instincts told him to do the opposite of what was expected. But he didn't know what was expected, except that he was supposed to be going north to Raheny. 'Head for Wicklow.'

'They'll have blocks up by now,' the driver warned.

'Keep off the main roads.' Callan slid the gun under his jacket but kept it pointing towards the driver as they came into the city centre. 'And don't try anything stupid.'

Fourteen

The message arrived at Keerins's home just ahead of him. 'There's been a shooting,' Deirdre said from the kitchen door as he stepped into the house.

'Who?' He stopped.

'At Sandymount strand. You're to go there.'

'Who is it?'

'I don't know,' she sniffed. 'He didn't say. Nobody tells me anything.'

He hurried back to his car without thinking and drove fast, headlights on and clearing his way with a forceful palm on the horn. He sped through Merrion gates as the level-crossing's warning lights flashed and the barriers began to dip. There was no point wondering: whatever had happened had happened. And was bound to be bad. Then he was alongside the strand and saw the motorcycle garda waving curious cars away.

Keerins shoved his identity card out of the window and told him impatiently to move the motorbike blocking the entrance to the car park. He drove in.

The first thing he saw was Amber's green Granada with a 'do not touch' sign propped against the back window and a fingerprint man dusting the driver's door. The back of the parking area was a jumble of garda cars, their radios cackling in unison like a collection of excited insects. An ambulance stood by silently, its warning lights off. A flat routine hung over everything, the routine that followed in the wake of anything sudden and violent.

The superintendent was off to one side in the middle of a group of plain-clothes men. Keerins saw Pursell watching him from the edge of the group and he turned away. He stepped over the scene of crime tape strung between the bushes and went up to the pathway. A couple of detectives were parting the bushes and peering carefully into them. Keerins looked down, fearing the worst.

The tape continued down the rocks and marked out a rough square on the sand. A detective was bent over the rocks, easing a bullet case from a deep crack with the tip of a pen. He dropped it into a plastic bag and chalked the rock. Along the path in both directions, uniformed policemen held back small groups of onlookers.

'Fuck's sake,' a voice beside him said. 'Don't move your foot.'

Keerins glanced down and saw another bullet case by his toecap. The man who had spoken bent down and drew a circle round it. 'Watch your step, will you?' he said irritably. Nobody paid any attention to the uncovered body on the sand.

Amber's body had the discarded look of a piece of broken furniture tossed away in a hurry. His arms and legs lay at haphazard angles and his body was partly on its side. The blood had darkened and seemed to merge with the damp seeping from the grey sand into his clothes .His face was twisted into the sand, the visible eye a bloody mess where the first bullet had hit him. Keerins felt sick.

He took a deep breath and forced his gaze up to the horizon and the blue haze hanging over the sea. He turned and looked at the bushes, part of his mind trying to identify their dark-blue flowers. Trying to divert him from the sight that refused to turn away from his inner eye.

He went back to the car park, stepping over the tape carefully in order to steady himself mentally as well as physically.

Pursell was waiting for him and said in an urgent whisper, 'You can't tell him now.'

'This is all your fault,' Keerins retorted, not looking at him.

'Don't be ridiculous.' Pursell reddened.

'It wouldn't have happened if you'd played it straight. Instead of trying to be too smart.'

'What the fuck's wrong with you?' Pursell grabbed his arm. 'It was his own fault. We didn't get him into this. He knew what he was doing.'

Keerins shook his arm free angrily. 'He'd be alive now if we'd done what we should have done.' If I'd done what I should have done, he amended mentally. Christ.

'The bastard was double-crossing us. Can't you see that? He was supposed to pass on information to us, not take on Callan himself. It's his own fault. He's the one who wasn't playing it straight.'

Keerins looked at him with disgust, seeing the mangled face on the sand.

'Well, that's the truth,' Pursell retorted defensively. 'He tried to go it alone. And he lost. And it served him right.'

'I thought he was a friend of yours,' Keerins said.

153

Pursell shook his head. 'He was a spy. OK, OK,' he added when he saw the look on Keerins's face, 'I'm sorry he got shot. But it was his own fucking fault. It wasn't anything to do with us. Can't you see that?'

Keerins walked away, feeling nauseous again. Pursell's transparent self-interest repelled him. But he was right, up to a point: Amber had known what he was doing. Still. It went against all his instincts as a policeman. He was supposed to prevent crime as well as solve it. And this death was one he could have prevented. If he had acted like a policeman.

The superintendent summoned him with a wave and Keerins changed direction, suddenly conscious of his own self-interest. Pursell tagged along behind. But the superintendent was intercepted by an officer from the press office, seeking details of what to tell the media.

'Victim's name is John Amber,' he barked impatiently. 'British national. Businessman of some sort. Shot four or five times. We're looking for two men. Descriptions later. That's all.'

Keerins and Pursell waited to one side. 'We're in this together,' Pursell whispered. 'Remember that.' Keerins did not reply.

The press officer noted the brusque details and then said, 'The press says he was a British agent.'

'What?' The superintendent glowered at him. 'What are you talking about?'

'The IRA has claimed it,' the press officer said with a helpless gesture as if to point out that it wasn't his fault. 'They say he was a British agent.'

The superintendent grunted and dismissed him with a wave. He wheeled round to Keerins with a face as abrasive as unpolished granite. 'Is this true, Inspector?'

Keerins swallowed and said, 'I don't know.'

'Well, what do you know?' the superintendent demanded.

'It's possible,' Keerins said slowly, trying to be as truthful as possible while being as careful as possible. He could hear Pursell breathing heavily behind him. 'I was trying to check him out. He was a contact of my informant's. I thought at first that he might be my man's IRA contact but he didn't match any of the likely knowns.'

'And what did you find?' The superintendent glared at him suspiciously. 'Was he a British agent or not?'

'The possibility occurred to me,' Keerins said, hoping his caution would be interpreted as normal carefulness. 'Especially after you had raised the possibility that my informant might have been working for the RUC as well. But I hadn't come up with anything definite.'

The superintendent sighed heavily and glanced round as a car arrived and a man got out and opened the boot. He took out a black case and looked around. The superintendent signalled to another detective who went over to the pathologist and led him towards the body.

'He was armed,' the superintendent said. 'He'd left a Smith and Wesson under the driver's seat.'

'I asked for a tap on his phone,' Keerins revealed, feeling more confident. 'You should have seen the request today.'

The superintendent shook his head as if that was one more in a series of cock-ups.

'I asked them to put it on anyway,' Keerins added. 'Pending the paperwork.'

'And did they?' The superintendent brightened up.

'I don't know,' Keerins admitted. 'They didn't send me anything.'

'You can't wait for those two-fingered typists,' the superintendent retorted. 'You've got to keep after them.'

As if to illustrate what he meant, he marched off to his car and pulled out a radio. Keerins leaned back against a squad car and tried to get his story straight. It'll be all right, he told himself. Tell him everything, except that I followed Amber and caught Pursell. Nobody knew that part of it; the rest hung together.

He felt cold suddenly. The sun had dipped down low and the shadows stretched over them. Fuck Amber, he thought suddenly; why did he have to go and get himself killed?

'You didn't tell me about the tap.' Pursell shifted from one foot to the other, accusingly. 'When did it start?'

'After he called you the other day.' Keerins felt tired, his energy sapped by a mixture of underlying guilt and the need to lie to his superiors.

'That's all right, then,' Pursell nodded to himself. 'We're OK.'

Keerins restrained himself. Fuck Pursell too. But there was no point. It was all a shambles. He had cocked it up. Well and truly.

'So what do you propose we do now?' he demanded.

155

Pursell shrugged helplessly and watched the superintendent return. A detective called to the ambulance men from the top of the steps and they went over with a stretcher slung sideways, one of them carrying a grey blanket.

'A couple of things on the tap,' the superintendent said. 'Callan called him and set this up. Amber had offered him some kind of deal.'

'It was definitely Callan?' Keerins inquired. He had assumed that all along but had hoped at the back of his mind that it wasn't him.

'No doubt. He was one of them. There's a good description from witnesses as well. Down to the American accent.' He shook his head. 'Cool customer. Talked to one of the witnesses afterwards.'

Keerins shook his head. 'But why? Is this what he came back for?'

The superintendent gave him a curious look. 'That's hardly the point,' he snapped. 'The point is that we have to take him out of circulation. As quickly as possible. He's been roaming free far too long. And this,' he waved towards the sea as if the scene was a personal affront, 'is too much. Broad daylight. People everywhere.'

Keerins took the implied criticism stoically. He had failed time and again to get Callan and Amber's murder highlighted that fact more dramatically than anything else. He could hardly defend himself: he had no defence.

'Right,' the superintendent said as if to break through Keerins's mental recriminations. 'What've we got?'

'Blinker's the one behind this,' Pursell offered decisively. 'He's obviously controlling Callan.'

'Right,' the superintendent repeated. 'What else?'

Archie, Keerins thought tiredly. He's my only card again and he had double-crossed me too. 'My informant,' he said.

'He's on the tapes as well.' The superintendent nodded. 'There's no doubt he was dealing with Amber. Where is he?'

'I don't know. But I've got a tail on him.'

'Well, find out,' the superintendent snapped. 'Get to it and stop hanging around like lethargic teenagers.'

He marched away and Keerins sprang into action at last. He went to one of the security section's cars and asked the radio controller to put him through to the surveillance unit.

The ambulance men carried the covered stretcher down the steps, followed by the pathologist who stopped to talk to the superintendent.

156

They slid the stretcher into the back and the ambulance left with its blue lights revolving.

'Where is he?' Keerins echoed when he got through to Paul on the surveillance detail.

'Busaras,' Paul said.

'What's he doing?'

'Waiting for a bus,' Paul said. What else would he be doing there, his tone implied. 'Don't know his destination yet.'

'What has he been doing? Has he been more agitated than usual?'

The radio crackled with a laugh. 'Hard to tell,' Paul said. 'He's always agitated. Called on the house he visited the other night. Then came straight here. Hold on.'

Keerins waited. Some garda cars began to start up and leave. What I need, he thought inconsequentially, is a long, hard run. Clear my mind of all this shit. The superintendent stopped by to tell him they were having a conference at headquarters in an hour. 'Have a full report on everything we know about Callan,' he ordered.

The radio came alive again. 'Got his destination,' Paul said. 'The Liverpool ferry.'

The little fucker, Keerins thought. 'Pick him up when he gets there,' he ordered.

'On what?'

'The Offences Against the State Act. Suspicion of having firearms and complicity in murder.'

'Got it.'

'And don't let him out of your sight,' Keerins ordered. 'He's not to get on that boat. Under any circumstances.'

They came up the hill from Ballinteer and Callan saw a sign for a wood. 'Up there,' he pointed. The car climbed steeply up the narrow road and the city's sprawl fell away behind them, bathed in the low evening sunshine. He glanced back and focused on the power station chimneys rising like markers between the spread of buildings and the edge of the peaceful blue bay. A faint line of smoke still ran from one of them.

The trees closed in around them and he directed the driver into a picnic area and then to a corner of the car park. The driver switched off the engine and they sat in the silence while Callan examined their surroundings carefully. There appeared to be nobody around.

'Out.' He indicated with the gun. 'Slowly. And put your hands on the roof.'

The driver did as he was told and Callan stepped out quickly and walked round the car, the gun hanging casually by his side, his eyes on the young man. The driver watched him; his face was pale and he was breathing heavily.

'Relax,' Callan said behind him and remembered Amber saying the same thing when he feigned nervousness. Amber had been very casual, he thought. Which was what convinced him that he himself was the target the moment before the biker fired and Amber fell. 'Don't worry. I've got no argument with you.'

He ran one hand down the man's sides and across his back and stepped away. 'Empty your pockets on to the seat.' The man tossed down a bunch of keys, a used tissue, a half roll of mints, loose coins, a couple of pound notes and an envelope. Callan told him to open the envelope and the man took out a letter.

'OK,' Callan said. 'Take everything back except the money.'

The man gathered up his belongings.

'Take a walk,' Callan said. 'And take your time.'

The man moved away backwards, hesitantly.

'It's all right,' Callan said, shoving the gun into his belt. 'I don't want you reporting back for a while. That's all.'

Callan sat into the car and started the engine and swung round by the man standing in the middle of the clearing.

'You're making a big mistake,' the man shouted as he went by.

It was all a big mistake. I should never have come back, Callan thought. I should have got out when they first sprung the trap. I shouldn't have let myself be sucked into it all again. I shouldn't have let Blinker con me. I shouldn't have been shocked into inaction.

He went down the hill and cruised through a thicket of suburban houses. He eventually found a phone box near a shopping centre, as shuttered as a fortress, its car park as deserted as a free fire zone. He dialled the number Blinker had given him.

'Where the fuck are you?' Blinker shouted.

'I'll ask the questions now,' Callan retorted, barely containing the anger that had built up within him. 'Why'd you pull that stunt?'

'You weren't going to do it.'

'Yes, I was. Until that lunatic opened up and nearly blew me away too.'

'Oh no, you weren't. You had a sitting target and you didn't take it. Sitting in his car waiting for it. And you,' Blinker added with cold menace, 'you tried to walk him out of the frame.'

'That cretin,' Callan gasped. 'He told you that! Jesus Christ!'

'That's the way it happened.'

'Listen,' Callan said in a fury. 'I don't give a fuck whether you want to believe this or not. If I had done it my way, we'd all have been well clear before anyone knew what happened. Instead of which there was a stack of witnesses and the cops arriving as we left. We barely got clear and' - his voice rose to smother Blinker's attempt to butt in - 'and all the witnesses can identify me. Which was the whole object.'

'You're out of your fucking tree.'

'Fucking right I am. You set me up in Connemara. And you tried again now. Very neat. Leaving me beside the body.'

'Grow up, will you?' Blinker shouted. 'We're trying to fight a war while you're piss acting . . .'

'I'm not surprised you're losing it if that's the way you operate these days.'

'You've lost your nerve,' Blinker sneered. 'Go back to painting houses.'

'That's what I'm going to do,' Callan said, trying to still his seething anger. 'But what I want to know first is, is it army policy to set me up? Or are you the informer you're supposed to be looking for?'

A string of curses erupted in his ear and the line went dead.

Callan slumped against the wall of the airless phone box. His heart was racing and his shirt was wet again. He ran his hand hard down his face and over the scratchy stubble on his jaw.

The fat fucker hasn't changed, he thought vindictively; he still can't take anybody arguing with him. But that offered little satisfaction, much less a solution. He told himself to think but he was tired of thinking. He had been thinking too much. Thinking slowed his reactions, had almost gotten him killed.

I need somewhere to rest up, he decided. But where?

He stepped out of the kiosk and looked at the deserted shopping centre and the empty road. He didn't even know where he was.

Fifteen

The cells were full and all the interview rooms occupied. Detectives milled about, drawn into the Bridewell from different units to help process the people picked up in the early morning raids. A perspiring station sergeant emerged from the cell block and collided with Keerins. Keerins stepped back and was thanked with a vicious look.

Keerins went into the block and asked someone which room Maire Callan was in. The detective jerked a thumb over his shoulder. Keerins opened the door a crack and the policewoman inside slipped out.

'Anything?' he asked.

She shook her head. 'She hasn't said a single word.'

Keerins shrugged and went in anyway. He was curious to see her, knowing her reputation as an implacable republican, one of the most uncompromising among the IRA's leadership.

She was sitting upright on a hard chair, her knees together and her arms folded. Her eyes were fixed on something to one side of the detective who stared at her from behind a scratched table. Keerins went round behind him and faced her. She took no notice of him, her eyes withdrawn and dead to all around her.

'Where's your husband, Mrs Callan?' he asked quietly.

She gave no indication that she had heard him. Keerins studied her face, memorising it, looking for something that would give him a clue to Callan. What he had seen in her, perhaps. What she had seen in him. He saw nothing.

'Where's my son?' she said suddenly.

The detective shifted in his chair, as if her unexpected question was a major breakthrough and they could now get down to business. Keerins stood still and said, 'He's being looked after. He's all right.'

Maire showed no reaction.

'He's at school,' Keerins added.

That seemed to surprise her. Her eyes flicked towards Keerins and met his for an instant before she went back to her private world.

'One of your neighbours took him to school,' Keerins said. 'She'll collect him after. Look after him until. . .' He stopped and let the unfinished sentence hang in the air like the threat of eternity.

'Where's your husband?' he asked again, after a time.

160

'I don't have a husband,' she said flatly.

'Your former husband, then. Why did he come back?'

She did not reply. A muffled laugh came from beyond the door but the room was frozen in silence, like the fade-out tableau of a play.

'I don't understand,' Keerins said in a conversational tone, 'why he came back. And why he's gone back on active service.' He stopped as though a thought had just struck him. 'Are you that short of volunteers that you're bringing people out of retirement?'

She stared without moving at the wall to his right. She doesn't look like a hard woman, Keerins thought. You wouldn't give her a second glance if you were asked to pick a terrorist out of a crowded street. But, then, you'd find very few of them that way. Not even Callan.

'I can't imagine what would have brought him back,' Keerins said, as if the idea troubled him. 'He has to know that his chances of getting away again are nil. It must be something very, very important. Much more important than shooting an English businessman.'

It was like talking to oneself. There was no agreement or disagreement from Maire. No hint that she even heard him.

'And you know what it is,' Keerins went on. 'You can't expect us to believe otherwise. One way or the other, he's got to have been in touch with you. You can put a stop to it before it gets even further out of hand.'

That was weak, he told himself. But the whole thing was pointless. She had given him one answer in return for the answer he had given her. And that was all he was going to get.

She gave no more sign of being aware of his departure than she had of his presence.

'Well?' the policewoman asked as he emerged.

'She says she doesn't have a husband,' Keerins sighed.

'Lucky woman.' She gave him a sly smile as she went back into the room.

Pursell emerged from another door and Keerins waited for him. 'Archie?' he inquired.

'Fucker makes me itchy,' Pursell nodded, scratching his armpit and moving his shoulders under his jacket.

'You didn't say anything to him?' Keerins checked.

'Not a word. Stared at him for ten minutes.' Pursell groaned with relief. 'Nobody's said a word to him. But it's hard work. He makes you want to sit on him, to keep him still.'

'Is he ready?'

'Leave him another while. He'll be crawling up the walls. Sing his head off by then.'

Keerins gave a bleak smile in spite of himself. The prospect of Archie singing was not something to look forward to. It was the usual feast or famine: they couldn't shut Archie up and they couldn't get a word out of the Provos.

'Cup of tea?' Pursell asked and Keerins agreed. Pursell seemed to have recovered his spirits now that he had something to do. Keerins envied him his apparent ability to put all the pressures of the last few days behind him.

They went out of the cell block and made their way upstairs. 'Just had word from Shannon,' a detective greeted them. 'That Air Canada return charter to Toronto. One passenger failed to show. A Canadian called Graves.'

Keerins nodded absently. He hadn't expected anything else. They knew how Callan had come in but that was all history now.

'You want his address?' the detective asked. 'Will I have it checked out?'

'Why not,' Keerins agreed although it wouldn't lead anywhere . 'And circulate that name to the other airports and ports.'

'What about Blinker?' Pursell asked him.

'No trace of him,' Keerins said. 'He's gone to ground.'

'One thing I'm sure of,' Pursell said as if it were a consolation. 'Archie doesn't know Amber's dead.'

'Blinker,' Callan demanded into the phone.

'Who wants him?' a heavy voice replied.

'Just get him.'

'He's not here.'

'When will he be there?'

'I don't know. Leave a message, if you want.'

'I'll call later. Tell him to be there.'

Callan hung up, opened the door of the phone box and hefted the backpack on to his shoulders. He stepped into the stream of purposeful pedestrians as if he too knew where he was going. He waited to cross the road at College Street and a blue garda car went by.

There was safety in numbers but walking the streets was dangerous too, he told himself. He could be recognised at any time. And not even know it until it was too late. He had to find somewhere safe, somewhere outside the IRA network, away from public places.

He had spent the night uneasily in the guesthouse and left once the city had woken up fully. There were one or two possibilities now but it was too early to check them out. And if they didn't work out, he'd have to take to the open and rough it. He had to prepare for that eventuality too.

He regretted his impetuousness with Blinker on the phone last night. It had served no purpose except to release his anger. It hadn't helped his situation at all. Not that Blinker had had any intention of helping him. He knew that now. They had used him, that was all. He wasn't trusted. He wasn't one of them any more.

Callan crossed the road and went round by the grey front of Trinity College. A group of American tourists waited at its gates, identifiable by their cameras and long raincoats. On the spur of the moment, he turned in through the archway to the cobbled calm of the interior. After all, he reminded himself, you are a tourist.

Keerins marched into the room and stood his briefcase on the table. 'Jesus, Mr Keerins.' Archie almost pranced off his chair. 'Am I glad to see you? Why am I here? Nobody'll tell me anything.'

Keerins stitched him back to the chair with a cold glare and looked around the room as if he was a surveyor searching for structural problems. The table was scratched and scored, the floor covered in faded tiles. The walls were a scum green, the plaster chipped in places. There was a wire cage over the grimy windows and the glimmer of sunshine outside seemed far away.

'What the fuck's going on?' Archie pleaded, his relief undeterred by Keerins's distant attitude. 'This place is like a home for dumb cops.'

Keerins turned his attention back to Archie as if a nasty smell had made him aware of his presence.

'Nobody'll tell me anything,' Archie repeated. 'What's going on? Why am I here?'

Keerins gave a shrug that said those were neither relevant nor interesting questions.

'OK, OK,' Archie said with irritation. 'What do you want?'

'Nothing,' Keerins said blandly. 'It's too late for that now.'

'Too late for what, for Christ's sake.'

Keerins settled the briefcase on to its base, slowly snapped the catches open and raised the lid. Archie's eyes darted from the lid to Keerins and back to the lid. Like a child watching a magician's trick, half terrified, half thrilled.

Keerins took out a newspaper and let it unfold. Then he turned it round so that Archie could read the heavy headline. 'MURDERED MAN BRITISH "SPY@rdquo;, IRA CLAIM,' it said.

Archie went rigid and his naturally pale face turned a greyer shade of white.

'You had your chance,' Keerins said.

'Oh, fuck,' Archie breathed.

'Of course,' Keerins continued, almost sadly. 'I didn't know when I gave you that chance. That you were part of a conspiracy to murder him.'

'What?'

'That you've been in the IRA all along. Playing the bait to see what you'd catch. Appropriately, I suppose. Acting the worm comes easily to you.'

'You're off your head.'

'No, Archie.' Keerins gave him a sickly grin. 'It's your head that's in the noose. And I mean that literally. You might be up for capital murder. Did your comrades not tell you? This man might've been a diplomat.'

Archie stared at him with his mouth open and Keerins feared for a moment that he had overdone it.

'He's a fucking talent scout,' Archie protested. 'For a record company.'

'He was a talent scout, all right,' Keerins agreed drily. That was what they said in London, too: Amber worked for a small agency. Neither the Foreign Office nor the Ministry of Defence had any knowledge of a John Amber, so the newspapers reported. 'A talent scout for a spy network. Which is why you had him murdered.' Keerins turned the newspaper to himself. 'You want me to read out what your comrades said about him?'

'Hold on. Just hold on, will you?' Archie rubbed his forehead with one hand and waved the other in a halting motion. 'Can I have a fag?' he muttered.

'I don't smoke.'

'They took mine away.'

Keerins rooted in the briefcase as if it contained all the important aspects of Archie's life. He found the cigarettes and tossed them to him with a disposable lighter.

'You've got it all wrong,' Archie spluttered as the smoke hit him.

Keerins shook his head. 'We've got it all wrapped up.' He reached into the briefcase again and held up a sheaf of photographs in one hand and a blank cassette tape in the other. 'Pictures of you and Amber together. A recording of your phone call arranging to meet him. And,' he added in a hard voice, 'warning him about me.'

Archie flinched.

'And then you don't turn up but someone else does. Shoots him in cold blood. While you head off for the B and I ferry.'

'I did turn up,' Archie pleaded. 'He didn't.'

'It's all wrapped up.' Keerins put the photographs and the tape and the newspaper back into the case and closed it slowly. He lifted it by the handle and stepped back from the table and took a last look at Archie.

'He's really dead,' Archie said, partly to himself, partly a question.

'No mistake. You put five bullets in him.'

'But I wasn't there. I swear to God.'

'A technicality.' Keerins turned towards the door, satisfied that he had tightened the screw sufficiently. 'You're as guilty under the law as your friend who pulled the trigger.'

'Don't you want to know the truth?' Archie demanded in a shocked voice. 'What really happened?'

'Save the excuses for the judges.' Keerins shrugged impatiently from the door.

'I'll tell you everything,' Archie offered desperately. 'Everything that happened.'

Keerins looked at his watch. He sighed and came back as if he was doing Archie a favour. 'Make it quick,' he snapped as he sat down behind the table. 'And don't leave anything out.'

'Yeah, yeah,' Archie nodded eagerly. 'The fucker was blackmailing me. Said he'd tell the Provos I was your informer unless I helped him find Callan.'

Keerins felt a surge of anger towards Pursell. That was his doing, the real extent of his treachery: he had turned Archie into Amber's informer and deprived him, Keerins, of his information. Of the chance to catch Callan. He kept his face sceptical.

165

'So you told him where to find Callan.'

'I hadn't any choice had I? He'd have had me killed.'

'Why didn't you tell me?' Keerins asked, more in sorrow than anger.

'I told you twice,' Archie protested. 'And you missed him.'

'Why didn't you tell me about Amber?' Keerins corrected his question.

'Because there was nothing you could do about it,' Archie shifted uneasily. 'I mean you couldn't protect me against those fuckers, could you?'

'Where was Callan?'

Archie avoided his stare and told him the address he had given Amber.

'And who gave it to you?' Keerins demanded.

Archie wriggled on the chair and fished out another cigarette and lit it. He shook his head.

'You said you were going to tell me everything.'

'About Amber,' Archie muttered.

'Everything,' Keerins repeated.

'I can't,' Archie pleaded. 'It's more than my life's worth.'

'Which is not a lot.' Keerins stood up with a brusque movement.

'I've given you everything else,' Archie said quickly. 'You've got to stop all that shit about me been involved in killing him.'

'All you've given me,' Keerins countered, 'is another reason why you had him killed. Because he was blackmailing you.'

'Jesus Christ.' Archie hung his head towards his knees. He didn't watch Keerins leave.

Outside the door, Keerins repeated the address he had got to two detectives. 'That was Callan's safe house,' he said. 'Search it and pull them in.'

The detectives left in a hurry, passing Pursell as he entered the cell block. 'You got something?' Pursell asked Keerins, his face glowing red as if he had been running.

Keerins brushed past him without a word.

Callan folded the evening paper to cover up the lead story and placed it beside his coffee. He lit a cigarette and glanced at the two young women sharing his table. They were engrossed in a low-voiced conversation, one punctuating the other's earnest narrative with expressions of shock.

The activity of the past few days had left him drained, even of adrenalin, and he felt dangerously lethargic. The description of himself in the news report was not enough to enliven him. It was accurate but too general: it could apply to half a dozen men in the crammed café. No casual reader would pick him out from it.

Around him, the clatter of the café and the babble of conversations were fused in the dead heat. He watched people in groups talking to each other; couples talking or being silent with each other; people on their own, restless or relaxed. They were all waiting or resting or hurrying. None of them were apprehensive about being there, being discovered. He felt apart from them, so far apart that he might not really be there at all.

Callan shook off his incipient self-pity and finished the coffee. There was no point indulging in what might have been. It was time to move.

Outside, he found a phone box and called Blinker's number again. It was answered by the same heavy-voiced man who demanded to know who he was.

'When will he be back?' Callan asked in reply.

'Will anyone else do?'

'No.'

'Try later,' the man suggested.

Callan replaced the receiver, wondering if the man was a cop. Anyway, he decided, that was the end of that. He couldn't expect any help from Blinker. They had cut him off.

He made his way up Grafton Street, setting his pace by the slow drift of a group of window-shopping tourists. People swarmed in both directions, swirling around a large group of chattering Spanish students outside McDonald's. A series of buskers provided a constant accompaniment of lilting tin whistles and old Bob Dylan songs.

He turned into a side street and the crowds thinned out. The narrow road was lined with cars and he tried to remember the name of the boutique and exactly where it was. There was another shop where his memory said it should be but he found a likely place farther on. The name seemed unfamiliar and he glanced through the window as he passed. He couldn't see inside but it was the only one there. He doubled back and went in.

The shop was small and empty and he stood inside the door, conscious of his bulk among the delicately sparse clothes racks. Then a woman came through an open arch from the back.

'Jenny?' Callan asked doubtfully. Her brown hair fell in curls around her tanned face. Her shoulders and arms were bare and brown and she was wearing a halter top over a long, loose skirt.

'Good Lord!' she said in a strong voice. Her arms folded under her breasts in an automatic gesture of surprise and defiance.

Callan smiled with relief at having found her and eased it into an apologetic shrug. 'Hi,' he said.

'An hour late I could understand. Even two could be put down to misfortune. But,' she paused to think, 'ten years. That has to be classed as carelessness.'

'Something came up,' he smiled.

'It must have been some thing, all right.' She gave a deep-throated chuckle and he joined in. She hadn't changed. Her south-east England accent was as unadulterated as her sense of humour. 'That you couldn't even send a postcard.'

'That was out of the question too, I'm afraid.' She didn't appear to have aged at all: she was no longer the older woman he had once perceived her to be. Their age difference didn't seem as great to him now as it once had. he decided.

'So, what are you now?' she inquired. 'A boy scout?'

'An impecunious traveller,' he offered, shrugging off the backpack and lowering it lightly by his foot. 'Doing Ireland on ten dollars a day.'

'Ah,' she said. 'Ambitious.' A benign smile still hovered . around her mouth but he could see from her eyes that she was thinking, now that the initial surprise was wearing off.

'Too ambitious,' he prompted ruefully. 'The mighty dollar ain't what it used to be.'

The door opened behind him and Callan lifted his bag and edged to one side as two women came in. Jenny directed him silently through the archway. 'Help yourself to some coffee,' she whispered as he passed into a windowless room. There was a neat desk and a notice board on one wall and a coffee machine on top of a low fridge in the opposite corner. The room was so small that Callan could almost touch all four walls from the centre of the floor.

He poured himself a cup of coffee, gone bitter with time, and idly examined the postcard views of Venice, Miami and somewhere eastern on the notice board. Jenny was talking to the two customers and he listened to her voice rather than her words. She used her accent as a positive advantage, a superior class of saleswoman who cloaked her persuasiveness in an air of indisputable authority. Which had always been her way, he remembered: even in a country where her imperious accent and manner could be a disadvantage.

He had found it amusing the first time they met, watching her stir the foot-shifting, silent irritation of the queue waiting for the motor taxation office to re-open after lunch. 'Bloody Irish,' she had declared loudly. 'One can't abide by the law even when one wishes to.' He was waiting patiently behind her to get a driving licence in a false name and she turned to him. 'Is this why nobody in this country bothers to tax their cars?'

'And sure why doesn't your ladyship do the same,' he suggested, exaggerating his accent into a slurred brogue. 'They'd never prosecute one of the quality.'

She looked at him then and her quick grin revealed that she was also acting and said touché. 'And who are you, my man?' she asked, keeping up the pretence while lowering her voice to a conversational tone. 'A member of the Abbey Theatre company?'

'I rescue damsels in distress,' he reverted to his normal voice.

'What a fascinating occupation. Does it keep you busy?'

'It has its moments,' he smiled. 'Would you like to be rescued?'

'Am I in distress?'

'Definitely,' he whispered. 'You're facing an irate mob about to avenge eight hundred years of oppression.'

'Lead on,' she said, mock-startled.

They went to a dingy pub where the walls were the colour of nicotine-stained fingers and the atmosphere was as dead as ash. A line of men at the bar drank vacantly and a few flustered lawyers from the nearby courts had hurried conversations over liquid lunches. They claimed a table in the emptying snug and continued their sparring banter.

Callan found her company refreshing, enjoying her stage Englishness, partly because she carried it off with such theatrical deliberation. It also suited his mood: he was in Dublin for a rest, opting out of the closed circle of the movement for a time. It was salutary to rediscover the world outside occasionally, now that its disinterest in the national struggle no longer angered him automatically.

'Are you a gunman?' she asked after he had lost count of the number of drinks they had had.

'What?' he replied through a haze, aware that he was drunk. She still seemed as sober as she had been in the queue.

'You Irish are all either gunmen or gougers,' she declared. 'Killers or only interested in a quick kill. And you don't appear to be a gouger. I can tell them at a hundred yards. They'd gouge your eyes out for a quick buck. I know. I married one of them.'

He laughed to cover his uncertainty and sudden suspicion. 'I'm only a trainee gouger,' he suggested.

She had given him a shrewd look and never raised the question again, even after they had become part-time lovers. But he presumed that she knew he was involved in the IRA: it didn't seem to bother her although he had never discovered what she really thought of it. Neither did his long disappearances, known euphemistically as his 'travels', interfere with their relationship. He had always assumed that the arrangement suited her.

Callan grimaced at the sour aftertaste of the coffee and heard the door close behind the two customers. Jenny came into the airless office and sighed as if she had just undergone an ordeal.

'Another successful sale?' he inquired.

'Bloody women who don't know what they want.' She paused. 'So. You want somewhere to stay?'

'If it's convenient.'

She smiled and nodded.

'Are you sure?' he asked tentatively. 'Will that be OK with Harry?'

'Oh, yes,' she said. 'Harry's on the Costa del Sol, his new spiritual home. Can't stand the climate but he can't resist all the hot money sloshing about there. Not to mention the scent of suntan lotion on young bodies.'

He moved out of her way as she re-tidied the already tidy desk and looked at her watch. 'Home time,' she said brightly. 'Shall we go?'

Home turned out to be a modern pastiche of once elegant styles in the foothills of the mountains, a large two-storey square with white columns by the entrance, its red bricks still unweathered.

170

'Wow,' Callan exclaimed as they went up the tarred drive- way, passing a series of plastic light standards.

'Your travels have made you very polite.' She gave him a disapproving glance. 'It has rather less aesthetic appeal than a brick shithouse. Harry thinks it's very grand, of course.'

Callan felt suitably reproved, bracketed among the peasants. He retrieved his backpack from the boot of the Volvo and looked down on the city, vague under its sweaty haze. A fresh breeze came into the hills from the distant sea and the mountains ran round the area in a protective semi-circle. Around the house, the fields were a rich green and the hill rose steeply behind into a darkly shaded pine wood. The silence was immense.

He followed Jenny into the kitchen and out on to a patio at the back. A couple of chairs stood at odd angles to a round table and a neat lawn, broken by two triangular flower beds, ran away to a railed-off paddock.

'You're into gardening?'

Jenny shook her head. 'One of Harry's minor acquisitions takes care of it. Justifies its losses, he says.' She straightened the chairs and invited him to sit down. 'Drink?'

'Beer,' he nodded.

Callan lit a cigarette and exhaled into the cool stillness. He closed his eyes and felt the tension drain away. This was perfect. He was safe here.

Jenny put a tray on the table and he took the cool can of Heineken and poured it into a glass. She unscrewed the top of a gin bottle, half filled her glass and completed it with tonic.

'Thanks,' he said, in gratitude for more than the drink. 'I really appreciate it.'

'Here's to . . .'she raised her glass, 'what? The past? The future?'

'The present.'

'The present,' she agreed.

They drank in silence and then she said, not looking at him, 'I hope you're not still involved.'

'Involved,' he repeated in surprise. Did she mean with the IRA? Or herself?

'In terrorism.'

Her directness and her seriousness took him aback. 'No,' he said, suppressing the automatic urge to add that he had never been a terrorist.

171

'Good.' She gave him a smile. 'Because you couldn't stay here if you were.'

'You've changed your mind,' he prompted, curious to hear the views that she had never revealed during the year they had known and loved each other.

'I've been in Ireland long enough for the scales to have fallen from my eyes,' she said. 'To realise that it's not an age-old, romantic freedom struggle. But a nasty little sectarian power struggle.'

It's both, Callan thought: romanticised history always grew out of individual nastiness. Every victor had to have a victim but people tended to forget that until their sensibilities were rubbed in the bloody realities.

He was about to ask her why she had changed her mind but decided against it. He didn't want to discuss it and, anyway, he thought he knew the answer. The war had gone on so long that the grand design had been submerged by the attrition. The IRA was being cornered and defeated by the very factors that had recreated it.

'You live in America,' she said, as if she too had decided to drop the subject.

'How can you tell?' he smiled.

'Your square shoes. They're a dead giveaway.' He laughed and she pointed to a barbecue on the edge of the patio. 'Does that mean you can work that apparatus?'

'As long as you have enough fuel to start a medium-sized forest fire.'

'There's enough of everything here to create an excess of anything,' she said.

He wheeled the barbecue out of its corner and busied himself with the charcoal and the lighter fuel. She watched him for a while and then went inside and brought him another lager and disappeared into the house again. Callan watched the coals whiten slowly and wondered idly at his capacity to live off other people's lives. That's what I've always done, he thought; one way or another. He felt totally at ease, as if this barbecue and this house and this woman were natural and normal parts of his life.

Jenny returned with two steaks and an assortment of relishes and they talked desultorily, like old companions, while the meat spat at the coals and the evening grew cool and the trees above the house merged into a dark, impenetrable mass.

Keerins tiptoed into the darkened room and slipped quickly into the bed. It was after midnight and he was both tired and alert, his mind's worries grating off his physical exhaustion. He felt a sudden flush of added resentment towards Deirdre who was lying rigidly on the far edge of the bed.

'Are you asleep?' he sighed quietly, knowing from the tight stillness of her body that she wasn't.

He lay on his back, watching the details of the room come up as his eyes adjusted to the yellow half-light from the silent suburb. The window was open and he could hear the rush of cars on a distant main road.

'I'm sorry,' he said. He didn't feel sorry but he said it anyway, irritably determined to go through the proper motions.

'It doesn't matter,' she said quietly.

'It does,' he retorted, although he didn't mean it in the way she assumed. He felt angry that she should give him the cold shoulder at a time like this. 'Things are very difficult at the moment.'

'So you say.'

'What does that mean?' he demanded of the back of her head.

She sighed: 'It means that you don't tell me anything any more.'

'I can't.'

'You used to before,' she said with the certainty of someone who had already rehearsed this conversation. 'When I was just your wife. Before I became a security risk or something.'

'Oh for fuck's sake,' Keerins groaned.

Deirdre rolled over and looked at him, ready to forgive if he met her half way. 'Well, that's the way it looks from here. You used to trust me enough to tell me what you were doing. But you haven't said three words to me in as many days.'

Keerins looked back at her in surprise and tried and failed to come up with the proof that she was wrong. 'I'm sorry,' he repeated, meaning it this time. 'Things have become very complicated. I didn't realise.'

She moved closer and he reached out his arm and she lifted her head into the crook of his elbow. His fingers stroked her shoulder and he sighed deeply. 'It's become a right mess.'

'The Callan case?'

He closed his eyes and nodded and she put her arm over him and moved closer until the heat of their bodies merged. She waited and he prepared to tell her a simplified story, leaving out the details of his own duplicity.

Sixteen

Callan woke with a start, conscious that there was somebody in the room. Jenny was sitting on the bed, offering him a cup of coffee and wearing a black tee shirt and black trousers. He pulled himself up on one elbow and asked her what time it was.

'Eight-thirty,' she chortled. 'I thought you'd be up at six. Like a real American. Out for a jog, that sort of thing.'

'Old habits die hard,' he grunted, shifting his body cautiously to avoid uncovering the automatic under the pillow. The room glowed orange from the sun coming through the bright curtains.

'How true.' She watched him drink some coffee. 'Do you want to come into town? Take a sightseeing tour or some- thing?'

He looked into the coffee as if his brain was functioning slower than it was. 'You're welcome to stay here if you wish,' she added.

'I think I might do that.' He nodded slowly. 'Being a tourist is very tiring.'

'Yes, I can see that. You won't be disturbed.'

'Thanks.' He touched the back of her hand. 'Again.'

'There's more coffee in the kitchen.' She stood up and he noticed that the ends of her hair were damp. 'Make yourself at home. There's food in the fridge and freezer. If you want a shower, use the one in my room. It's got a better spray.'

He nodded gratefully and she bent down and kissed him on the cheek. 'See you later,' she said from the door.

'Have a good day,' he called and her laugh hung in the air as she went down the stairs. He heard the front door close and the car start up.

Keerins turned over another page and his eyes were half-way down it before he realised that his brain was not taking any of it in. There was too much of it, too many names, too many random details. And too little of significance.

He looked up as the door opened and said good morning, more alertly than he felt, to the superintendent. 'Well?' the superintendent inquired.

'Just going through the reports,' Keerins said. 'Nothing very definite, I'm afraid.' In fact, nothing at all: a big fat zero. Or, at any rate, nothing that he could see.

'Wasting our time,' the superintendent said.

Keerins wasn't sure whether that was a question or a comment. 'Oh, no,' he replied with the determined enthusiasm of a salesman who knew he was peddling a dubious product, 'I wouldn't say that. We've been keeping the pressure up. And one of this morning's crop had a box of timers and fuse wire under his bed.'

The superintendent gave a snort of derision and crossed to the window and looked down at the Bridewell's yard. Keerins sighed quietly behind his back, knowing that he was right. The raids had only produced an administrative headache and the mound of paperwork in front of him. They were a waste of time. The general intelligence product was minimal, specific information about Callan non-existent.

'Blinker?' the superintendent asked, still studying the movements in the yard.

'No trace either,' Keerins admitted. 'The border divisions are checking all the likely haunts but I haven't got anything back yet.'

'And your informer?' the superintendent turned round to face him.

'I've left him alone for the last twenty-four hours. Let him sweat it out before I try again.'

'His forty-eight hours are up when? Tonight?'

Keerins nodded. Time was running out, taking with it the chances of catching Callan. And his own career prospects.

'And what do you propose to do then? Release him?'

Not if I can help it. Keerins thought. Archie wasn't going to walk away from this, scot free. 'I'd like to have him charged,' he said aloud. 'With something.'

'What?'

'We could make a case for involvement in Amber's murder.'

'No, we can't,' the superintendent snapped. 'I have no desire to be carpeted in the DPP's office. Given a lecture on the rules of evidence.'

'But he was giving information to a foreign agent,' Keerins moaned. 'We can't let him away with that.'

'We don't know that Amber was a foreign agent,' the superintendent said coldly. 'Not officially. And that's the way it stays. In everybody's interests.'

Keerins accepted the order with stoicism, recognising the logic and official convenience behind it. It would only serve the IRA's propaganda to confirm their claim publicly, to make a highly visible diplomatic crisis out of it. So Amber would remain a talent scout. Just as Archie said.

'I know how you feel.' The superintendent eased his tone into sympathy. 'Archie's left you hanging in the wind. But there is no room for personal vendettas in this work. Or for people who try to be too smart for their own good.'

Keerins stiffened at hearing his own description of himself.

'The other thing that still concerns me,' the superintendent added, 'is who was feeding Amber, assuming for the moment that Amber was the only British agent dealing with Callan.'

'Archie,' Keerins said, trying to cover his unease with a look of perplexity. This was the conversation he had been dreading, knowing it was inevitable but still half hoping that Amber's death had closed that episode.

'He admits that?'

'Yes. Says that Amber was blackmailing him. Threatening to tell the Provos about him.'

The superintendent nodded sagely and clasped his hands behind his back. 'So he confirms that Amber approached him after he had given you information.'

'He didn't say that,' Keerins said, realising too late that he had walked into a trap. 'Not explicitly.' Did the superintendent know it was a trap, he wondered with a sick feeling. 'I'm afraid I haven't questioned him closely about Amber. I was too concerned with Callan.'

'Of course.' The superintendent pursed his lips. 'Perhaps I should talk to him myself.'

I should tell him, Keerins thought suddenly as the silence lengthened. Make a clean breast of it and clear the air. Then I could concentrate on Callan. But then I'd be in deep shit. Off the case, probably out of security. There was no easy excuse for his failure to do what he should have done in the first place.

'Has Pursell ever mentioned Amber to you?' the superintendent asked casually.

'Pursell?' Keerins repeated, startled.

The superintendent nodded vaguely. 'Before his death. Amber's.'

Keerins shook his head once, involuntarily, not wanting to answer the question, not knowing how to avoid it. But the superintendent took his gesture as a reply which seemed to shake him out of his reverie.

'Just thinking aloud,' he said as if he needed to explain himself. 'Pursell has come up with a few unrelated pieces of intelligence recently that had no obvious source.'

The superintendent turned abruptly to the door. 'Keep after Callan,' he instructed.

Keerins watched the door close after him and felt his shirt stick to his back. He knows everything, he thought bleakly. He stood up to relieve his confusion and realised his hands were shaking. He had to know, he told himself, that's what he was telling me. But he was also telling me it didn't matter. As long as I get Callan.

He looked out the window at a squad car poking its bonnet into the narrow entrance to the yard. I wouldn't last five minutes in a real interrogation, he decided with disgust. Five minutes of Deirdre turning her back on me and I confessed everything. Almost.

Callan stood unmoving under the shower, watching the water collect between his chest and his folded arms. He had been there for a long time, letting the spray wash away the tiredness and then restore his energy. Everything seemed to have happened a long time ago, now that a secure day of rest stretched out before him.

He raised his arms slightly and the pool of water sloshed down his stomach and legs. He turned off the shower and towelled himself lightly. His second cup of coffee had gone cool but he finished it as he padded barefoot across Jenny's bedroom, leaving a faint trail on the pink carpet. Outside, the sharp sunlight picked out the green tops of the trees in the wood.

Back in his room, he drew open the curtains and the wide vista of the bay and the huddle of the city spread out beneath him. The horizon was a clear, sharp line between the full blue of the sea and the soft blue of the sky. As sharp as the edge of the world.

Callan emptied his backpack on to the bed, sorting its contents into three piles. He took the automatic from under the pillow and laid it alongside the Kalashnikov on top of the camouflage jacket and trousers he had bought in separate army surplus stores the previous day. Just in case. The patterns didn't match properly but they were close enough. With any luck they wouldn't be needed anyway.

He dressed in a teeshirt and jeans and rolled the other dirty clothes into a bundle. Then he sorted through the useless passports, counted the remaining traveller's cheques and looked at the unused Air Canada ticket. He should have been back in Boston now, waking up with Sharon this morning, resuming his other life. Although that had been compromised, too. He'd have to leave Boston. Persuade Sharon to go to California, maybe. If she'd have him back.

There was no point worrying about that now, he thought as he shoved the automatic into his waistband. He had to get back there first. And he had no idea how he was going to do that. There was no hurry, however: he had to let the dust settle first.

He took the bundle of dirty clothes downstairs, found a washing machine in a room off the kitchen and studied the dial before selecting the simplest looking programme. Water coursed in and the motor clicked on and Callan watched it nervously for a moment and then decided to leave it alone.

He picked an apple from a bowl of fruit in the kitchen and munched it as he wandered slowly through the ground-floor rooms. Of all the hideouts he'd ever used, this was certainly the most spacious. At the other end of the scale from the dark border bunkers he'd squatted in during a few emergencies.

The living room occupied one corner of the house, from two windows at the front to a French window opening on to the patio at the back. A vase of wilting flowers stood on a polished table, dropping petals between a half-circle of framed photographs. One showed an elderly, couple in front of a sunny hedge, the man with a conspicuous moustache sitting, the white-haired woman standing and resting one hand on his shoulder. Another was of Jenny and a balding, round-faced man in evening dress. Callan assumed it was Harry and he examined him more closely. A real mick face, he thought. He looked pissed.

A portrait of Jenny hung over the marble fireplace and Callan unconsciously copied her pose. Her head was tilted, a faint smile illuminated her face and her right eye was slightly closed. She looked as though she was about to wink, lewdly, and he smiled. It caught her perfectly.

There was a hi-fi system beside the marble fireplace, a compact disc in the player. Callan pressed the play button and a gentle drumbeat filled the room followed by a declamatory violin and the rest of the orchestra. He sank on to the couch and stared at the portrait and let his thoughts and memories mix and mingle with the feints and revelations of the music.

They kept coming back to the same theme. Sharon.

He got up suddenly and went into the hall and flicked through the phone book to find the international code. Then he punched out the thirteen digits quickly and waited for the connection to catch up. It rang once and the wait seemed interminable. I've missed her, he decided, she's gone to work. But he let it ring on like an extension of his thoughts, visualising the phone on the wall of the empty kitchen.

Sharon picked it up with a breathless 'hi' after the third ring.

'It's me.' He imagined her brushing her blonde hair back from her free ear, as if he was there watching one of her telephone mannerisms.

'Bobby?' she breathed heavily.

'Are you OK?' he asked, suddenly concerned. She sounded flustered, not her normal composed self.

'Fine,' she said. 'I was on my way out. Had just locked the door.' She took a deep breath. 'Where are you?'

'Ireland.'

'Ireland?'

'I had to come here in a hurry,' he said, relieved that she hadn't hung up. As she had every right to do. 'I'm sorry . . .'

'I was so worried,' she broke in with a hint of anger. 'I spent two days calling casualty departments. I was about to report you missing when they told me at your work that you were on vacation.'

'I'm sorry,' he sighed. 'I should have told you. But I couldn't explain it. I had to come here for a little while.'

'You could at least have told me,' she said and he could see her adopting her confrontational pose. The image was so strong that he could almost smell the kitchen and feel the fan stirring the humid heat. He felt a desperate need to reach out and touch her. 'That you wanted out.'

'Oh, no,' he said quickly, pushing away a sick sense of despair. 'I don't want out. That's the last thing I want. Absolutely the last thing in the world. I had to come back here. There was something I had to do. That's all. Nothing to do with us.'

'I don't understand,' she said neutrally, suspending judgement.

'I don't know if I do either,' he admitted. 'But I'll try and explain. When I see you.'

'How could you disappear like that?' she demanded. 'Get up and go without a word?'

How could I, he wondered, lost for a meaningful answer. 'There was a reason,' he offered lamely. 'What seemed like a reason at the time.'

'You want to know what it looks like from where I am?'

'I know,' he said. 'I know. But it's not like that. You've got to believe me. I will explain when I get back.'

'You're coming back?'

'Yes,' he insisted. 'Of course. As soon as I can.'

'When's that?'

'I don't know,' he sighed, suddenly conscious of who might be listening but not caring. That was of minor importance now. 'A couple of days. A week. Maybe more. I can't tell.'

'You're in trouble,' she said quietly.

'Yes,' he sighed again. He tried to visualise the way she was standing now but he found he couldn't. He had lost her. 'I love you,' he said into the silence. 'I miss you.'

'Me too,' she replied after a moment.

'See you soon.' He closed his eyes, willing it to come true.

'I'll be here,' she said.

'I'll tell you everything then,' he promised, as much to himself as to her. Yes, I will, he thought, straighten it all out; put an end to all the subterfuge, to all this crazy compartmentalisation. Start again from scratch. And if it changed her mind, then so be it.

'OK,' she said. 'We'll talk it through.'

'We will.' There was nothing more to say but he didn't want to let her go. 'I'll call again if I can,' he added. 'Let you know what's happening. But if you don't hear anything for a while, it won't mean anything. I'll still love you.'

'I've got to go,' she said apologetically. 'I'm running late.'

'I know. You hang up.'

'I love you too, Bobby.'

The phone clicked and Callan put it down, feeling strung out, his emotions stretched. As if the phone's illusion of closeness had actually distanced them, cut them off for ever. I might never touch her again, he realised with a dull shock, never again hold her, never again make love with her. Worse, I might never be there again, never be with her.

He sat on the stairs, his head in his hands, and watched her locking the door behind her and reversing the Honda on to the road and driving away between the open lawns and the sprinklers and the children's swings. He looked back and glimpsed the edge of the house, as if he was seeing it disappearing through the rear window of the car and he was leaving on a long journey.

How could I, he wondered. How could I have risked what I had there for some vague dissatisfaction, some residual scum of sentiment? Why do I let myself be defined by whatever situation I'm in? Why did I let my life in Boston be poisoned by hiding from the past? Why did I become a gunman again because I spent a night with Blinker?

He pushed the palms of his hands into his eyes. Why do I never know what I really want until it's too late? Why can't I be content with where I am? With who I am? Whoever I am.

A haunting violin melody came from the living room, caught his mood and lifted him slowly back into the present. He listened to its steadily building tempo, the violin leading the other instruments, and it carried him along to its joyous and sudden climax. It's not too late, he reminded himself, his resolve buoyed by the music and strengthened by Sharon's forgiveness and understanding.

I will make it.

'Seen this?' Pursell held out the Evening Press as Keerins came back from lunch. 'TOP IRA MAN SOUGHT FOR "SPY@rdquo; MURDER', the thick headline said over a smudged, single-column picture of Callan.

A leading IRA man who fled this country after the unsolved murder of a Garda officer almost ten years ago is now being hunted in connection with the killing of alleged British spy John Amber, Keerins read. Gardai investigating the latest killing want to question Fergus Callan (38) who, they believe, returned recently from the US where he had been in hiding since Special Branch . . .

Keerins looked up, belched on his beer and sandwich and demanded, 'Where did they get this? Picture and all?'

Pursell shrugged.

'Did you leak it?'

'No,' Pursell looked affronted. 'Of course not.'

'Somebody did.' Keerins tossed the paper on to his desk. 'Fucking hell.'

'What's the matter?' Pursell asked, taken aback.

The matter, Keerins thought, was that the whole bloody country now knew about it. Knew as much as he knew himself. He sat down and stared vacantly into the middle distance.

'It won't do any harm,' Pursell suggested. 'Might even do some good. Increase the pressure on him. Anyone who hides him now can't say that they don't know who he is and what he's done. Like that pair of so-called innocents.' His voice grew heavy with disgust and he mimicked the couple who had sheltered Callan. 'But he seemed like such a nice young man, sergeant. We never thought he was like that.' He paused. 'Like fuck.'

Keerins wasn't listening, letting his frustrations build up into a satisfying self-abuse. The only pressure that was increasing was the pressure on himself. Looking for somebody who could be anywhere, who had a seemingly endless network of helpers and supporters. Who could dodge and weave through this broad stream, some kind of hero, probably laughing his head off. And there was nothing he, Keerins, seemed to be able to do about it. Except plod along after every lousy lead, more for the necessity to do something than in any real expectation of success. He felt defeated.

'Like fuck,' Pursell was saying and Keerins stared at him, suddenly seeing himself in the older man. That's the way I'm heading, he thought. I'll end up the same: full of righteous anger and outraged impotence, ground down by the relentlessness of all this: frustrated, polarised.

'Do you have any concrete suggestions?' Keerins demanded, his determination to avoid that fate adding irritation to his tone.

Pursell shook his head, a flash of surprise giving way to a blank defensiveness.

'Has the Super talked to you about Amber?' Keerins went on, turning the screw.

Pursell shook his head once more.

'He hasn't given up.'

'What'd he say?'

'Nothing much. But he's still trying to find Amber's contact.' Pursell licked his lips. 'What'd you say?'

'Nothing.'

Pursell searched his eyes warily. Keerins looked back, giving nothing away.

'If you've got any favours to call in,' Keerins said stiffly, 'I'd appreciate you calling them in now.'

'Nothing that'll lead us to Callan,' Pursell said. 'Nothing at that level.'

'Try them anyway.'

'Sure,' Pursell shrugged. 'But they're low level.'

'Who's got the best IRA contacts around here?' Keerins asked.

'Hard to say,' Pursell said. 'Some of the lads are very cagey with that sort of information. Besides, I'm sure they've all tried. The Super will have made sure of that.'

'Tell me anyway,' Keerins ordered. It would be useful to know things like that for the future. And he needed to break into this case from another angle. Any other angle.

Callan heard the car drive up and went quickly to the front of the house, the automatic loose in his hand. He caught a glimpse of Jenny getting out and he was back on the patio, turning the steaks, before she came in the hall door, the gun tight against the small of his back.

'Good evening, madam.' He held out a silver salver with a gin and tonic as she came through to the back.

'Bit old to be a houseboy, aren't you?' She unhooked her shoulder bag and left it on the kitchen counter. 'Or, perhaps, a bit young.'

'Dinner is almost ready.'

'Give me ten minutes,' she pleaded and disappeared upstairs with her drink. Callan pulled open a lager for himself and pottered lazily around the barbecue. The meat spat at the coals and teased the hot evening with the drifting smell of its grilling. He had nothing more demanding on his mind.

When she came back she had changed into a white mini-dress and she lay into one of the chairs and stretched her neck to the sun. 'I'm beginning to think all this talk about the greenhouse effect must be true,' she said, her eyes closed. 'It's wonderful. If one didn't have to work.'

'But you don't.' Callan slid the meat on to the plates and sat down opposite her. 'Have to work. Do you?'

'I have to do something.' She sat up and helped herself to some salad. 'I can't rattle about Harry's mausoleum all day. Much as he would like that.'

'Oh, I don't know,' he said, curious about her life but reluctant to question her. 'I can think of worse.'

'What have you been doing all day?' She gave him a quizzical grin. 'Tippling the gin?'

'Looking down on the city. Watching the steam rise.'

'And cooking,' she added, cutting a piece of meat. 'I never knew you were so house trained.' She chewed thoughtfully for a moment. 'Can you bark as well? Scare the burglars?'

'You want to hear my wolf howl?'

'Not at this precise point in time.' She smiled. 'It would make me feel more like a carnivore than I want to be.'

'You haven't turned vegetarian?'

'No.' She stretched the word out. 'I'm still partial to a good piece of flesh.'

He laughed at what he presumed was her double meaning and it struck him suddenly that she had changed. She had grown older or lonelier or something: there was a raw edge behind the familiar veneer. Maybe it had always been there and he never noticed. Maybe I'm the one who has changed, he thought.

But, then, they had never sat around like this in the old days when, for one reason or another, they had usually been in a hurry. They had always met in the city, moving through a succession of places to make love. Most belonged to Jenny's friends and Callan tried now to remember some of their names. He could picture two of them, brash women who seemed to hover on the edge of some frenzy, but their names eluded him.

He asked her about them and a casual domesticity settled around them while the sun slewed away to the west and the shadow of the hill spread down the fields. Jenny shivered eventually and went in to get something and Callan balanced the glasses and bottles on the plates and carried them in to the kitchen sink.

'Leave my glass,' she said when she returned, a white shawl over her shoulders. 'And dump the rest in the dishwasher.'

He smiled and left his own glass alongside hers on the counter between them and bent down to slot the plates into the rack. He heard her pour another drink behind him and when he straightened up she handed him a folded newspaper.

'I presumed you'd want to see this,' she said.

He glanced at her with sudden apprehension and unfolded the Evening Press and didn't recognise his picture at first. He looked back at her and held her steady gaze and said, 'I didn't kill him.'

'Which of them?'

'Amber.' He tapped the paper.

'And the rest?'

He looked back at the paper in confusion and glanced through the suggestive story.

'Eight or ten people,' she said. 'A Special Branch officer here. Three soldiers in Northern Ireland. Two policemen and,' she shrugged, 'whatever.'

I don't know anything about half of those, Callan thought clinically: they're just throwing shit at me. He left the paper down on the counter and said nothing.

'You told me you weren't involved any more.'

'I'm not.'

'You've a gun under your shirt,' she said, as matter of factly as if she was telling him his zip was undone.

'Because of this.' He laid his hand on the paper. 'Because they're blaming me. And I didn't kill him.'

'Then why are they blaming you?'

Because I was there, he almost said, half wanting to explain, to begin the talking he had promised Sharon, end all the subterfuge. 'Because they found out I was back,' he said.

Jenny raised her glass at last and took a drink without taking her eyes off him. It had gone dark outside and the glass door turned the room back upon itself, locking them into position on either side of the counter.

'You want me to leave,' he said.

She shrugged and the shawl slipped slowly off one shoulder. She tugged it back into place.

'Can I have a drink?'

She nodded and he opened the refrigerator and took out a can of Heineken. He pulled the tab off and poured it slowly, all the time aware of her unwavering scrutiny. Fuck it, he thought tiredly. There was no escape.

'What's it like,' she asked as he sipped the lager, 'to kill somebody?'

Leave, he told himself. It's over.

'Tell me.'

Callan lit a cigarette. That question was way out of bounds.

'Please,' she insisted.

'Easy,' he said, partly to shock and dissuade her.

'Yes, but what does it feel like?'

'It's a necessity,' he said. 'Sometimes.'

She snorted at him.

'It's a war.' He shrugged, reluctant to do what he knew he should do. Reluctant, too, to let this fragment of his life end in sterile recrimination. 'That's what you're trained to do. That's what the enemy is trained to do.'

'Balls,' she said.

He shook his head. 'No,' he said slowly. 'That's what it comes down to. You join up and it's all a bit of an adventure at first. While you're trained. And then it becomes real.'

She looked sceptical but said nothing.

'It's like checking in at an airline desk,' he said. 'Once you do it you're slotted into a system, moved along from one point to another until you're funnelled into a plane and it takes off.'

'I don't follow,' she said. 'You're saying that once you join up you can't get out?'

'No, no.' He flicked the ash off his cigarette into the sink. 'You're trained to use a weapon. Other things too but principally that. It all seems like a game, shooting at targets, that sort of thing. And then it evolves that there is only one purpose to all this. That once you take up a gun there is only one thing to do with it. Sooner or later.'

'But why join up in the first place?' she demanded. 'And why stay in it if you don't have to?'

'That's a different set of questions.' Callan rested his elbows on the counter and stared into his beer. 'Another set of inevitabilities.' He paused. 'Why check in at an airline desk at all? Because you want to get somewhere. From one point to another.'

'Through the use of terror.'

'That's what all armies are for. To achieve objectives through the use of force.'

'Blowing up people in pubs,' she exclaimed. 'Shooting farmers in the back.'

Callan sipped at his beer. Killing and maiming children with plastic bullets, he thought. Endless harassment as an inevitable birthright. Sudden death for people found in the wrong place at the wrong time. Not an inch and our day will come. Force and counter-force. Terror and counter-terror. Inevitable casualties.

'Well?' she demanded.

'I don't want to argue with you.' He looked up at her.

'You mean you can't.'

'No,' he said. 'I mean I don't want to. We could argue the propaganda war back and forth all night. And it wouldn't change anything.'

'You disappoint me.' Jenny turned away and sat down at the table. 'I assumed you had all the answers.'

'I'm out of it. Like I told you.' He held the cigarette butt under a tap and dropped it into the garbage bin. Then he moved round the counter and leaned his back against it, facing her. 'I don't even know the questions any more. Never mind the answers.'

'And you still haven't answered my first one,' she reminded him. 'What does it feel like?'

Callan shrugged, remembering the first time, sighting the target, squeezing the trigger. The thrill of doing it for real contained by the imposed ritual of getting the shot right. Then he had wanted to throw up, toss the gun away, discard what he had done, run. But he hadn't done any of those things. He had slid away, as the plan and the training had taught him. Intent on survival.

'Whatever I would tell you now,' he said, 'wouldn't be what I would have told you then.'

'You're still evading the question.'

'We're all wriggling on the pin of history,' Callan sighed. 'Individually. And collectively.'

'Only if we choose to,' she said.

Callan said nothing. It wasn't as simple, as academic, as that. You only have a choice if you can see it. And what choices do I have now?

Jenny drained her glass and asked him to pass the bottle of gin. 'Could you shoot me?' she inquired as she filled up her glass again.

'No.' He gave a surprised laugh. 'Of course not.'

'But I am your enemy.'

'No, you're not.'

'I'm an imperialist Brit,' she declared. 'Of the class that has subjugated you honest toiling peasants for centuries.'

Callan smiled wanly, wondering if she was getting drunk or steering their relationship back on to its normal course. Or both.

'That's what you told me the first time we met,' she added as if she too was reluctant to let it end abruptly.

'And you told me I was a ham actor. And so were you.'

'And I said you were a gunman. And so you were.' She took a large mouthful of gin. 'Would you use your gun now if I went to phone the police.'

He shook his head, watching her warily.

'What would you do?'

'Run,' he said.

'Run?'

'Like fuck,' he nodded.

She laughed lightly and got to her feet. 'Aren't you getting a little mature for running?'

'At least it's downhill from here.'

She stood before him, drink in her hand.

'It's been very nice seeing you again,' Callan said. 'It would have been even nicer if the circumstances could have been different.'

They stood in silence, looking at each other for a long moment. Another bridge burned, he thought wearily. I seem to be ridding myself of them with increasing speed.

'Thank you.' He held her arm and kissed her gently on the cheek. 'For your hospitality. And friendship. Everything.' He stepped back and gave her an apologetically faint grin.

'Bloody hell,' she sighed and grabbed his hand and led him from the kitchen, flicking off the lights as they went.

Seventeen

Keerins assumed an impassive stare from behind the table as Archie was brought by the arm into the interview room. The uniformed garda released him at the table and left.

'I want to see a lawyer,' Archie demanded.

'Later,' Keerins snapped.

'No.' Archie raised his chin defiantly. 'I want a lawyer now. I know my fucking rights. If I want a lawyer you have to get me one.'

'All right,' Keerins said. 'Sit.'

Archie looked at the chair behind him as if it might be a trick and sank on to it. He pulled out a packet of cigarettes and lit one, blowing the smoke at the ceiling in a cloud of unconcern.

'One question,' Keerins said.

'When do I get the lawyer?' Archie interrupted.

'After the question,' Keerins said, trying to quell his growing exasperation. 'This is your last chance. Once it's with the lawyers, it'll be too late. There'll be no going back.' He paused. 'Who is your informant?'

'Fuck's sake,' Archie groaned. 'How many times do I have to tell you? There's no way. No way.'

'OK,' Keerins sighed to himself without surprise. He hadn't expected anything else.

'What about the lawyer?' Archie demanded. 'I have a right

'You don't need a lawyer.'

'I know my rights,' Archie insisted.

'Go and get one if you want,' Keerins growled. Who the fuck had put him in a cell with one of the know-all brigade, he wondered. 'You're not in custody any more.'

'What?' Surprise made Archie sound shocked.

'You're free.'

Archie didn't move, trying to figure out the catch.

'Get the fuck out of my sight,' Keerins roared at him.

Archie got up and sidled towards the door, still suspicious that this was a trick. He half expected the door to burst open and a crowd of policemen to pile in and beat the shit out of him.

Keerins watched him, regretting that he had ever come across the little fucker. All my problems flowed from him, he told himself. With any luck I'll never see him again. But that was probably too much to hope for. 'D'you have a passport?' he demanded as a thought struck him. It wouldn't do to have him disappear altogether, in case something cropped up.

Archie shook his head.

'Don't try and get on the ferry again,' Keerins warned.

Archie stopped with his hand on the door knob. 'But you said I was free,' he said accusingly.

'Yes, but not to leave the country.'

Archie's face screwed up into a look of anguish. 'But I've got to,' he protested. 'I'm dead if I stay here.'

'That's your problem,' Keerins said without interest. 'Fuck off.'

'I'm serious.' Archie bounded back across the room and leaned on the table as if he were the one who was now interrogating Keerins. 'They'll kill me. I haven't a fucking chance out there.'

Keerins leaned the side of his face on to the palm of his hand. I'm never going to get rid of him, he thought. He's going to hang around me for ever like some family skeleton reminding me of this cock-up.

'Sending me out there is like tying me to a tree,' Archie insisted. 'And waiting for the red Indians to come and scalp me. I haven't a chance.'

Keerins grimaced at the image, vindictively hoping the cavalry didn't make it in time to rescue him.

'It's not fucking funny,' Archie howled. 'You might as well kill me yourself. You'll be just as responsible.'

'Who's going to kill you?' Keerins tried to shake off his mental tiredness. The garish light in the room hurt his eyes. It had been another long frustrating day. Culminating in the demeaning fact that he had to let Archie go.

'The Provos, of course.'

'Why?'

'For being an informer.' Archie looked at him closely as though he was worried about the state of his health.

'Well, you should have thought of that before, shouldn't you?' Keerins suggested sweetly. 'Before you took Amber's money.'

'But I didn't know he was going to be killed, did I?'

'What's that got to do with it?'

191

'Everything,' Archie groaned in exasperation. 'The Brits are going to tell the Provos about me, if anything happened to him.'

Keerins let his weight tip his chair back and swung his feet on to the table. 'You didn't tell me that before,' he said.

Archie shifted from one foot to the other.

'Did you?'

'I'm telling you now,' Archie muttered.

'One of the many things you haven't told me.' Keerins shook his head with something akin to admiration. 'All the trouble you've caused me. All the bullshit you've given me. And now you want me to help you. You have some fucking neck.'

'It's a matter of life or death.'

'Your life and death,' Keerins retorted. 'Amber's didn't keep you awake at night, did it?'

'I didn't know the fucker was going to get himself killed,' Archie whined as if Amber's death was yet another deliberate ploy to cause him difficulty.

Neither did I, Keerins admitted to himself. We have something in common. He fixed an unseeing stare on Archie and tried to work out the possibilities of this new turn of events. The remains of Amber's bloody eye stared at him from the dry sand and he knew he had no choice but to help. He couldn't allow a second murder to take place. Not even of Archie.

'Well, now,' he said with the slow certainty of someone coming to the satisfying realisation that he had the upper hand, 'what is it you want?'

'You've got to let me out of the country.'

'Out of the question. You're a witness in a major murder investigation. There's no way you can leave the jurisdiction.'

'You can't let me hang around until they pick me up,' Archie pleaded. 'You know what they'll do. Torture me and everything. Before they shoot me.'

Keerins nodded sanguinely, as if he relished the prospect. 'You'll answer all their questions too, won't you?'

'I might even have to tell them about you,' Archie warned desperately.

'That's the least of my problems,' Keerins laughed.

Archie lit another cigarette.

'The situation is very simple,' Keerins suggested, dropping his feet from the table. 'If you want our help, you've got to help us. Make a clean breast of everything.'

Archie gave his cigarette a jittery pull. 'I don't know,' he said. 'It's not as easy as that.'

'Yes, it is.' Keerins stood up.

'There's two more places,' Archie offered. 'Where Callan might be hiding.'

Keerins took out his notebook and jotted down the addresses. 'That's not enough,' he said. 'Not any more.'

'You don't understand,' Archie moaned.

'What?'

Archie shrugged.

'OK,' Keerins said, tiring of Archie's agonising. 'You stay here tonight. Sign a statement saying that it's at your own request. And make up your mind. Before morning. Or you're out on the streets. First thing.'

He left Archie in the room and went upstairs to the detective unit in search of Pursell. Some things were becoming clear. Callan must have gone after Amber to find out who was informing on him. That made more sense than any other theory: he couldn't have come back on active service again.

Pursell was talking to a young detective, in the middle of a lengthy tale about some past operation. He broke off to ask what had happened.

'We're keeping him overnight,' Keerins said. 'Protective custody.'

'What?' Pursell demanded.

Keerins gave him a short summary.

'I'll go and sort him out,' Pursell offered for the other detective's benefit. 'There's only one way to handle these characters. You won't get anywhere with your kid-glove treatment.'

'No,' Keerins ordered, tearing the page of addresses from his notebook. 'See if these have been checked out. If not, get someone on to them.'

'Waste of time,' Pursell snorted. 'You know fucking well he won't be there now. If he ever was.'

'Do it,' Keerins insisted. 'Now.'

Pursell cast his eyes upwards behind Keerins's back to prove the point of his story to the young detective that officers never knew anything.

'Where's the Super?' Keerins yawned.

'Gone home.'

Keerins reached for the phone, wondering why Archie was still so reluctant to reveal his IRA source. That didn't make sense any longer. They could only kill him once.

Callan slid the automatic under the bed, dropped his clothes on the floor and stretched out on top of the duvet. The room was bright with the gun-metal glow of the moonlight and a dog barked somewhere, the sound muffled by distance and the silence. The heat of the day still lingered, thickening the enclosed air. It felt cool on his naked body.

The toilet flushed and a moment later Jenny was framed in the bathroom door. She turned off the light and came to the bed, trailing an open kimono. She let it fall from her shoulders and lay down on her side, propped her head on her hand and looked at him.

Her pose and the sepia colour of her body in the half light made him think suddenly of an old photograph. This situation had the same quality of distance, of belonging to a different time, of unreality. He didn't understand it but he didn't question it.

He rolled towards her and put his arms round her and their bodies closed together loosely and they stroked each other without haste. He heard the deep satisfaction of her heavy breaths in his ear and felt her body warm and steady beneath his hands. The tingle of her hands on his back was like the afterglow from her warmth and he surrendered himself totally into the comfort of their closeness.

He found her lips and then kissed her eyelids and ran his kisses down her neck and along her shoulder and down on to her breasts and she twisted slowly with him and against him.

After a while she eased him away with a hand on his shoulder and held up a finger to his surprised look. She turned to the bedside table, opened a drawer and took out a condom.

She tore off its wrapping and held it between two fingers and got on to her knees and parted his legs and settled in between them. Her palms came down on his thighs and moved steadily upwards as she leaned forward over him. She caught his erection between her breasts and eased back and forth and he stretched into a long, breath-catching groan. The doorbell chimed.

All his senses switched. His eyes opened and the clock showed almost midnight and the night light from the window was undiluted.

194

His ears strained to catch any sound beyond her sighs as she lengthened her movements and the tip of his penis caressed her throat.

'You expecting visitors?' he asked in a thick whisper.

'Huh,' she murmured and half opened her eyes, still moving back and forth.

'Are you expecting visitors?' he repeated.

Jenny shook her head drowsily, not comprehending, still adrift on the intense intimacy he had abandoned.

The doorbell chimed again and she heard it this time and shook her head as if to say it didn't matter. But his face said it did and she drew back slowly. 'They'll go away,' she whispered.

Callan threw his left leg over her and rolled off the bed, his hand reaching underneath for the automatic. He ran silently from the room towards the front of the house and into the room he had occupied the previous night. He peered out, keeping back from the window.

There were two strange cars outside, one with its parking lights on, the other dark. The one with the lights on had the hump on its roof of an unlit 'garda' sign. He couldn't see anybody.

Callan grabbed the backpack, opening it as he hurried back to Jenny's room. She was still kneeling on the bed as he came in, pulling the Kalashnikov from the bag. The look of mild confusion on her face solidified into shock. He dropped the bag and shoved a magazine into the rifle and the muzzle came up pointing at her.

'Fergus,' she exclaimed, in a hoarse, startled voice.

She did it, he thought, his mind running through the possibilities. No, she didn't. There were only four of them, two uniformed, two armed. They'd be here in force if they knew for certain.

'Fergus,' Jenny repeated urgently. 'What is it?'

He turned the gun away and looked out the window at the back. The moonlight lit the lawn and he cursed its brightness, already planning. There was no sign of anyone. It's all right, part of his mind reassured him, they don't know. It's routine. Maybe something else altogether.

The door knocker slammed three times.

'Who is it?' Jenny demanded, a frantic edge to her voice, knowing the answer to her question. 'I didn't tell them.'

Callan dressed quickly, his mind made up. There was no time for thinking, for persuading himself that they weren't looking for him. He couldn't afford to be trapped here.

'I'll send them away,' Jenny said with an air of determination, getting off the bed.

'They won't go.' He pulled the backpack over his shoulders. He shoved the automatic into his waistband and took the Kalashnikov in one hand.

'You can hide here,' she suggested, looking around desperately. 'I'll get rid of them.'

Callan caught her by the arm and she reached for her kimono.

'No,' he said and pulled her away.

She tried to hold her ground. 'They'll go away if we don't answer,' she said. 'Think there's nobody here.'

'Your car's outside,' he said, increasing the pressure on her arm. Time was running out. His only hope was speed. And aggression.

'You hide here,' she pleaded as he led her out of the room. She still had the unwrapped condom in her hand. 'And I'll get rid of them. I promise.'

He shushed her and took her across the landing. From the hall they heard the metallic flap of the letter box as someone let it close.

'Fergus,' she said, half-resisting his hold again. 'What are you doing?'

He guided her into the front room and glanced quickly out of the window. He couldn't see anybody.

'Oh my God,' Jenny whispered. 'What am I going to tell Harry?'

'I broke in. Held you at gunpoint,' he said.

'What are you going to do?'

'Stay here,' he ordered. 'In this room. No matter what. Until it's over.'

'What are you going to do?'

He put his hand on her back and she shivered violently. He pushed her up to the window. 'Scream,' he whispered.

'Oh Jesus Christ.' She shook her head, dropping one hand between her legs as if she had suddenly become conscious of her nakedness.

Callan rammed the muzzle of the rifle through a window pane and fired a clattering burst through the breaking glass. The noise in the room was deafening. A line of bullets ripped into the bonnet of the farther car. Jenny screamed.

'Tell them to keep away,' Callan said.

'Keep away,' she shouted.

'They've got guns,' he prompted.

'They've got guns,' she screamed.

'Keep screaming and don't move,' he told her and hesitated a moment. Jenny had her hands over her ears and he gave her quivering body a quick hug and muttered 'sorry'. She didn't hear him.

He ran across the landing into another room and from the window saw a figure running towards one of the cars. He broke the window and aimed a short burst at the tarmac. Jenny screamed again and he went quickly down the stairs, covering the door, his ears ringing from the automatic fire. He crossed the hall and sidled into the living room.

The room was bright and he thought he could hear a voice outside and the crackling of a police radio. He moved round by the walls, keeping an eye on the windows at both ends and straightened up by the patio door. He released the catch and eased the door open with his foot. It rolled back soundlessly.

He stepped back into the room, took a couple of deep breaths, checked behind him and ran. He came through the door fast, bent low and weaving. He had gone almost twenty yards when there was a shout from the back of the house. He swung sideways and his foot sank into the edge of a flower bed. He squeezed off a low, unaimed burst on the run. Another window smashed and a bullet toppled the barbecue on to the patio.

There was no other sound from behind and he kept going, the bag bouncing on his back, aware of the pained breathing of his bursting lungs. He reached the fence at the end of the lawn and threw himself sideways and rolled over its top. He landed on his side and swung round until he was facing back the way he had come, the rifle covering the lawn. There was no one in pursuit.

He rested for a moment and then set off at a jog across the rising field, heading for the thick shadows of a ditch. It ran uphill towards the dark mass of the wood but he decided against that: it was too obvious. Down to his right, the yellow lights of the city winked and blinked like a distant universe. That was where he had to go.

He knew now who had betrayed him. Who was behind everything.

Eighteen

Keerins swung fast into the driveway and swerved on to the grass to get around a hurriedly parked car. The house was ablaze with light, the area in front of the open hall door a jumble of cars. He left his car on the grass and strode quickly inside.

The scenes-of-crime man he remembered from Amber's murder stopped him in the hall, his face flushed with exasperation. 'Are you in command here?' he demanded.

Keerins nodded absently.

'Well, put some order on this fucking mess,' the man growled. 'How are we expected to do our job with people trampling everywhere?'

'Where did it happen?' Keerins asked.

'Everywhere,' the man waved his hands. 'It's like there was a small battle. And your people are . . .'

Keerins stepped impatiently round him and went into the kitchen. Three detectives were lounging about with the air of stragglers reluctant to leave a party that was long over. They stirred themselves and melted away under his glower. Pursell stood at the open patio door, gazing out like a landlord surveying his estate. He had a cup of tea in his hand.

'Which way did he go?' Keerins joined him.

Pursell pointed up the hill.

'How much of a head start?'

'Half an hour.'

'What?' Keerins demanded. 'Nobody went after him for half an hour?'

'The situation was confused,' Pursell shrugged. 'The lads who were here first thought there were more of them in the house. They had to wait for reinforcements.'

'For fuck's sake,' Keerins groaned.

'Well, that's what the woman said,' Pursell said with an air of reasonableness.

'You mean nobody even gave chase.'

'One of the lads who challenged him was lucky to escape with his life,' Pursell protested.

Keerins stepped out on to the patio and looked up the hill. The moon shone over it, lighting the fields like they were an invitation to enter the dark mass of the wood. The overturned barbecue had spilt ash on to the patio and a bullet had gouged a hole in the brick near the door. 'There'll be hell to pay over this,' he said.

'What'd you expect him to do?' Pursell asked aggressively. 'Go after him on his own? Take on an assault rifle with an Uzi?' He shook his head. 'It'd be fucking suicide.'

'Over the whole thing, I meant,' Keerins said.

Pursell raised his eyes in a dismissive jerk as if to say that was nothing new, they'd get over that. 'We did it by the book,' he said, satisfied that he had all the answers. 'We did everything we could.'

'Except catch him,' Keerins said, remembering Pursell's certainty that Callan wouldn't be at either of Archie's addresses. But he could hardly complain; he hadn't expected anything either.

'We flushed him out.'

Wonderful, Keerins thought, staring at the ominous wood. And now he's disappeared. While I'm back at square one. Trying to explain to the Super why I've let him get away again. 'Is there anyone up there now?'

'No point.' Pursell shook his head. 'We're waiting for first light to comb it out.'

'He'll be gone by then.'

'You want to go up there? Off you go.'

Keerins stifled his irritation: Pursell appeared to be almost happy that the whole thing was a fuck-up. As if it confirmed his predictions. But he wasn't the one who would have to account for it.

'We've got road blocks up,' Pursell offered. 'Patrols out on all the roads.'

'He's on foot, isn't he?' Keerins sighed and turned his attention to the spacious kitchen and the wide hall beyond. He tried to imagine Callan here, a couple of hours ago. He certainly used a better class of safe house: no hiding out in poky flats in Ballymun or Darndale for him. My whole house would fit into just this much, he thought.

'How long was he here?' he asked.

Pursell backed into the room and put his cup on the draining board. 'Could've been a few days,' he said. 'The woman claims he was waiting when she got home from work last evening.'

'What about her? Any form?'

Pursell shook his head and filled him in on Jenny's back- ground, age, occupation and husband and what they had found in the house. 'She's sticking by her story that he forced his way in at gunpoint,' he concluded. 'Held her hostage.'

'There's no way that's true?'

'It's bollocks,' Pursell sniffed, almost delicately. 'She was in bed with him.'

'Why?' Keerins asked, wondering why somebody like her had harboured Callan.

'Why d'you think?' Pursell let out a lewd laugh 'They weren't saying the family rosary.'

Keerins felt his face colour and asked where she was. He left the kitchen purposefully and followed Pursell's directions into the living room.

Jenny was sitting upright in an armchair, her knees together and her arms folded tight over her stomach. She was wearing her kimono and staring at nothing. A detective was wandering idly around the room.

Keerins surveyed the room quickly, taking in her portrait and the door through which Callan had escaped. 'How long have you known Fergus Callan?' he asked, towering over her.

'I'd like a drink,' she said in a dull voice.

Keerins told the detective to get a glass of water.

'Something stronger,' she said.

'Later,' he said. 'Perhaps.' He stared at her but she refused to meet his eyes. She looked guilty as hell, he thought as he lowered himself on to the coffee table in front of her. She still avoided his eyes. 'How long have you known Fergus Callan?' he repeated.

'Who?'

'The man you were hiding here.'

'I wasn't hiding him. He forced his way in. He had a gun.'

'Are you saying you don't know who he was?'

'He was a man with a gun.'

'You had a newspaper with his photograph.'

'I didn't look at it.'

'You had a meal together. Drinks.'

'He demanded something to eat.'

'A barbecue?'

'Yes.'

'He demanded that you make him a barbecue,' Keerins said with heavy sarcasm.

'Yes.'

'Out in the open?'

'Yes.' She glanced at him, a quick flare of defiance. 'In full view of anybody up the hill?' The detective came back with a glass of water. She took it and sipped at it.

'He stood outside with a gun trained on you,' Keerins continued in a deadpan voice. 'In full view of anybody who might be passing. While you cooked a barbecue.'

'He had the gun in his belt.'

'A rifle in his belt?'

'No. He had a small gun.'

'How many weapons did he have?'

'Two. That I saw.'

'Then you went to bed.'

'Yes.'

'Together.'

'No.'

'You went to bed. Where did he go?'

'He came into my room. Told me to go to sleep.'

'What did he do?'

'He sat in a chair.'

'Did you sleep?'

'What do you think?' she snapped, her irritation finally breaking through.

Keerins leaned back and studied her coldly. Bitch, he thought. Lying as determinedly as any common criminal behind her haughty accent. 'You helped him get away.'

Jenny shook her head. 'You said there was more than one.'

'That's what he told me to say.'

'And you said it.'

'He had a gun.'

'Did he tell you to take off your clothes?'

'Yes.'

'When?'

'When the doorbell rang.'

'How did he know who was there?'

'He went to look.'

201

'And he left you alone.'

'For a moment.'

'What did you do?'

'Nothing. It only took a few seconds.'

'You didn't try to run.'

'Run where?'

'Or shout a warning.'

'I didn't know who was there.'

'You're not telling me the truth.'

She sighed.

'Not the whole truth.'

'He had a gun. He forced me to do everything I did.'

'You were his willing accomplice,' Keerins said. 'And I can prove that. The evidence is lying all around the house. You could be charged with harbouring him, possessing firearms with intent to endanger life. Even attempted murder.'

Jenny raised her glass and an involuntary shudder knocked it against her teeth.

'Do you support the IRA?'

'No.'

'Sympathise with them?'

'Of course not,' she snapped.

'Then why did you help him?' 'I've told you. I had no choice.'

'How long have you known Callan?' he asked, starting all over again.

'I don't know him,' she said wearily. 'I never have.'

Keerins let himself into the silent house and closed the door quietly. He paused for a moment in the cramped hall as a jaw-wrenching yawn took hold.

The dawn's grey light illuminated the kitchen as he pulled back the curtains. He plugged in the electric kettle, dropped two slices of bread into the toaster and opened the refrigerator. He took out two eggs, looked at them and then put them back again. He couldn't be bothered.

He stood by the window, waiting for the growling kettle to boil. The sky was brightening to the east, the milky light seeping up into the departing night. The back lawns lay cropped and tiny in the stillness, their symmetry broken by garden sheds and random bits of furniture. The windows of the houses behind were shrouded by closed curtains.

The toaster popped and he buttered the slices and poured the bubbling water on to the teabags. He sat at the table and munched methodically through the toast and drank a cup of tea and poured himself another. What a way to make a living, he thought tiredly.

He had got nowhere with Jenny but it was doubtful if she knew anything useful. Callan would hardly have told her where he was going. He had used her and she had allowed herself to be used - which was the part he couldn't comprehend. The part that filled him with anger.

Pursell was right: there was nothing more despicable than a Brit Provo-lover. Life was complicated enough without them, and without the well-off, so-called respectable native supporters. Like the old couple who had hidden Callan. All shifty and embarrassed when they were caught. Claimed to know nothing, didn't realise what he had done. But they knew enough not to have helped him in the first place. What the fuck did they think IRA men did anyway? Provide meals on wheels?

The glamour of violence, he thought idly. That's what it was. Automatic respect for a gunman. An ambiguity of fascination and revulsion. You could blame it on history but it was more than that: that was only the peculiar local background. You could see it everywhere: the glorification of armed men, from the ceremonial precision of armies to the beauty of war cemeteries. Except they always left out the bits in between. Like Amber's dead face. They never showed you those.

I'm a man with a gun too, he realised suddenly, easing the Smith and Wesson out of its holster. He turned the revolver over in his hand as though he had never really seen it before.

Is that why I'm a policeman? He had never fired it outside of the occasional visit to the range. No, he shook his head, it's just a job. A job I used to enjoy.

Don't take it personally, he warned himself. Not any of it.

He replaced the revolver and rinsed his plate and cup and went into the living room. He sank into an armchair, feeling exhausted. Not the clean exhaustion of physical exercise but the gritty unsatisfying exhaustion of endless hours achieving nothing under pressure. He dozed intermittently.

When he woke the sun was streaming in the window and he feared he had overslept and everybody was up. He had to get out again, avoid any discussion with Deirdre who had been on the edge of another huff at his sudden departure last night. Get things moving before the official inquests into the night's fiasco began.

It was just after six o'clock and he splashed some cold water on to his face from the kitchen sink. He left the house resolutely, easing the door closed with his key to avoid waking anybody.

The streets were empty and clear, brushed by the soft sun and warming up to another hot day. The city centre was still shuttered like a ghost town, the odd pedestrian bowling along like tumbleweed, and he turned down the quays towards the Bridewell. A truck careered round the corner at the Four Courts, heading for the markets, and Keerins cautiously crashed a red light in its wake.

In the Bridewell, the night shift was coming to an end and he asked one of the detectives who had been in Jenny's house if there were any developments. 'They're due to start searching the wood about now,' he said, checking his watch.

Keerins found the jailer, a portly sergeant who hadn't chased anybody for a long time, and asked him to open Archie's cell. The jailer looked at his watch pointedly.

'Come on,' Keerins urged impatiently. 'He's not in custody.'

The cell was gloomy and stale: it smelled of urine and disinfectant. Keerins shook Archie by the shoulder and he stirred and muttered in his sleep. He shook him again and Archie opened his eyes and looked vacantly at him. 'What time is it?' he groaned thickly.

'Time to stop fucking about,' Keerins said, pulling him by the arm. 'Sit up.'

Archie dragged himself upright, taking the blanket with him to cover his thin chest in an automatic gesture of protectiveness.

'Listen carefully,' Keerins said slowly, bending close to his face. 'I'm only saying this once. You have a choice. Tell me what I need to know and I'll put you on the ferry to Liverpool this morning. Don't tell me and I will personally drive you to South Armagh and dump you in the main street of Crossmaglen. Tied up, with a sign pinned to you saying you're a British informer. Right?'

Archie looked at him dully, his eyes flicking left and right at the anger in Keerins's stare.

'You understand?' Keerins shook him.

Archie went to say something but a dry cough came out.

'Right?' Keerins repeated.

Archie nodded.

'OK.' Keerins released his hold and sat on the side of the hard bunk. 'Who is it?'

Archie reached for his jeans and scrabbled in the pockets for his cigarettes and his lighter. Keerins knocked them from his hand with a sudden blow. The lighter skidded across the floor and bounced off a wall.

'Who is it?' Keerins repeated, noting the flash of fear widen Archie's sleepy eyes. He felt a grim satisfaction.

Archie looked at his hand in surprise and muttered: 'I don't know.'

'OK,' Keerins stood up grimly. 'Get dressed. We're going for a long drive.'

'But I don't know,' Archie pleaded.

'Don't know what?' Keerins demanded.

'Don't know who he is.'

'What the fuck are you talking about?' Keerins growled with menace.

'I've never met him,' Archie said to the blanket, his head hanging in defeat. 'I swear to God. He uses a messenger. A go-between.'

'Who?'

'A woman.'

'Who?' Keerins demanded again.

'Her name is Maire.'

'Maire who?' 1

'I don't know.'

'Where does she live?'

'I don't know.'

'What does she look like?'

Archie shrugged. 'Sort of middle-aged. Dark hair.'

'A Northern accent?' Keerins felt the sudden excitement churn his empty stomach. He sank down on to the side of the bed again.

'Yes.' Archie looked up as though he was relieved to be able to tell him something positive. He saw the change in Keerins's demeanour but didn't understand it.

Would you believe it, Keerins was thinking. The oldest motive in the book. The woman scorned. He turned part of his attention back to Archie, determined to get everything out of him. 'Where'd you meet her?'

'At the gigs,' Archie said eagerly. 'Met her a couple of times and one night she told me about this friend of hers. He's in the IRA but wants out and wanted someone to pass on some stuff to the guards. She never told me who he was. I swear to God.'

'Why you?' Keerins asked automatically, his mind concentrating on what he had already learned. I still don't believe it, he thought euphorically. 'Why'd she want you to pass it on?'

'Can I have a fag?' Archie pleaded, recovering some of his confidence.

'Answer the fucking question,' Keerins snapped. Why she wanted to get even with Callan didn't matter. What mattered was that she would find him. And that was only a small part of it, of what she could tell him.

'I don't know,' Archie was muttering. 'Because we were friends.'

'Why'd she think you'd do it?'

'Because I'd told her once that I had a thing going with the guards,' Archie admitted sheepishly.

'What kind of thing?' Keerins turned his full attention back to Archie for a moment.

'Over the drugs.' Archie shifted uncomfortably. 'A deal, like. That they'd leave me alone.'

'You little fuck,' Keerins snorted. 'You mean you told her you were bribing guards or something?' 1

Archie scratched his chest vigorously. 'Well, I was only trying to impress her. Sort of.'

'You fancied her?'

'Oh no,' Archie said quickly. 'She hangs around with some tough characters. Though she isn't one of them. But you wouldn't want to get on the wrong side of them like.'

'But you did,' Keerins said. A thought struck him. 'Did she tell you about the arms shipment a few months ago?'

Archie nodded.

That wasn't revenge, Keerins thought, confused. 'And about Callan?'

Archie nodded again.

'Where to find him for Amber?' It had to be something more than the woman scorned, Keerins told himself.

'She didn't know anything about Amber.' Archie pursued his itch up the back of his neck, clawing at it loudly.

'Why was she doing it?'

'To help her friend.'

'And why was he doing it?'

'I told you. Because he wanted out.'

'Then why didn't he come to us directly?'

'Because he's a very cautious fucker,' Archie said with a hint of exasperation. 'Like I told you before. He won't move till the time is right. And he didn't want you lads to know about him until he was ready. Because of all the informers in the guards.'

Was that her own thinking, Keerins wondered, or just a story she spun Archie? He stood up and stretched himself slowly, as if he was awakening from a long and satisfying sleep. I can find out soon enough, he thought. He didn't feel tired any more. It had worked. He had got what he wanted at last. And it had turned out much better than he could have expected.

'I've told you everything,' Archie reminded him nervously. 'Every fucking thing.'

Keerins grunted and checked his watch. I can have her hauled in now, he thought. Or I can go to her myself.

'I know where you can find her,' Archie offered, anxious to talk now that it was all out in the open, disconcerted by Keerins's evident happiness.

Go to her myself, Keerins decided. That held out endless possibilities. Keep her in place and I can get a continuous supply of top-grade information. Really set myself up.

'Don't you want to know?' Archie implored him.

'What?'

'Where to find her.'

'I know where to find her.' Keerins revelled momentarily in the power of his superior knowledge. He moved towards the door.

'Hey,' Archie called. 'What about the ferry?'

'I'll see about it,' Keerins said, idly kicking Archie's cigarettes across the floor to the bed.

'But I've told you everything,' Archie whined. 'The whole works.'

Keerins kicked the lighter after the cigarettes. 'I'll have to check with your friends in the drugs squad.'

'What've they got to do with it?'

'You're on bail,' Keerins said sweetly from the door. 'On drugs charges. I can't help you jump bail.'

'But we've got a deal,' Archie moaned.

Keerins smiled at him and went out.

Nineteen

There was no one about. The houses looked deserted, their windows blank but for the clock cards ordering milk deliveries. Most of the short driveways were empty of cars. Nothing disturbed the suburban torpor of the mid-morning.

The sun was high in the sky behind him and Callan felt out of sympathy with the new morning. He moved past the lawns at a steady pace, neither fast nor slow, alert to every detail around him. The neutral façades of the similar houses, the emptiness of the road, the insubstantial shadows cast by the young trees spaced along the footpath, the silence outside the soft fall of his steady footsteps.

This was risky, highly risky. But it had to be done; he had to know for sure. And he had the advantage of surprise. They wouldn't expect him to come looking for Maire. Not now.

He found what he was looking for at the end of the estate where the road swung into a tight circle before a blank concrete wall. A narrow lane ran between high concrete walls towards the neighbouring cul-de-sac, towards the end of the small housing estate where Maire lived. He turned into it.

He wondered what was behind the wall on his left as the lane turned slightly, blocking both ends from his sight. Then he could see the other end and he slowed as he approached it and let the backpack's straps slip down on to his arms. He paused at the opening, half in and half out of the lane. He looked quickly down the short road.

Maire's car was in her driveway and there was another car on the road outside. It was empty. He pulled the backpack up into place again and adjusted the straps, hoping to ease any casual observer's suspicions while he studied the road more carefully. There were no signs of life. Nothing out of place. Nothing unexpected. Except for the car outside her house.

Callan hesitated a moment longer, considering the car and the fact that she had a visitor or visitors. He couldn't delay, he decided and turned into the estate. He walked steadily towards her house, breathing shallowly, watching the blank windows, ready to change direction, break into a run between the houses he passed.

The house adjoining Maire's seemed unoccupied, the driveway blotched by an ingrained oil stain where a car should have been. He walked into the driveway as if he lived there and went along the side of the house and out the back. He crossed the back of the house quickly, glancing in the windows as he went by. He stepped over the low wall into Maire's garden.

Callan stood still against the wall beside the back door. He looked up and down the rear gardens and listened intently. There was nobody about, nothing to hear. He eased the backpack on to the ground and took the automatic from under his teeshirt and eased off the safety catch. He waited for a few moments and then stole a glance through the window in the door. The kitchen was empty.

He grasped the door handle and forced it down slowly. The door swung out when he pulled and he stepped in quickly and closed it silently behind him. He surveyed the room with the point of the gun, noted the unwashed dishes by the sink, the boy's hurley stick beside a football in a corner. He stepped quickly across the room, hearing the murmur of a male voice.

He sidled along the short hall towards the door of another room. It was ajar and the man's voice was coming from behind it. Callan listened to what he was saying for a moment. Caught in the act, he thought viciously. Red handed. He took a slow deep breath.

He stepped sideways through the door and flattened himself against the wall inside, his left hand supporting the outstretched gun.

Keerins sensed the movement behind him just as Maire's attention jerked suddenly to the door. He turned and the gun was aimed at his face. His body froze in shock. His brain stopped functioning.

'Is he alone?' Callan asked Maire. He kept his eyes fixed on Keerins, watching her with his peripheral vision.

Maire nodded.

'Anyone outside?'

'I don't know,' she said. 'He came in alone.'

Oh no, Keerins thought as his brain dislodged itself from the shock and went into a wild spin. It's a trap. I've walked into a trap. He's been here all the time. It was all set up for me.

'Anyone else in the house?' Callan asked.

'No,' Maire said. She sounded calm, matter of fact.

'Where's Shay?'

'Gone to school.'

'Take it easy,' Keerins said, trying to hold down a sudden feeling of panic, keep it out of his voice. 'I'm on my own.'

'Turn around,' Callan ordered him.

Keerins turned back towards Maire and his body tensed, not knowing what to expect. He's a cop killer, his mind reminded him. Nobody knows where you are. You've really fucked it up this time. Trying to be too smart.

Callan inspected the scene he had interrupted. The tall, almost gangly man standing there in a navy suit, making his earnest pitch. Maire facing him from the fireplace, her arms folded, like a reluctant housewife listening to a salesman. Except she wasn't reluctant.

'Close the curtains,' he ordered her. 'Not the whole way.'

She moved to the window, glancing at the gun as he covered her, and tugged the light curtains across the wide expanse of the window. The light in the room dimmed but remained clear. Maire stood by the window and looked at him impassively. He waved her down to the end of the room.

Callan jabbed the gun into Keerins's back and told him to spread-eagle himself against the end wall. He frisked him quickly and pulled the Smith and Wesson from the holster on his right hip and shoved it into his own belt. He emptied Keerins's pockets on to the floor and pulled a wallet from his jacket and shook its contents out, one-handed, on to an armchair. He picked up the identity card and read his name.

Callan glanced around the room, his attention caught by the framed photograph on the mantlepiece. He saw a boy's smiling face, an impression of eagerness, and resisted the urge to study it more closely. He stepped away from Keerins, turned his back on the picture and told them to sit on the couch.

They sat down side by side and stared up at him, waiting. Maire's face was neutral, Keerins's apprehensive. It's going to be all right, Keerins reassured himself. He'd have done it if he was going to do it.

'Caught in the act,' Callan said, partly to himself. All of a sudden, he didn't know what to do. He had come here for proof that Maire was behind the attempts to trap him. And he had gotten it. 'Is he your controller?' He inclined his head towards Keerins.

'No,' Maire said.

'No point lying about it,' Callan said. 'I was listening.' And I should have left then, he told himself. Slipped out again. I had all the proof I'd ever need. For all the good it would do me.

'I came here looking for information,' Keerins said hoarsely. 'To see what I could find out.'

Callan shook his head, as if it didn't matter any more. The incontrovertible proof had left him with a more immediate problem. What to do with this cop. How to get out of here.

'Give yourself up, Fergus,' Keerins suggested feebly, sensing the indecision in Callan's demeanour. The stubble on his jaw, the tired rings under his eyes gave him an air of desperation. Otherwise, Keerins thought dispassionately, he still looks surprisingly like his old pictures.

Callan ignored him, staring at Maire. She was wearing the same wine striped dress she had had on the day he met her in the supermarket. She seemed unperturbed but he knew it was a façade, a bland façade he remembered of old. She had always been good at hiding her true feelings. Why, he wanted to ask her. Why did you do it?

'You can't go on fighting a one-man war,' Keerins said, emboldened by Callan's lack of response. It's going to be all right, he told himself again.

'I didn't declare it,' Callan said automatically.

'But you can't go on like this for ever,' Keerins said. 'Give yourself up. Put an end to it.'

Callan ignored him. 'You're a tout,' he said to Maire. Even though he knew it for certain, he couldn't quite believe it. Not Maire, of all people.

She said nothing. Callan stared at her and she stared back evenly.

Keerins watched Callan, feeling there was something going on here that he knew nothing about. And didn't care about either. These were two of the most ruthless terrorists in the country. But the situation seemed unreal. Everything was happening too fast. He felt like he was an observer in the middle of a domestic dispute.

'Get me something to tie him up with,' Callan said, his mind made up.

Maire got up and left the room.

Keerins relaxed a little more, now that he knew Callan's intentions. He watched him closely, memorising his features. Keep him talking, he told himself, trying to find some saliva in his mouth. 'It'd make it easier on yourself,' he suggested, 'if you gave up.'

Callan moved quickly to the end of the couch and knelt down beside Keerins, placing him between himself and the door. He put the muzzle of the gun behind Keerins's ear. 'How long has she been your informer?' he asked quietly.

'She's not.' Keerins gulped, his certainty of what was about to happen shattered by Callan's sudden movement.

'I heard you,' Callan said, his eyes on the door, watching for Maire's reappearance. 'Saying you wanted to change the arrangements.'

'You've got it all wrong.' Keerins tried to shake his head but stopped under the pressure of the cold gun. Sweat broke out on his body.

'Was she informing on me only?'

'She isn't. . .' Keerins stopped as Maire returned, a ball of light string in one hand and a dishcloth in the other.

'That's the best I can do,' she said, holding out the string.

Callan got to his feet and put his free hand on the back of Keerins's neck. He pushed him forward off the couch and on to his knees. 'Hands behind your back,' he said and nodded to Maire.

She tied the end of the string round one of Keerins's wrists and wound it tightly round the other wrist several times and knotted it. 'Open your mouth,' Callan ordered. Maire pulled the dishcloth hard against his open mouth and tied it at the back of his head.

'Up,' Callan said.

Keerins raised one knee and got up, balancing cautiously and breathing heavily through his nose. Callan picked up the ball of string and indicated with the gun and Maire led them out of the room. He stopped them in the hall, told Maire to open the door of the cupboard under the stairs and ordered Keerins in.

Keerins bent almost double and stepped into the cramped space. Coats were hanging on pegs at one end and there was a jumble of household equipment where the stairs tapered down. 'Lie,' Callan said. Keerins eased himself down sideways between a vacuum cleaner and a folded deck chair and into a tight foetal position.

Callan handed Maire the ball of unwinding string and she bent down and bound Keerins's ankles and ran the string back up to his wrists. When she had finished, Callan leant in and put the gun to

Keerins's neck. 'I'm not going anywhere,' he said slowly. 'I'll be back to you in a while.'

He closed the door of the cupboard and motioned Maire back into the living room. Callan took Keerins's keys from the floor and pointed her silently towards the back of the house. On the way he stopped to pull the lead from the phone. The plug at one end popped out and he disconnected the other end and put the lead into his pocket.

Keerins sensed their movements along the hall through the floorboards. He could see nothing in the blackness, hear nothing beyond his own breathing. The dry smell of dusters tickled his nose and the fabric of the dishcloth made him feel like gagging. The thin twine cut into his wrists.

Callan handed Keerins's keys to Maire and picked up his backpack. He followed her round the side of the house, carrying the bag in front of him, his gun hand concealed behind it.

Nothing had changed in the estate. The sun shone down. The houses looked deserted. There were few cars left. There was no one about.

Maire unlocked the driver's door of Keerins's Mazda, sat in and opened the passenger door for Callan. He looked around the dashboard quickly and flipped open the glove compartment. There was no radio.

Maire looked at him inquiringly and he nodded. She started the car, swung it across the road into the driveway opposite, reversed and drove away. Callan settled the backpack in front of his feet, leaving himself room to jump out in a hurry. If Keerins had any back-up, they could be waiting at the main road.

The road wound in a gentle curve and straightened out as it met the main road. There were no cars there. Callan relaxed slightly.

Maire stopped and waited for his instructions. He looked up and and down the main road and then pointed right. She turned the car down the hill and he glanced sideways at the granite rock bearing the estate's name.

'Where are we going?' she asked as they came towards the junction with the Bray dual carriageway. She sounded as calm as if they were going for a Sunday afternoon drive.

'Out of town.'

'Wicklow?'

He nodded. They'll expect that, he thought. But he wanted out of the city, to get into the country. There was nothing else for it now anyway.

A green arrow pointed left at the traffic lights and Maire followed it out on to the two-lane road and accelerated. Callan wound down his window and felt the wind whip by. He checked the time and decided he had twenty minutes, maybe half an hour, before they'd know what they were looking for.

The road dipped down into Loughlinstown and rose again to narrow into Shankill. The traffic lights at the church had just turned green and they slowed behind a truck spewing blue diesel smoke as it clambered over the bridge.

Callan sat with his arms folded loosely, the automatic dangling under his left elbow. He didn't know what to think. He watched the village go by slowly: a couple of teenagers shifted impatiently at a bus stop, an old man waited to cross the road with a young boy, a woman came out of a newsagent's.

He turned to study Maire's sideface as if it would answer his unspoken questions. She looked ahead, intent on driving. 'Why?' he asked at last.

She changed gear and pulled out, overtaking the truck as the village ended and the road widened again.

Keerins balanced himself precariously against the wall of the cupboard. He took a deep breath and fell against the door. It burst open and he toppled heavily into the hall.

He lay still for a moment, biting his lip against the pain from his wrists and the ache from the shoulder he had landed on. There was no sound or movement in the house. Then he dragged himself along the hall, trying to ignore the pressure on his wrists and on his ankles from every squirm. Speed was all important.

'Revenge?' Callan demanded as they sped down the empty road. 'Is that it?'

'For what?' Maire glanced at him in surprise.

'For deserting you when you were in jail,' Callan shrugged. 'You knew about Jenny.'

'You left long before that,' she said without acrimony.

'What then?'

215

They came round a bend and were into the bottleneck of Bray. She stopped behind a line of cars and met his inquisitive gaze. 'Insurance,' she said.

He shook his head, baffled.

'Nothing to do with you. Nothing personal.'

'Tell me.'

The line of cars began to move and she turned back to driving, letting out the clutch a little too quickly. 'I was trying to take out some insurance for Shay,' she said in a tired voice. 'I don't want him getting involved. Ending up in the H-Blocks or Milltown cemetery. He's suffered enough already.'

Callan watched her and waited, not knowing what she was talking about.

'He's very withdrawn,' she said. 'Introverted. Doesn't mix with other children. Suffers terrible nightmares.'

'Why?'

'Because of me,' she sighed. 'Because of you. Because of everything.'

Callan shook his head, not understanding. Maire turned right towards Wexford before they got into the town centre and the traffic speeded up.

'He hasn't exactly had a stable family life.' She glanced at Callan.

'Your parents were looking after him,' he said, trying to catch up with her, get on the same wavelength.

'Yes.' She nodded absently and paused. 'He had a bad experience there,' she sighed. 'When he was about four. He was playing one day with a friend, in his house, when the loyalists attacked a pub next door. They drove up and sprayed the outside with bullets. Tossed a bomb into the pub. Killed a few.' She paused again. 'The family ran out the back of the house when the shooting started. But their young lad went out the front for some reason. And Shay followed him. The loyalists opened up again with a sub-machine-gun as they left. Cheering. A few forty-fives hit the other boy. Tore him apart.'

Jesus, Callan breathed. He tried to visualise the photograph on the mantlepiece in Maire's house but all he saw was an impression of a happy, smiling boy.

'He wasn't hit,' Maire added. 'God knows why.'

Callan watched the road ahead broaden into a dual carriageway, tree-lined hills rising on either side. All the horror stories came back to him, of people killed and maimed, of victims who were dismissed as survivors. The stories that were an adjunct to the grand ideals but ultimately more important. The stories that had fuelled his own commitment but had never touched him personally.

'My mother died shortly after that,' Maire continued. 'And my sister took him. But he never got over that. He still has the same nightmare. The two of them running out the front door. Kevin being shot.'

The engine whined loudly as the car climbed up a long hill and Callan closed his eyes. This doesn't touch me either, he was thinking. And yet it does. It must. He's my son. Even if I've never seen him. If all I've got is a vague impression of a smiling boy.

'Why didn't you let me know?' he asked, pointlessly.

'And what would you have done about it?'

Callan sighed. Nothing, he thought. What could I have done? 'But it's not your fault either,' he said.

Maire gave him a withering look, as if he didn't understand anything. They lapsed into silence and he watched her closely, imagining he saw the anguish behind her eyes. That was it, he thought. That was what had brought the changes he had seen in her at their last meeting. Not prison nor age nor running the armed struggle.

'I came to Dublin when I got out,' Maire said after a while. 'To get him away from it all. But it hasn't worked.' She sighed heavily. 'He's never had a chance,' she added, the edge of her voice cracking. 'Not a childhood. Nothing.'

He looked at her in sympathy and found he had nothing to say.

Keerins worked his way along the living-room window to the gap between the curtains. He levered himself on to his knees against the wall and tried to look out the window. It was too high.

He leaned back to raise himself on to his feet, overriding the agony with determination. He made it eventually, balanced on his toes, his forehead against the cool glass, and looked out. His car was gone: there was nobody in sight.

The window clouded under his hot breath and the glass became slippy from the sweat off his forehead. His body shook from the strain of holding the position and he feared he would unbalance before somebody came along. Then a young woman came into view, guiding an empty pushchair and holding a toddler with her other hand.

He waited until she was almost opposite the window and then banged his forehead hard against the glass, again and again. She looked at the house and her expression dropped into a slack-mouthed surprise. She gathered the child under her arm and hurried away.

Keerins fell away from the window and on to the floor. He lay unmoving, willing the pain to subside, waiting for the sirens. I'm going to get that fucker, he promised himself. Nothing is more certain.

The signs warned against overtaking as the dual carriageway ended and the road levelled out approaching Kilmacanogue. The Sugar Loaf rose into a brown pinnacle ahead, sharp in the sunlight. Callan checked the time and saw a sign for Glendalough. 'Turn right,' he said. 'Get off the main road.'

Maire slowed to a stop and waited for a line of cars to pass from the opposite direction. The indicator clicked in the silence. She turned into a narrow road and heavy hedges closed in around them as they began to climb round the mountain.

'So you told the guards about that arms shipment,' Callan said.

Maire nodded, almost imperceptibly.

'That was a very stupid thing to do,' he added, watching her. 'Whatever the reason.'

'I wasn't thinking straight,' she said. 'I was very depressed. And I thought that if I passed on one bit of information I could maybe protect him in future.'

Callan snorted. 'You can't take out that kind of insurance. You know that.'

'I had to do something,' she shrugged, a hint of pleading in her voice. 'It had been building up for a long time. Then Shay was suspended from school. For kicking a teacher who criticised the armed struggle.'

'And you turned into a full-time tout.'

'No.'

'They turned you.'

'No,' she repeated. 'I gave them nothing else.'

'Except me,' he shot back.

Maire said nothing.

'Why?' Callan demanded. 'You still haven't told me.'

'To protect myself.' She glared at him briefly, defiantly. 'And Shay.'

He grunted and looked past the flickering hedges. The road ran straight now and the countryside had flattened into a peaceful rural scene. Bright-green fields spread on either side and sloped gently away to the mountains on the right. He wondered why he didn't feel more angry at her.

'Blinker was conducting an enquiry into the arms leak,' Maire added, as if he deserved a fuller explanation. 'He came up with the idea that you might have been responsible. Asked me to get you back. I told him you wouldn't come at my invitation. So he got Willy to do it.'

'But you tipped off the guards,' Callan said dispassionately. He felt as if they were casually discussing someone else's predicament. Something of which he wasn't really a part.

'I didn't want Blinker to talk to you.'

'You just wanted me locked up for forty years,' Callan said automatically. It's because I don't care any more, he decided. That's why I can't really feel angry.

'No.' She glanced at him. 'I only wanted Blinker's inquiries stymied. I wanted more time.'

'For what?' He turned back to her. 'You know he's going to work it out sooner or later.'

'I'm sorry,' she shrugged. 'It was nothing against you. I assumed you'd escape. Get back to America immediately.' She paused. 'You were always good in a tight corner.'

'What's going to happen then,' he persisted, consciously trying to pay her back by demanding the answer they both knew was inevitable, 'when he finds out you're the informer?'

Maire said nothing.

'What's going to happen to Shay after they execute you?'

She did not reply.

Callan looked at her as if she was a stranger. Which she is, he thought. I don't know her any more. If I ever did.

The car hummed along, accentuating the silence. He shifted in his seat and unfolded his arms and let the gun dangle between his knees. He looked at a passing farmhouse without seeing it and his gaze swept casually over the fields. His attention narrowed in suddenly on a speck moving above the hills. A helicopter.

'You've got to get out,' he said, watching the aircraft heading south, following the main road. It might be nothing. 'America. Australia. Wherever.'

'We've got to finish it this time.'

'You can't.'

'We've got to,' she said. Her voice sounded determined, like a voice from the past and he turned back to her. 'Otherwise it's all been for nothing.'

'But you can't,' he insisted with the advantage of his detachment. 'They can't beat you. But you can't beat them. You can't force it to an end.'

'We've got to,' she repeated.

'You don't have to win the war single-handed.'

'We have to see it through. We can't just throw up our hands, leave it for another generation.'

'But that's what's happening,' Callan said, more irritated by her obstinacy than her betrayal. 'That's what you're worried about. With Shay.'

'There are a few years,' she glanced at him, 'before that happens.'

'You don't have a few years,' he said harshly. 'You have to get out now. For Shay's sake. If you're really worried about him.'

Maire said nothing.

'Or send him to me,' he added. 'When I get settled again.'

'No,' she said flatly. 'He's had too much disruption.'

This is pointless, he thought, turning back to the helicopter. It was coming inland in a wide circle. 'Fuck,' he muttered.

Maire looked at him quickly and he pointed to it. 'Searching,' he added.

The road ahead was straight, the land open. There was no cover.

'Where are we?' he demanded. The helicopter was still a long way off but straightening out. About to head north. Towards them.

'I don't know.'

Callan sorted quickly through the glove compartment, looking for a map. There was only a street map of Dublin.

'Take the next turn right,' he ordered. That was his only hope. Get into the mountain forests.

Maire accelerated down the empty straight and the helicopter grew larger. Callan flicked down his sun visor and rolled up his window.

They sped round a bend and into another straight. The gap between them closed quickly.

Callan sat back in his seat, unmoving, hoping the helicopter crew wouldn't see through the windows' reflections. He could hear its dull thump thump thump now. It passed half a mile to his left and he saw the green, white and orange roundel on the fuselage. There was no doubt about it: they were looking for him.

'Road to the right,' Maire said tersely.

'Take it.' Callan twisted in his seat to look after the helicopter. It was banking sideways into a tight turn to follow them.

Maire braked hard and swung into a narrow lane and the thumping noise became louder and turned into an engine whine as the helicopter roared overhead. They passed a sign for a forest park and the lane twisted and then they were between dense dark trees.

'Slow down,' Callan said.

She slowed to a halt and looked at him. Callan listened to the helicopter approaching, hoping they'd see the car stopped. It passed over and he nodded to her to go on.

'You have a plan?' she asked.

'No.'

'Make for Dunmore East,' she said as they came out of the trees and the road climbed. 'There's a friend of mine there who'll get you on to a trawler. They'll put you on to a Basque boat, take you to Spain.'

She told him a name and an address and he sat rigidly as the helicopter passed over again. They were staying with the car.

'I won't tell them,' Maire promised. 'Any of them.'

Heather and gorse covered the sides of the hills as they went higher. Another wood was coming up on the left. The helicopter was sweeping towards them from the left and he watched it carefully. It went overhead and turned and started back as they passed by the wood.

'Let me out,' he said quickly. 'As soon as it goes over.'

He waited until the machine was overhead, then stuffed the automatic into his belt and gathered his backpack with his right hand. He had the door open as the car slowed.

'Keep going,' he said. 'As far as you can.'

Maire nodded and their eyes met in a glimpse of mutual understanding.

Callan stepped out as the car halted and slammed the door. Maire accelerated away.

He tossed the backpack into the trees, leaped over a loose barbed-wire fence and dived under the low branches as the overhead clatter rolled over the wood and passed overhead in a deafening crescendo.

Twenty

'We've found him.' The detective burst into the kitchen of Maire's house.

'Where?' Keerins looked round from the hard chair where he was sitting, jacket off, sleeves rolled up. One of his raw wrists was held out straight while a colleague wrapped a gauze bandage round the ointment. The other was already bandaged.

'Near Roundwood,' the detective said. 'The Air Corps picked up a red Mazda. It's trying to run for it.'

'Both of them?' Keerins signalled to the other detective to hurry up.

'I don't know.'

The other detective split the end of the bandage and tied it.

'Does the Super know?' Keerins stood up and gathered his jacket and hurried from the house.

'Yes,' the detective said, following in his wake. 'The search party's been diverted there. The army's on its way.'

We've got him this time, Keerins thought happily. Caught him in the open. He paused on the footpath, looking at the four cars drawn up there. A small group of people had materialised from somewhere and watched from across the road. He didn't notice them.

'This one,' the detective led him to a car. 'The helicopter was already involved in the other search,' he added. 'Only took it a few minutes to get down there.'

'Move it,' Keerins snapped impatiently as he sat in. The radio chattered, heightening his excitement. 'Move it.'

The roar of the helicopter dropped to a steady thumping as it swung out over the hillside and dipped round into a swooping turn. The sun flashed off its windscreen and it circled back, farther up the hill. Following the car.

Callan gave a brief smile. They hadn't seen him leave the car. He retrieved his backpack and settled it on to his shoulders and set off among the trees. The sound of the helicopter faded further, like a receding headache.

The going was easy. The earth was brown and bouncy and sloped downhill. There was little undergrowth. The tree trunks were bare near the ground, their foliage thick at the top. An odd shaft of sunlight worked its way through a gap in the trees with the precision and power of a spotlight. He breathed deeply on the resin-scented air and felt at ease again, for the first time since Jenny had produced the evening paper.

Everything was looking good. All he had to do was to get some distance between himself and them. Which depended mainly on Maire. On how far she got.

A twinge of suspicion flashed through his mind and he dismissed it instantly. I can trust her, he decided. There's no reason not to. In spite of everything.

He ducked under a stray branch, thinking about her dilemma and her apparent refusal to confront reality. Her chances of survival were next to nil. Unless she got out immediately. All she had done for the movement wouldn't save her, couldn't save her. Her years of total dedication, constant hardship, on the run and in prison, all betrayed. By what? Some kind of maternal guilt?

He shook his head in an involuntary gesture. You could never foretell how things would catch up with you.

Maire came over a rise and saw the two cars in the distance, coming along the bare hillside, fast. She slowed down.

They kept coming and turned into the straight ahead of her. Then the first car swung across the narrow road and stopped and she saw the doors open. Four, five, six figures leaped out. Two of them jumped over the low ditch and ran a little way towards her and dropped into the heather.

She touched the brakes and put the gearshift into neutral and the car coasted slowly towards them. She stopped more than fifty yards from them and shut off the engine. Every minute mattered. She sat with her hands on the top of the steering wheel and waited. Nobody moved.

One of the detectives shouted something but she couldn't hear what he was saying. Then two more detectives ran out from behind the cover of their car and jumped the opposite ditch. They began to make their way cautiously towards her on either side of the road.

'Out of the car,' one of them shouted when they were close enough.

She opened the door and stepped out. They stayed low in the meagre cover.

'Come forward,' the same man shouted. She stepped forward, alongside the bonnet. The wind tugged her black hair from behind her ear and tossed it across her face. She stood perfectly still, her arms hanging by her side, facing up the road, ignoring the detectives' movements.

Two of them came out on to the road in front of her while the other two ran along the hill until they were alongside the car. They looked into it quickly, Uzis at the ready.

'Where is he, Maire?' One of them stepped round her and ran his hand around her body quickly.

'Who?' she asked, not focusing on her questioner.

'Don't fuck about,' the man in front of her warned.

'I don't know,' she said. 'He got out in Bray.'

'And you're just out for a drive in the country,' the man in front snorted, 'in a hijacked car.'

She said nothing and the man behind her cocked his Uzi with a menacing click. 'You've got five seconds,' he said quietly.

The wind swept up from a shadowed valley below them and on over the empty hillside above. There was no trace of human habitation, nobody and nothing in sight. They stood in an enclosed group, lost in the deserted landscape.

'I want to see Inspector Keerins,' Maire said, looking her questioner in the eye at last.

'He's not here,' the man retorted.

'I'll only talk to him.'

The man sighed and turned away to summon their cars with a wave. Maire suddenly became aware that the helicopter was gone. Had left her before she had seen the approaching cars.

Callan saw the sunlight between the trees and headed towards it, realising that the wood wasn't as big as he had hoped. Unless it stretched away farther to one side. He wished he had a map, at least some knowledge of the terrain.

The trees shifted gently in the wind as he came to the edge of the wood and the countryside opened out before him. The hill fell away gradually into a green valley which split into two offshoots and ran off into the mountains. Houses were scattered in the valley below, cattle grazed in the fields and a car moved silently along a road.

Beyond, the mountains reared up behind each other, the nearer ones brown, the farther ones purpled by distance. The sun glared down, casting dark patches of shadow on their slopes and glinted on a wedge of water between them.

He shook off his backpack and sat down against a tree, taking in the peace of the scenery like a resting hiker. He relaxed slowly, feeling his eyes grow heavy and realised how tired he was. He yawned and remembered the way he had felt in Connemara after he had escaped from the trap and the roadblock. He felt as easy and confident now. As though he had come through the worst.

What lay ahead was almost as inviting as a holiday. Move due south across the valley and work his way through the mountains and on down to the south coast. He relished the long hike across country, away from the tension and claustrophobia of the city and the uncertainties of the last few days. He was in control of his own destiny again.

It wasn't as simple as that, of course. They'd search this area but they'd have to cover so much ground it would be pretty cursory. It shouldn't pose any problem.

Callan leaned his back against the tree, closed his eyes and emptied his mind. He felt the warm wind on his face and the heat of the sun brushed his cheeks as the branches of the trees in front of him swayed.

He had lost his sense of time when his ears picked up an alien sound. His brain resisted the information for a moment and then he opened his eyes and the helicopter was sweeping down on the hill from behind the trees on his right.

He rolled to his feet, gathered his bag and crouched behind the tree in one movement. The grey undercarriage of the helicopter passed by, angled into a wide arc. It was gone from his sight in seconds.

How fucking stupid can you be, he asked himself furiously. You can't relax for a second. Not one. Not ever.

He stayed still, controlling his surprise and anger. Had they seen him? Doubtful, he decided. He had been back from the tree line and their angle of vision was against them. They were too high to see under the trees.

He turned into a sitting position and opened the backpack. Their reappearance meant they had caught up with Maire. Are they back-tracking, hoping to pick me up, he wondered. Or do they know where I left the car.

226

He took out the Kalashnikov and shoved the unused magazine into place. I'll know which it is soon enough, he thought. Then he pulled out the camouflage jacket and trousers, slipped off his jeans and dressed quickly. He went through the back- pack, retrieving his passports and money and buttoning them into the pockets of the combat jacket.

He dug his fingers into the loose earth and rubbed it hard on to his forehead and cheeks and neck. Preparing for the worst.

'There they are,' the driver said as they sped along the hillside.

Keerins grunted, his attention on the radio. It kept fading in and out as the mountains blocked the signal but he could follow the movements. The helicopter was circling the wood where Callan had gone, the crew certain he hadn't emerged: police and army units were converging from three directions.

They came up to the two cars parked by the roadside and stopped alongside Keerins's Mazda. Four detectives stood around like men who had broken a long journey to stretch and relieve themselves. One of them pointed to their car as Keerins stepped out.

He opened the driver's door and sat in sideways. Maire was sitting in the centre of the back seat, her handcuffed wrists on her lap. She looked pale, strained.

'Well?' he demanded sharply.

'I want to do a deal.' She stared past him, out the wind- screen.

'I'm listening.'

'I'll give you the location of some arms dumps, I and my son leave the country. With new identities.'

Keerins gave a derisive laugh.

'Some of the arms dumps you haven't been able to find in years of searches.'

'You'll have to do better than that,' Keerins said. 'What d'you think we are? A fucking travel agency?'

Maire said nothing.

'The stakes have gone up,' Keerins said, raising a bandaged wrist. 'I can put you away for ten years minimum now. No problem.'

'What'd you expect me to do,' she retorted. 'Disarm him?'

'You didn't have to co-operate so fully,' he said with an air of petulance. 'As I will point out to the court.'

227

Two military jeeps went by, their long aerials tied down, heading for the wood. Keerins felt impatient to follow them.

'There are other things I can tell you,' Maire offered resignedly.

'Like what?'

'What I won't do' - she looked at him - 'is give information or evidence against anyone. I won't become a supergrass.'

'What other information?'

'Operations that are being planned.'

'And will be abandoned as soon as you disappear,' he snorted.

'Supply lines. Things like that.'

'I don't know.' He shook his head, feeling euphoric. She's a mine of information, he was thinking. A veritable gold mine. And she's my catch. 'I'll have to put it to my superiors.'

Maire nodded.

'I wouldn't hold out much hope,' he said. 'I can't see them liking the idea of someone with your record getting away scot free.'

'I want my son taken to a safe place,' Maire said.

Keerins nodded vaguely, thinking about how he was going to present this to the superintendent. Nothing to it: tell him straight. It was a major intelligence coup to turn a member of the army council into a defector.

'Immediately.'

'OK,' he agreed, anxious to get on to the next business. 'I'll have him picked up from school.'

Maire shook her head decisively. 'I want to collect him myself.'

'OK. Where's Callan?' he added as an afterthought.

Maire looked past him.

'That's not evidence of a co-operative attitude,' he said.

'We don't have a deal yet, you said.'

'I'll talk to you later.'

Keerins stepped out of the car and signalled the sergeant in the group to follow him over to his own car. 'She wants to do a deal,' Keerins told him. 'Take her to collect her child from school and bring them somewhere safe. And keep this quiet,' he added. 'Nobody but nobody is to know. She's under arrest officially.'

The sergeant waved his men back to their car and Keerins got back into the car in which he had arrived. 'What about your own car?' the driver asked.

'Later,' Keerins said, his attention already on the radio. 'Let's get down there.'

The creaking of the trees was the only sound now. The muffled thud of the helicopter had gone but it had passed round often enough to confirm his suspicions.

Callan stopped and hunkered down and surveyed everything around him. Nearby, the trees seemed well spaced but their trunks gathered into an opaque wall with distance, resisting his vision. He tried to detect any movements, any sudden shifts, but there were none. There was no sound but the slight shifting of the trees.

He moved on again, the rifle pointed at the ground ahead, his index finger on the trigger guard. The ground sloped down and there were small patches of jumbled undergrowth here and there. He reckoned he was moving parallel to the road but there was nothing to guide him except for the falling ground.

He changed direction, deciding to take another look into the valley. The glow of the bright sun began to appear among the trees and he stopped to scan his surroundings again. He eased the backpack off one shoulder at a time and left it by a tree.

He moved forward warily, from tree to tree, watching the ground for brittle twigs, watching the tree line. He stopped short of the edge of the wood, lowered himself to the ground and wriggled forward on his arms to look out.

A platoon of soldiers was strung across the hill a hundred yards away. They were moving steadily, the last man stopping off every forty yards or so. Surrounding the wood.

A fox shoot, Callan thought, remembering being one of a group of children beating through a wood to flush the raiding foxes into their fathers' waiting guns. The farmers' retaliation for the losses of their lambs.

That's what they were going to do. Sweep through the wood once their cordon was in place. Flush him out.

The dwindling line of soldiers moved outside his sight and he watched those left behind. They faced the wood, making no effort to conceal or cover themselves. They were just a deterrent, already beginning to look bored.

I could make a run for it now, he thought. Take out a couple of them easily. Punch a hole in their line. They wouldn't expect that. And then what? I'd be out in the open. A long way from any cover. Fuck-all ammunition left.

He raised himself slowly on his elbows to look over the bulge of the hill. The long grass and heather bent submissively before the wind and the bottom of the hill levelled out gently into the valley. Over to his right, a thick ditch ran straight downhill. That was the place to do it, he thought automatically. Only have to worry about one flank.

Ideally, I should wait for dark, crawl between them, risk their night sights. But it wouldn't be dark for ten hours, maybe longer. Too long.

The only alternative was bad weather, low cloud and an impenetrable mist. But there was no chance of that either. The sun shone down determinedly and the blue sky was marked only by a few wisps of cloud, as delicate as a child's curls, on high.

You've got to do it now, he told himself. If you're going to do it.

He lowered his elbows and rested his forehead on the rifle's hard stock. As though he was trying to summon up energy that he couldn't find. The trees sighed in the wind above him and he smelled the musty earth and the gun oil.

No, he decided at last. There's no point. My war is over. It's all over.

He raised his head and took a last, lingering look beyond the soldiers at the sun on the slopes and peaks of the far-off mountains. He slid backwards into the wood, aware of what he had decided.

They parked at the end of a line of cars and military trucks and Keerins hurried down the last stretch of the hill. Small groups of armed soldiers and policemen stood about, their radios chattering like demented crickets. Nobody seemed to be doing anything.

He saw Pursell leaning against a loose stone wall and sucking on a stem of grass. He looked like an unconcerned farmer who had wandered up to see what all the activity was about.

'Is he in there?' Keerins reached him and nodded towards the trees. 'Definitely?'

'So the Air Corps says.'

'But has there been a definite sighting?' Keerins persisted anxiously.

Pursell shook his head. 'Process of elimination.' He took the grass stem from his mouth. 'They say he was in the car and then he wasn't. And this is the only place he could have jumped out unseen.'

Keerins cursed under his breath: that wasn't at all as certain as he wanted it to be. 'What's everybody doing?' he demanded.

'Getting into position.'

Jesus, Keerins thought. Don't they have any idea of what a slippery character they're up against? 'Is the Super here?' he asked, curbing his impatience.

'Haven't seen him yet. Unless he's down there.' Pursell inclined his head down the road towards another jumble of cars and armed men.

Keerins continued towards the second group, thinking irritably that this was precisely the kind of fuckology that allowed Callan to get away time after time.

Callan stepped forward cautiously, encouraged by the spread of undergrowth across the floor of the wood. The trees had thinned out a little and brambles spread treacherous trails through the rough grass. Here and there they built into small clumps which he examined closely.

None were big enough or dense enough to burrow under, he decided. Anyway, his camouflage wouldn't be good enough to withstand more than a cursory look. And there weren't enough places to hide to make a proper search difficult. If only I had a ghillie suit, he thought. Maybe the other wood would have been better.

If. Maybe.

He shrugged off all the might-have-beens and stepped over the trunk of a fallen tree. He squatted on the ground behind it and looked back the way he had come, the rifle resting on the tree. Spots of sunshine dappled the rising ground and the trees and motes hovered in the beams. An animal scurried quickly through the undergrowth to one side.

He felt tired and thought about staying here. Making a last stand. Like it was a game. Shoot-out at the OK corral or something. The cowboys and Indiana he used to play with Brendan in the woods near the farm. He tucked the butt of the rifle into his shoulder and traversed the trees through the iron sights. The gun was real and it wasn't a game. And his field of fire was too limited.

He moved on again, not bothering to take so much care any more. He had a while yet. They wouldn't come until they were ready. They didn't need to hurry.

He came to a large tangle of briars and kicked back a hole in it. He took off the backpack and shoved it into the gap and forced the clinging briars back into place with his foot. He stepped back and looked at the backpack. It would escape a passing glance.

Up ahead he saw a widening patch of sunlight and made for it with renewed caution. It turned out to be a small clearing, one half in the sun, the other shadowed. Weathered tree stumps were dotted amid the long matted grass and low outcrops of brambles and nettles.

He stepped through the sunshine into the shadowed half of the clearing and looked around. A part of his mind suggested he might just get away with it. They wouldn't expect him to be in the open. And his camouflage gear was the right mixture of dull greens and browns. They might pass by with a perfunctory look, intent on seeking hiding places.

Another part of his mind said it was as good a place as any.

He picked a spot in the shadow and settled down on the ground, flat on his back. He lay still for a moment and then shifted slightly to move his back to a more comfortable contour. He breathed deeply, staring up into the infinite blue of the sky, relaxing his body.

Time seemed to lose its relevance and his mind drifted free of its immediate concerns, floated backwards and forwards like a piece of wood on a turning tide. He thought about all that had happened and what might have happened in the future. The new life he could have had with Sharon. A truly new life this time, finally freed of all the shackles of the past. Could that really have been, he wondered. Can you ever escape the legacy you build up, uncaringly, unthinkingly, for yourself?

A jet came into his vision above the swaying tips of the trees, cutting westward through the blue like a barbed arrowhead. He watched its trail unravel like a thin braid of stretched cotton wool and he remembered the day on the farm, lying by the stream, the pinkeens darting.

Why did I come back at all? Was it some immutable law of nature? Foretold by that dream on the plane? Like a salmon returning to spawn and die.

He thought of his mother waiting for his letter and her ticket to America and the last sight he had had of her, standing by the side of the house. And of his father, his memorial card still in the pocket of his jeans, in the bag hidden in the clump of briars. And of his unknown son, the vague smiling child to whom he'd helped give a hard legacy without the happiness of a childhood.

An overwhelming sense of regret overcame him. For what had been and for what might have been and for what would never be. He blinked away the tears. There was no escape.

The jet was gone, its trail dissolving rapidly, leaving the sky unmarked.

He waited.

Twenty-one

'Come on,' Keerins called, his patience finally giving way before the inactivity all around him. Groups of detectives and soldiers were still standing about with the indecisive air of people who had been locked out of some place and could think of nowhere else to go.

'Where?' Pursell did not stir from his wall.

'We're going in there.' Keerins handed him a strip of white ribbon. He began tying another strip round his own arm.

'Who?' Pursell eyed him suspiciously.

'Us,' Keerins said, tightening the knot. 'You and me.'

'You're out of your fucking mind.' Pursell jolted himself away from the wall with sudden outrage.

'We're going in.'

'The Rangers are in there,' Pursell protested. 'The fucking place is crawling with armed men.'

Keerins nodded. He had seen the army unit go in, two squads in combat dress, faces smeared with camouflage cream. 'This is our operation,' he said. 'We should be in there. On the spot.'

'What does the Super say?' Pursell asked desperately.

'Hasn't arrived yet,' Keerins paused. 'Look,' he said slowly. 'I'm sick to death of waiting to have everyone who's supposed to catch Callan come back to me with a load of excuses about why he got away. I don't want to hear any more. I've had enough of them. I'm going in. I want to see this myself.'

A young lieutenant listening nearby glared at him. 'I don't think it's a good idea,' he offered. 'You'll only confuse the situation.'

'This is a police matter.' Keerins turned on him. 'You're only here in a support role.'

He strode away to the detective who had driven him to the scene and asked to borrow his gun. Pursell threw his eyes to heaven and followed, tying the ribbon round his left arm. 'Fucking glory merchants,' he muttered to the lieutenant.

The trees closed round them quickly, cutting them off from the brightness and the outside certainties. Keerins moved forward quickly, Pursell a short distance to his right and slightly behind. They had their revolvers in their hands.

The trees teased their prying eyes, letting them see so far and then no further. The perspective changed with every step, creating an illusion of movements as the relative positions of the bare trunks shifted.

Keerins slowed down to stop his eyes darting from side to side with every change on the edge of his vision. His anger gave way to a brittle nervousness at his sudden awareness of the hostility of the wood, the expectation of a sudden burst of gunfire. Forests, in his experience, were places for gentle family walks along sign-posted trails. Not for pursuing a dedicated killer.

Maybe this wasn't such a good idea, he conceded mentally. But it had to be done. He had to know. He couldn't go back now.

He wasn't convinced that Callan was here at all, half-hoped he wasn't. The helicopter crew's certainty didn't seem to be based on anything other than guesswork. Or covering their ass for having found him and lost him again. Like everybody else involved with this case.

At least, he thought, I've got Maire to show for it all. Which was worth the humiliation of having been disarmed and tied up and virtually ignored by Callan. The fucker didn't even see me as a threat. In fact, he realised, he hardly saw me at all.

He wondered about that. Why Callan had seemed so preoccupied. He had never met a wanted man who seemed so uncaring about the presence of a policeman. But he knows now that I'm after him.

A twig snapped under his foot, startling him out of his satisfaction. He glanced over at Pursell who gave him a smug look. Keerins resisted the temptation to go over, seek his advice.

They went on down the sloping ground, no method in their advance. The wood seemed to be deserted. The trees towered over them, aloof. The light had a sepia-tinted gloom. The silence was accentuated by the slight creaks of the trees and the sighs of branches. As if nature too was holding its breath, waiting to see what would happen.

Keerins caught a sudden movement away to his left and turned towards it but there was nothing there. He moved on, conscious suddenly that they were being watched, seeing nobody. This is pointless, he thought, covering another outcrop of undergrowth with his gun as if he expected it to leap up and run. Where were the bloody Rangers?

What if one of them jumped up suddenly? Jesus. They could end up shooting each other. He hadn't thought about that, about what the Rangers were going to do. He had vaguely assumed he'd meet up with them, moving in a search line and follow them. But there was no sign of them at all.

A splash of sunshine caught his attention and he veered towards it automatically. Like it was a light on a dark night.

He came upon the clearing suddenly and saw the sun shining down on the far side of it. He was about to step out into it but hesitated. It looked so exposed. Then the gun caught his attention.

He thought at first that it was lying on the ground. And then he made out the camouflaged figure under it. He froze.

The waiting had seemed endless and now it ended too soon. Callan sensed their arrival through some subtle change in the surroundings. He tensed his body and tightened his grip on the Kalashnikov without moving, preparing for the challenge.

He looked up into the azure sky with a calm detachment. The past was all gone. Like the future. There was only the here and now. He knew what he was going to do. It was all decided.

This is it, he thought.

Keerins signalled Pursell over to him and put a finger to his lips. He pointed to the armed figure and they looked at each other. Pursell nodded silently.

It's not him, a part of Keerins' mind reassured him. He wasn't dressed like that. It's a soldier resting.

But he knew it was Callan. Where was the fucking army, he wondered desperately. But there was nothing else for it. They had to go forward. Do it.

He stepped into the clearing, revolver held high, its blunt sight covering the figure. Pursell moved alongside, a couple of feet to his left.

Callan heard the graze of their footsteps on the grass.

They stopped about ten yards from him. Keerins nodded to Pursell and licked his lips. 'Police!' he shouted. 'Throw the gun to one side.'

Callan didn't move. He closed his eyes, took a deep breath and took a last look at the pines fringing the sky.

'Throw the gun away,' Keerins repeated. 'Now!'

Callan moved before he had finished. He raised the gun above his head and rolled over twice in a fast continuous motion. Pursell fired twice. Keerins once, automatically. Their bullets thudded into the ground where he had been.

The rolls brought Callan round with the rifle pointed towards them, amazed he was still alive. There's only two of them, he thought, recognising Keerins. Some instinct for survival, and a residue of all his experiences and training cancelled his decisions, took over. You can get out of this, it told him. You can make it.

He loosed off a short burst to one side of them. Empty cases flew from the breech, cordite filled his nostrils. The bullets splattered into the trees and one smashed the bone in Pursell's shoulder, swinging him back on to the ground, and ricocheted away. A Ranger kneeling by a tree, his Steyr steadied against the trunk, cursed silently. Keerins was blocking his aim.

Keerins swung his revolver towards Callan, his hand shaking, aware that Pursell had gone, hearing nothing but the terrorising clatter of the Kalashnikov. He fired wildly.

Then Callan was on his feet, firing another unaimed burst. I can make it, he thought, running low, picking up speed. I can make it.

The Ranger fired.

A tight line of bullets caught Callan along the side and back and seemed to lift him up and pitch him violently into the tangled grass. The gun fell from his grasp.

Keerins stood where he was, shaking uncontrollably, his mind a blank. Soldiers suddenly seemed to be everywhere.

One bent over Callan, feeling for a pulse. Another knelt by Pursell, cutting away his shirt, a field dressing at the ready. A third was talking into a radio.

'You all right?' a soldier asked him.

Keerins stared into his painted face and nodded after a moment. 'Sure?'

Keerins nodded again, his brain slowly coming back into action. He turned round and dropped on to the ground beside Pursell. His face was a white sheen of sweat and he had his teeth dug into his lower lip.

'He's OK,' the soldier said to Keerins, tearing open a syringe of morphine. 'He's in no danger.'

Keerins took hold of Pursell's hand and muttered, 'Sorry.'

Pursell unclenched his teeth for a moment. 'I told you,' he grunted.

Keerins squeezed his hand and let it go. He stood up. Everything seemed surreal. The soldiers stood about, talking quietly. One of them carried Callan's Kalashnikov. They didn't pay any attention to Callan any more. A couple of them watched silently as Keerins wandered unsteadily over to his body.

He was lying on his back. A thorn scratch on his dusty cheek was congealing into a dark-red line. Blood was still spreading darkly around the tears in his jacket, altering the camouflage patterns like a chameleon changing its disguise. His eyes were open, staring towards the sky.

The ambulance carrying Pursell moved off down the hill with a toot of its siren, its blue lights revolving. Keerins watched it until it disappeared and then turned his attention back to the steady stream of men coming and going from the wood. There must be a well-worn path into the clearing by now, he thought casually.

Passing detectives nodded to him, the man of the moment. Cars were beginning to move off, leaving a haze of exhaust fumes on the road. The action was over. It was just after midday.

The superintendent strode up and extended his hand. 'Well done, George,' he said. 'Excellent day's work.'

'Thank you, sir.' Keerins shook his hand formally.

'Take a few days off. If you like.'

'No, thanks,' Keerins said with determination.

'Are you sure?' the superintendent inquired solicitously. 'That must have been a frightening experience.'

Keerins shook his head. It wasn't frightening any more. 'I'd like to talk to Maire,' he said. 'Get moving on that.'

'If you're sure.'

Keerins nodded. Sure I'm sure, he thought wryly. She's my catch. I'm not going to hand her over to anyone else. After all this.

'Good,' the Superintendent said. 'She's in headquarters. We'll have to move quickly. Before they realise what's happened.'

'We can say she's been detained,' Keerins suggested. 'Section thirty. Give us forty-eight hours before they know.'

'They'll know sooner,' the superintendent said. 'When they hear the child is gone. We can't let her drag things out. She's got to give us whatever she has immediately.'

238

They stopped to watch as four soldiers emerged from the wood, carrying Callan's body in a sagging bag. They stepped carefully over the loose wire fence, raising the bag.

'I'm sorry it had to end in bloodshed,' Keerins said.

'Nobody'll shed any tears over him,' the superintendent shrugged.

The soldiers put the body bag into the back of a green army ambulance and the driver climbed into the cab. No, Keerins admitted to himself, I'm not sorry it ended like this. The shoot-out had left him with a heady euphoria, a clean sense of invincibility at having survived a violent action that had killed one person, wounded another. The ambulance moved off slowly, followed by a Land Rover.

'Pursell will pull through,' the superintendent said, his mind on the next business. 'Get compensation. Go out on a disability pension. He'll be all right.' He paused as if he was about to impart a confidence, a small gesture of equality between them. 'He used to be a good man. Until he let the frustrations of the job distort his judgement. A lesson to us all.'

He knows all about Amber, Keerins thought dispassionately. But that was of no consequence. It doesn't matter to me any more.

'Perhaps it's all for the better this way,' the superintendent shrugged. 'I better get someone round to his family. Inform them.'

And I should call Deirdre, Keerins told himself as the superintendent walked away. He settled back against the wall, reluctant to move, to break the sense of well being. There is no need, he decided. She'll hear all about it on the lunchtime news.

The high sun was hot on his face and the wind swept warmly overhead and on up the curving brown hill behind him. He felt wonderful.

Printed in Great Britain
by Amazon